FIRST-TIME
MOTHER

BOOKS BY AJ CAMPBELL

My Perfect Marriage
Did I Kill My Husband?

Leave Well Alone
Don't Come Looking
Search No Further
The Phone Call
The Wrong Key
Her Missing Husband
The Mistake

FIRST-TIME MOTHER

AJ CAMPBELL

bookouture

Published by Bookouture in 2025

An imprint of Storyfire Ltd.
Carmelite House
50 Victoria Embankment
London EC4Y 0DZ

www.bookouture.com

The authorised representative in the EEA is Hachette Ireland
8 Castlecourt Centre
Dublin 15 D15 XTP3
Ireland
(email: info@hbgi.ie)

ISBN: 978-1-83618-626-7
eBook ISBN: 978-1-83618-627-4

For my amazing friend Christine Henderson.
Thank you for your continued support with my writing.
Love always.
Amanda X

PROLOGUE

Lola's incessant fussing grates on my ragged nerves. It's endless. I cut my shower short. As I step out onto the bath mat, the room spins. I grasp the side of the sink, squeezing my eyes shut tightly, waiting for the feeling to subside. I shouldn't have had the water so hot.

But I needed distraction. I always do around this time of the day. An escape to get me through to bedtime. Only a new mum would understand.

My body is heavy. So very heavy. I glance up at the ugly popcorn-like ceiling and mutter silent prayers of despair. 'Please, God, give me a break. Let me sleep.' I bend down and gently rock my daughter's car seat. 'Be quiet, darling,' I murmur, shivering.

After slipping into my dressing gown, I unstrap my baby and run the tip of my thumb along the smooth skin of her cheek. 'Baby girl, please, please, be quiet.'

I lay her over my shoulder and stumble into the bedroom. The bed looks so inviting, like a warm, cosy fire on a cold winter's day. 'Come on, baby girl. Help me. Help your mumma.' My disheartened whisper is lost among her whiny breaths. 'Shh... shh... let's lie down together.'

I drop down onto the firm mattress, my baby's face squished against my chest. A quick lie-down, that's all I need. Then I'll get up and put that casserole in the oven.

Lola quietens as I gently rock us from side to side. A deep, encompassing stillness calms my senses, it's mesmerising; like a magnet, it pulls me closer to unconsciousness. I'm powerless, unable to fight it. Perhaps I can have forty winks. No one will ever know. My vision blurs. My eyes close...

But it's over in a flash. Before I know it, I awake drenched in sweat and disorientated from the usual faceless soul that appears like the devil in my dreams.

My baby.

Where is my baby?

My stomach turns three-sixty, a spin of nausea I can't control. I jump up and run to the en suite, one hand over my mouth, the other reaching for the light switch.

The blinding LED lights ignite in the darkness. I stop. Scream. But nothing comes out. I'm fixed to the spot, staring at the lifeless body. This can't be right. I must still be dreaming. I slap my cheeks, dragging my hands down my face.

But this is no dream.

I reach out to touch her hand.

I stop.

I'm too late.

She's dead.

ONE

BEFORE

Tears spring from my eyes and fall down my face like two fat raindrops as I slice the knife through an onion. Chop. Chop. Chop. I wipe them away with my hand, resisting the urge to blink. I rock my daughter's bouncy cradle with my foot.

She's not settling. Again.

Her whimpering escalates. I know the pattern. I don't have long. Within minutes, her fussing will morph into persistent crying that only circling the streets in the car will soothe. My foot twitches, picking up speed, trying to buy me time to finish what I'm doing. It's been a while since I managed to make dinner. I need to get this right. 'One minute, darling girl. Just give Mumma a minute.'

Chop. Chop. Chop. I throw the onion into the burning oil. Now for the rice. The rice. I can't remember what I did with the rice. I had it somewhere. It's in the sieve on the sink. Lola's crying continues. Again I stick out my foot to rock her bouncy cradle. 'I won't be long,' I tell her. 'I'm nearly there.' I pick up the sieve but drop it. Grains of rice splatter across the floor like tiny beads from a broken bracelet. I swear repeatedly as I grab the dustpan from the cupboard and sweep up the mess. I drop my head to my chest. All I seem to do is make mistakes these days.

As I pick up the knife to chop vegetables for a salad, Lola lets out an almighty scream. Her fists tighten into angry balls and her face contorts, cutting through me. I stab the tip of the knife into the chopping board and bend down. Unstrapping her from the cradle, I gently place her over my shoulder. I don't know who suffers more from these relentless episodes. 'Shh... shh. Let's try you with some milk.' It sometimes works.

I pat her back. 'How about a walk?' This works sometimes, too. I pace up and down our open-plan kitchen. Our kitchen? No. Their kitchen. Even after a year, this place still doesn't feel like home. It suffocates me despite its size. I feel like a guest here – an intruder who replaced the wife and mother who passed on. It's a morbid thought.

The shabby wooden cupboards make the room dark. The whole house could do with a makeover, not just the kitchen. It's dismal and dreary, like a neglected garden in the middle of winter. It doesn't seem to bother Max or the twins, but I would've ripped the whole lot out and started again long ago. That was the plan when he and his first wife got married, Max told me. They'd made a start with the patio doors and knocking through the kitchen and dining room. Then she died. A subject he won't talk about. He says it's too painful. But he has promised lots of changes to the house when the money from the sale of his business comes through.

If we stay here.

Lola's crying continues, clouding my thoughts. This is what it's like. Night after night her screams echo endlessly around the room.

It's driving me crazy.

I never imagined it being so damn difficult. I had visions of contentment – happy days walking my baby in the park and serene evenings cooking a family dinner. Instead, every day is a slog, every evening a disaster.

I just need to get through these difficult few months, everyone tells me.

I'm trying my best.

I really am.

But I can't help wondering if it's karma.

Payback for what I've done.

TWO

Each step across the tiled kitchen floor resounds with my escalating anxiety. My eyes flit around the room, searching for anything that will soothe my baby's endless wailing, but I don't find anything among the clutter. It's such a bloody mess in here.

I sing to my baby, gentle ballads my mother sang to me many years ago. And then I remember 'The Happy Song'. According to the mums in the local baby and toddler group I sometimes drop into, this song is meant to be the mother of all baby silencers. It always works, they declared. Every time. Not that it has for my daughter. But my daughter isn't like their babies.

I continue to sing, pacing the length of the kitchen. My phone rings. It's Max.

'I'm going to be later than I thought,' he says after asking how we all are. 'At least another half an hour.'

I squash my lips firmly together to stop myself from reacting. What that really means is he could be another couple of hours. I hear my sister Samantha's voice in the background. She is one of his business partners. 'We've had a request from the States that we need to deal with,' Max adds.

These days, he spends more time with my sister than with me.

'I'll be back as soon as I can, darling.'

I take a sip of the vitamin juice that I started drinking after the birth. My friend Nisha recommended it to help me heal from the trauma. It's mandarin and berry flavour tonight, one of my favourites.

A voice startles me. Jacob, my stepson, is standing at the kitchen door in his coat, his backpack hung over his shoulder. He must have just got in from one of the many afterschool music clubs he belongs to.

'Where's Dad?' His hands are lost in his trouser pockets, and his tall frame is hunched over itself.

'He should be home soon.' One-handedly, I refill the sieve with rice.

The light shines on Jacob's face, accentuating the red wine birthmark, shaped like a map of the world, that spreads from the right of his nose to the lobe of his ear. He removes his hand from his pocket and sweeps aside his mop of dark curls. 'He's late again.'

Lola lets out a cry. I pat her back. 'I know. But he's very busy.' I try to sound upbeat. 'Once the sale of the business goes through, he'll be around much more.'

I ask him about his day, but he doesn't answer. When I turn around, he's gone.

I glance at the clock above the sink. I've been singing for ten minutes, but Lola is still awake. I look down. And my tired heart melts. For once, my baby is entranced, staring back at me with her beautiful pale blue eyes. She has Max's soulful eyes. Perfect round balls like the colour of the ocean in shallow waters.

Footsteps thunder down the stairs, missing the bottom two before landing with a thud. My stepdaughter always descends the stairs this way. She never used to, Max tells me. Not before I moved in. I asked him once if she does it intentionally to irritate me, but he just laughed and told me not to be so silly.

'What's for dinner?' Jasmine asks, the usual air of disdain in her voice that Max insists is another spectre of my imagination.

'Chilli con carne.'

She sweeps across the kitchen and takes a can of Coke out of the fridge.

'Would you like a—' But she's gone. Give it five seconds, and the sound of her thumping back up the stairs will echo through the house. I count to five. There we go.

Lola quietens. I don't believe it. Her eyes are droopy; I lower my voice to a gentle hum until they close. Yawning, I tiptoe to the armchair wedged into the corner by the patio doors. The sound of Lola's gentle snores are a soothing relief. It's never usually this easy. I recline in the chair and raise my legs onto the low coffee table. Her face is pressed against my breasts, squashing her cheek into her perfectly formed pink lips.

My body sways in time to the soothing melody of my voice. 'Please stay asleep, baby girl. Please. I'm desperate.'

THREE

'Annie, wake up!'

At first, I think I'm dreaming, finally able to float on soft clouds of endless oblivion. After so long without the sweet relief of sleep, it's beautiful. I want to stay here, but the consistent yelling and panic jolts me awake.

I blink several times. My head is foggy. I don't know what day it is or where I am.

Lola stirs on my chest. My daughter, asleep on me? The memory weaves its way through my muddled mind. I was trying to console her. We must have both fallen asleep.

Startled, I look into my husband's urgent eyes. A dreadful odour fills my nostrils: an intense burning smell like charred toast. He smacks my shoulder. His usual placid features are alarmed with fear.

'Annie.' He grabs hold of me and pulls me out of the chair. 'Get Lola out of here. Go. Go.'

I glance behind me, confused. Crackling flames roar from one of the saucepans on the cooker. 'What happened?'

He wraps an arm around me and our baby, protecting us like a shield, as he marches us away from the fire and towards the small utility room on the other side of the kitchen. 'You must've left something on the cooker.' Max's eyes are wide with alarm or is that accusation? He tries to open the side door leading to a walkway to the back garden. It won't budge. He tugs hard, his face bright red. 'Where's the key?' he barks.

'The key?' I ask blankly.

'The key that opens this door. It's always in the lock.' He glances around despairingly. 'Think. What have you done with it?' He tugs at the door handle, a last frenzied attempt to free his family. 'Where's the key, Annie?'

'I can't remember touching any keys.' My voice is garbled, confused at the turn of events.

He gives me that look. The one he has thrown my way a lot lately – ever since Lola was born. 'Annie! We've got to get out of here,' he shouts. 'What have you done with the key?'

'I don't know.' I'm panicking now and, sensing the turmoil, Lola lets out an ear-splitting scream. I cringe as it thunders through me.

'Get with it.' Max grabs Lola from my arms and pushes me back into the kitchen.

My legs won't connect with my brain. Lola's wails are going right through me. The flames are getting bigger, roaring towards the ceiling.

'Move!' Max pushes me.

The smell is worsening. I remember now. I was cooking a chilli. Max's favourite dish, and the twins'. It's one of the few dishes I make that they collectively like. So the twins complain I make it too much. And, then, I sang to Lola and managed to get her to sleep, and I sat down to rest. But what happened to the key?

When we reach the front door, Max forces a screaming Lola back into my arms. 'Get out. Now.'

'You come, too,' I plead.

'I need to get the twins. And I need to put this fire out before the whole place burns down.'

'No, Max,' I scream. 'No. Call the fire brigade.'

He is insistent. 'Just get Lola out of here!' His pleading tone further scares our baby daughter. Her screams intensify, piercing through me. I follow his orders, stumbling to open the door. He yells up the stairs, 'Jasmine. Jacob.'

The weight of Lola feels like a barrel of bricks in my arms, and my legs are still so heavy and weak, as if they are about to buckle. I yank open the heavy front door to the frosty night. The chill bites into my skin. It's too cold for Lola out here. I cradle her in my arms, enshrouding her in my cardigan. She's still crying – angry tears. So many tears. So much anger.

I stand on the doorstep. My heart is pounding, pulsating in my head. I need to know if Max is OK. I flounder across the wet grass and around to the back of the house. Lola is still screaming. I hold her close to my chest, one arm wrapped around her, the other holding her head. 'It's going to be OK, baby girl,' I whisper, wondering who I'm trying to convince.

'Max!' My yells dissolve into the night air as I turn the corner, heading through the gate to the back garden. 'Max!'

When I reach the patio doors, my yells morph into wails. Inside, the flames lick at the sleeve of my husband's shirt as he whirls around in pain.

FOUR

Desperation shoots through me. This is all my fault. I bang on the glass door. 'Max!'

He drops a flaming tea towel onto the floor and urgently stamps on it. It flares up again, precariously close to his trouser leg.

Reversing my steps, I rush back to the front door and push it open, but stop. I can't take Lola back in there. But I need to make sure my husband is all right. I stare intently at my crying baby and make a rash decision. Taking her back into the house isn't an option. I struggle out of my cardigan and wrap it around her, tucking the sleeves behind her back.

Retrieving her car seat from inside the front door, I lower her in and leave the seat on the doorstep, wedged between the brick-work and an empty ceramic planter. It seems the logical place.

I rush into the house. The twins are now downstairs. One of them has located the fire extinguisher and set it on Max. Someone has dampened the fire with a saucepan lid.

'What the hell, Annie!' Jasmine shouts. 'You could've burned the house down.'

Three sets of eyes glare at me like embers from the fire.

Jasmine points a finger of accusation in my direction. 'You could've got us all killed.'

I ignore my stepdaughter and stare at Max as he asks, 'Where's Lola?'

I wish sometimes he would defend me against his daughter. 'I left her outside.'

Max looks at me as if I'm mad. 'Outside? Where?' He storms past me.

'I couldn't bring her back in here.' I grab his arm as he passes. 'On the doorstep. She's safe. I'll get her.' But he is too quick for me. He's gone. 'Max, I'll get her.' I try to catch up with him, but my weakened legs won't move at his speed.

He reaches Lola before me. Scooping her up, he kisses her forehead. 'You didn't buckle her in.'

'I did.'

Didn't I? I don't know. This has become the norm, not knowing what I've done from one moment to the next. Mummy mind – that's what the other mums in the baby and toddler group call it. The temporary fogginess while my brain readjusts and adapts to my new reality: a constantly crying baby and a painfully endless lack of sleep. It's a killer. It's been four months now – hardly temporary. Four months of barely sleeping. It's hell. Pure hell.

Two figures appear, a sense of urgency in their countenance. It's two of the builders working on the renovations to the back of the house. 'What's happening, Mrs C?' asks Jigsaw, a name he earned after a carpentry accident that left his left hand without a middle finger.

'We've had a fire.' My frantic breaths fog the evening air.

'We saw through the doors,' says Cameron in his casual American accent.

I study my daughter's face as her wails soften to low moans.

I could swear I buckled her in. The cold, as well as the shock, sends shivers through me.

'Let's get you two back inside.' Max places a silent Lola over his shoulder. 'We need to get you warm.' Lines of worry that never existed when we met crease his forehead.

'Do you need a hand?' Cameron asks.

'We've got it under control,' Max says. 'Thanks, anyway.'

'We were just about to call it a day,' Jigsaw says. 'We've finally finished levelling the floor and have had to put out heaters to help the concrete dry. Otherwise it won't be ready in time for the floor layer. You can leave them on overnight. They shouldn't cause you any problems.'

'Is it safe to go back in?' I ask Max once the builders have gone. I don't know what else to say. This is all my fault. But I can't remember leaving that saucepan on. I must have, I know. But it doesn't make sense. I think back over the evening, but a familiar fog of confusion descends upon me. Max called to say he was going to be late home... again. And I turned the cooker to low, thinking the chilli would be cooked by the time he got home and all I'd need to do was cook the rice. The rice. I can't remember what I did with the rice.

'I don't think we should take her back in there.' Max puts his hands over our daughter's head. 'The room needs airing.'

I hold out my arms. 'I'll put her to bed.'

He manoeuvres his body towards the staircase, dodging my outstretched arms. 'It's all right. I'll take her up.'

He carefully climbs the dark oak staircase, rocking our baby girl in his arms. His voice softens as he turns to look at me. 'Why don't you order a takeaway, darling?'

'What do you fancy?'

'I don't mind,' he whispers. 'You choose. And see if you can find the keys and open the kitchen doors, can you? And all the windows. The place will stink for weeks if we don't give it a proper airing.'

In the kitchen, Jasmine and Jacob's heads are lost in the fridge, debating what to eat. The charred waft of burnt food lingers in the air, bitter and acrid like a pile of fresh ashes. I pick up Max's suit jacket from the floor, staring at the cooker with not one but two saucepans, both with their lids on. That's right, I left a lid on the chilli. I think I did, anyway. I rub my forehead. Oh, I don't know. I'm so bone-weary, it's all a blur. Everything around me appears twisted and contorted. I clutch my stomach. It's those cramps again. The ones that have regularly troubled me since my caesarean, not that the medical experts can find anything wrong.

Gingerly, I lift the lid of the other pan, releasing another waft of rancid odour. Burnt rice that caused the fire. But I can't remember even putting the rice on. I think I filled the saucepan with water. I look towards the sink. The strainer I used to wash and drain the rice is balanced across the half bowl, empty.

I must have started to cook the rice before I fell asleep.

But I could swear I didn't.

I need to get some air in here. I walk towards the doors that open onto a patio which stretches across to where the living room now joins the old extension.

But the key isn't in this lock, either.

FIVE

'Jasmine, Jacob? Have you seen the key to this door?' I'm growing more anxious. I have to know what happened to the keys.

My stepchildren turn in unison from the fridge. With Jasmine's dark bob and Jacob's black curls, it's hard to believe they're twins. Although similar in build, slight and slender, Jasmine appears taller than her brother because of his stoop. Jasmine places her hands on her skinny hips. Her blue eyes glare at me in disdain. 'Why would we touch the keys?' She pulls a packet of fresh penne from the fridge. 'I'll cook some pasta.'

I hold up a hand. 'I'm going to order a takeaway. Chinese?'

'Pizza,' she says.

'We had pizza last week.'

Jacob lowers his head, his curtain of curls falling across his face.

'Whatever.' She tosses the packet of pasta back into the fridge. 'I've got homework to do.'

Jacob follows Jasmine out of the room. I step to the door. Jasmine heads for the stairs, but Jacob wanders to the living room and over to the mini grand piano that once belonged to his mother. He lifts the lid and settles on the black stool. His fingers strike a set of chords. I shudder. He's a gifted lad. A talent passed down from his mother, who was a concert pianist. She played at venues around the world until the twins were born. And apart from a few snippets I've gained from the twins, I know very little else about her as Max doesn't like talking about her. This house is a shrine to her memory, though. I often feel I'm living in her shadow. The shadow of the woman they all deeply adored.

My phone rings. I take it out of my back pocket. It's my sister. 'Have you done it yet?' Samantha asks.

Jacob's fingers stomp along the keys of the piano as if he's angry.

'I can't talk at the moment.'

'You promised me.'

'I'll call you back later,' I whisper.

Jacob plays as if he has some kind of superpower. I used to find his performances mesmerising. His fingers glide along the keys in an almost feminine way – simply magical to watch. But since Lola was born, he has taken to playing dark and moody pieces, thumping the keys as if he is testing how far he can go before he breaks them.

Max's suit jacket dangles from my hand. I drape it over a stool at the breakfast bar as my stomach cramps. I stagger to the armchair by the patio doors and sit down, bent over double. The sound of the piano grows louder and louder.

I lift my head and lock my gaze onto the cooker as I try to work out what I did with the rice and the keys. But my thoughts are so jumbled, like a complicated puzzle with missing pieces. I pick up the photo of me and Max at our wedding that sits on the pedestal side table. We were so happy that day. I run my finger over the cold glass, touching his face, thinking about our whirl-wind affair.

We met in August last year at my sister's wedding. Along with Sean, the three of them own a software company they are in the final stages of selling to an American corporation. That wedding was a massive turning point in my life. Samantha sat me between Max and Sean's wife, Nisha, who has become a close friend.

Samantha denies she had any intention of trying to match Max and me, but as soon as I sat down, sparks flew between us like fireworks. A week later, he invited me for dinner and life as I knew it became a distant memory. We fell deeply in love. Then I discovered I was pregnant. Unplanned, of course. The result of an unlucky condom. Max moved me into his family home, this imposing Victorian double-fronted house with an in-out drive and a muddled layout which confuses me even now.

Sometimes, I wish we could rewind to our pre-wedding days. I was so ecstatically happy. The future was bright. I had the man of my dreams, and the baby I hadn't known I wanted was on the way. Max was as happy as me then. I know he was.

But as soon as I moved in, the twins kicked up a stink, making me feel like an interloper. Lola arrived, and an offer came in for Max's business. He changed. And so did my sister.

SIX

Max's reflection appears in the glass of the patio doors, startling me. He has changed into a pair of black jeans and a black long-sleeved top. He picks up his jacket from the stool. 'I'll have to chuck this out. My best suit, too.' He walks over to me, rests a hand on my shoulder and kisses me. 'What have you done with all the keys, Annie?'

I spin around to face him. 'I haven't touched them. Honestly, Max. I haven't.'

He rummages through the junk drawer by the kitchen sink, pulling out various items and tossing them on the kitchen counter. 'There's a spare set in here somewhere. Here we go.' He jingles a set of keys, holding them in my line of vision. 'I'm going to get another set cut.'

'I'll do it. I need to go shopping tomorrow,' I offer.

He snaps the keys in his hand as if he's playing a castanet. 'It's fine. I can pop out at lunchtime.' He marches across to the patio doors, opens them and flings his jacket outside. He walks around opening the windows, letting in the cold winter air and dispersing the smell of acrid smoke. 'What did you order?'

'Order?' I'm confused.

'Takeaway. You were going to order a takeaway, darling.'

'I thought I'd wait for you,' I lie. Something I seem to be doing more and more these days. I hate myself for it, but I can't admit I haven't even been able to perform the simple task of ordering dinner yet.

'I said I don't mind.' His phone buzzes. He slips it out of his pocket, takes a look and quickly puts it away.

'The twins want pizza,' I say.

'Pizza it is, then.'

Sighing, I find the Domino's app on my phone. I navigate the screens and order three large pizzas. I'll stick with the salad I made earlier. I'm still trying to shred the stubborn extra weight I gained during pregnancy.

Max checks the baby monitor on the side of the worktop before heading to the fridge. He opens the door and pulls out a beer. 'Do you want a drink?'

I shouldn't. My head is thumping. But I need something to calm my nerves. I open my mouth to ask for a glass of wine but he holds up a bottle of Chardonnay. It's half empty. 'Crikey, Annie. Did you drink all this tonight?'

I look from him to the bottle, confused. 'No, I didn't! ' Rewind to before I fell pregnant with Lola, and I wouldn't have thought twice about polishing off a bottle of wine with a friend when I fancied it. But I rarely touch alcohol any more. 'I was drinking a vitamin juice,' I say.

He throws me a look. A familiar one that questions whether he believes me or not.

'I'll have a glass of water,' I say.

'Have you seen the ceiling?'

My eyes follow his to where flames have browned the white paint. It could've been worse. A lot worse. The jarring sound from the piano grows louder. It's too much. My voice wobbles. 'I'm sorry.' I can't remember feeling so miserable in my life.

'Come on.' He places an arm around my shoulders.

My heart aches. We used to get on so well. But ever since Lola arrived, it's as if I've lost a piece of him to her. A piece that grows bigger and bigger as each dawn turns to dusk. I thought it was meant to be the other way around – men are the ones made to feel left out when their partners have a baby.

I never felt the gravitational pull towards motherhood I'd often heard other women describe. With friends aplenty and my thriving online clothing business, my life was full. Max said he didn't want more children, either. The twins were enough for him. And anyway, he was too old to be a father again, he said when we had *the talk* shortly after we met when we both knew we were for keeps. We firmly agreed kids of our own didn't feature in our future plans.

But then I fell pregnant, and I changed. Maybe it was because of my age, or because I'd finally met the man of my dreams. But I knew without a single doubt that I wanted the baby growing inside of me. And once Max found out, he came around without a fuss.

He squeezes my shoulder. 'Let's go to my office.'

I don't want to go to his office. It's always cold in there. I'd rather go to the living room, but with the racket Jacob is making we won't stand a chance in hell of hearing each other. 'Let's stay here.' Even with the doors and windows open, it's warmer in here than in his office. I pull out two stools from the breakfast bar.

Max hands me a glass of water and sits down, staring at his bottle of Bud. He takes a deep breath, his voice soft. 'What happened, then, darling?'

I shrug.

'I need to know, Annie. You could've killed both of you. And the twins.'

My bottom lip trembles. I want to cry out in frustration. He doesn't know how it feels to be bone-tired every minute of every day. I haven't had more than three consecutive hours of sleep since I was seven months pregnant. It could be even longer. 'I don't remember putting the rice on. I must've nodded off.'

Jacob's piano playing grows louder until it reaches a crescendo of intolerable notes.

'I'm sorry.'

I want to share my frustrations with him. The fear that has been growing in me. I didn't notice it at first. The minuscule seed his children planted the day I moved in was way too tiny for the human eye. But they have watered and nurtured it, and now I can see its ugly thorns of death. But what I can't determine is whether it's him or her – Jacob or Jasmine? Or perhaps it's both of them.

All I know is they want me to suffer.

And I'd go as far as to say, they would happily see me dead.

SEVEN

Max takes my hand. 'I think the time has come, Annie, don't you?'

I sigh. Not this discussion again.

He squeezes my fingers. 'It's nothing to be ashamed of, darling. People get depressed. Lots of people go to therapy. Phil's wife saw a counsellor after their youngest was born. She had postnatal depression, too.'

But it was Phil and Susie's sixth child. Susie had the right to be tired and grumpy and to walk around with a thunderous scowl on her usually perfect face.

I drop my head. I hate those two words used together. Postnatal depression. They sound wrong, as if they're a punishment from mothers who can't have children – like my sister. But I hate them more when my husband says them because they don't apply to me.

I'm not depressed. I've looked up this disorder, this condition, read every article I've come across. I even completed an online questionnaire. Yes, I'm tired. Who wouldn't be in my circumstances? The sleep deprivation of motherhood is a silent destroyer of any new mum's sanity and emotions. Everyone knows that. And I haven't bonded with my daughter. Well, maybe I have. I love her. I know that. And I'd never do anything to hurt her, but I don't feel the closeness I've read so much about – the strong attachment and warm glow whenever I look at her. But I'm not sad. I'm far too damn tired to be sad.

'Perhaps I can get you an appointment. I'll speak to Phil,' Max says, touching my face.

'No.' I'm adamant. 'I just need some sleep.'

'Then we need to hire some help.'

'We've had this discussion, Max. I can't have anyone else in this house. They'd just get in the way.' Enough people are doing that already what with him holding business meetings here, and the kids' friends and the bloody builders in and out all the time.

'You need help, darling. We need help. It'll only be a short-term solution until you get back on your feet. And to help you while I'm away next week.'

My silence conveys my reluctance. I know what he's thinking. He's worried about leaving me on my own when he flies out to Los Angeles to iron out the final details of the sale of his business.

I tear my hand from his grip and grab a bunch of my blonde hair, suppressing the urge to scream and shout at him. His constant suggestions of getting more help are driving me crazy. He even suggested a local nursery he'd looked into. Before Lola was born, he never interfered in what I did. He just let me get on with things. But lately, he seems to be making all the decisions. He has changed. But then I guess I've changed, too. That's what having a baby does to a couple. Especially one who doesn't sleep and constantly cries all the time. 'We just need to get through this rocky patch.'

'You can't work and look after a baby. It's impossible,' he says. 'And it's not good for you, darling.'

I had planned on taking six months' maternity leave. Everything was meticulously arranged. But I didn't even get a month.

When Lola was three weeks and five days old, the woman I employed to step into my business shoes didn't turn up. I couldn't get hold of her for three days. And then all I got was an email saying she was dreadfully sorry, she loved working for me, but she'd had a family emergency and wouldn't be coming back. I had no option but to return to my business, albeit on reduced hours.

'I just need some sleep.' The broken record keeps on playing.

Max sips his beer. 'Why don't I do the night feed tonight?' His voice is gentle, a solace in the chaos of parenthood. That's what attracted me to him in the first place. He has this soft, reassuring lull to his voice that makes me feel safe.

'What's the point? I'll still wake up, and then we'll both suffer,' I say.

He needs his sleep, too. I get that. He's got enough of his own stresses. The house renovations were meant to be finished by the time Lola was born. As soon as I fell pregnant, and he had got down on one knee with a beautiful diamond, he pulled out the plans he and his first wife had drawn up to renovate the house ready for the big family they'd planned to have. Within days of his proposal, he'd arranged for contractors to quote for the work. That's Max all over: super-efficient and super-organised… exactly how I used to be.

I'd have preferred to move. Get a place we could call our own. But he said he couldn't uproot the twins at such a crucial stage of their schooling. They were born in this house. By the end of the following week, he'd secured a firm of builders that started two weeks later. But then it all went terribly wrong. The company went into liquidation, delaying the start of the project by four months as Max struggled to source another set of reliable builders at a reasonable cost. He's still trying to recoup the fifty per cent deposit he paid to the original firm.

'The point is, darling, you could've died tonight. And I need to make sure it doesn't happen again. I love you all so much. I've been speaking to Cameron. He knows someone who is looking for some part-time work. Zoe, I think he said her name was. I'll arrange for her to come and meet us.'

He rattles on, but I'm not listening. I stand. I need to get out of here.

'And what's with the keys?' he says.

'Keys?'

He gives me a disapproving frown. 'What happened to the keys, Annie? Why are none of them in the doors? We always keep them in the locks.' He points to the cooker. 'For this very reason.'

I'm at a loss. 'I don't know.'

'I asked Jasmine and Jacob, and they haven't touched them,' he says. 'Wait a moment!' He pushes the stool away from the breakfast bar. It topples over with a loud crash, but he doesn't pick it up. He marches to the pedestal table where the photo of us on our wedding day sits, and beside it is the unsightly silver trinket pot shaped like a bird that was a wedding present from his parents. The lid sits askew. He picks it up. My mind is in overdrive as he picks up not only my car keys, but the keys to all the doors as well.

I must've put my car keys in there. But I don't remember doing that. And more importantly, I can't for the life of me explain why I would.

Max rejoins me and picks up the stool. He slides an arm around my middle, his breath in my ear. He kisses the side of my head. 'We need to do something, darling. We can't carry on like this.'

EIGHT

I turn into Bower Street, a quaint tree-lined avenue where my sister lives in a beautiful three-bedroom ground-floor apartment with her husband, Ezra. I tug Lola's car seat out of the car. It's an arduous task. The buckle catches. The belt gets caught. Everything's a struggle.

Samantha's working from home today, as she has done most days this past month since the company offices were flooded after someone left a tap running in the kitchen. The sink was blocked with leftover pasta, and the water flowed like a river across the majority of the ground floor. Another stress that has affected Max. They had to find temporary accommodation for their twenty workers, which proved difficult. Max searched high and low, but ultimately, they had to settle for premises that can't accommodate individual offices for the three business partners.

A gust of wind blows Samantha's red, untamed hair around her face in wild waves when she opens the door. She's a slender woman, her delicate build as graceful and composed as a Russian ballerina. Ever since we were kids I've felt like a large sack of potatoes beside her. Even more so since giving birth.

She kisses me. I love my sister. We've always been close. She knows everything about me. Everything! She reaches out, her thin lips broadening as she takes Lola from me. 'Now, now. Come and tell Aunty Samantha all about it,' she coos, gently tapping Lola's button nose with her bony finger.

My sister adores Lola. She treats her as if she's the baby she's never been able to conceive. After several gruelling rounds of medical evaluations at the beginning of the year, they discovered Ezra was infertile. She has silently struggled ever since, especially after Lola came along and turned her nightmare – what she'd never be: a mother – into a reality.

I step inside, savouring the familiar scent of the orange blossom potpourri she loves so much. There's something different about her today. I can't quite figure it out. Being a redhead, her complexion is usually pale, but today she looks completely wrung out. And she appears a little gaunt, as if she has skipped a few meals her skinny frame can't afford to miss. 'What've you been up to?' she asks. 'Anything exciting?'

Exciting? I remove my boots. There hasn't been any excitement in my life for a long time. Unless you'd call causing a house fire exciting. Before I met Max, my life was full of excitement – girlie weekends away, exotic holidays, and lazy Sunday brunches with friends. Not that I'd have it any other way. But however hard I try, the days looking after a crying baby are long and demanding. Any new mum would agree. It's practically impossible to make them sound interesting. I push these thoughts aside. They make the mother guilt even more pronounced.

I was told things would get easier as the weeks passed. My baby would get into a schedule. Righteous mums in the baby and toddler group report their feeding schedules are under control. They are breastfeeding with ease, and their babies' bedtimes have shifted earlier, they tell me as I stifle yawns at the mundane exchange. Smug-faced others claim they've cracked the sleep cycles, and their babies are now sleeping through the night. So how has the super-efficient, super-organised Annie, rarely frazzled by life's unforeseen twists and turns, made such a mess of things? Lola rarely sleeps, and her feeding regime is erratic.

'Did you hear me?' Samantha clicks her fingers. 'Earth to Annie.'

I turn to her.

'I asked what you've been up to?'

'Same old, same old!'

'Coffee?' she asks.

'Of course.'

I follow her along the narrow passageway, where vibrant artwork adds riots of colour to the otherwise whitewashed walls. It's such a contrast to the gloomy hallway of Max's house. I still do that – call it Max's house. It's become the norm. Perhaps it'll be different after the renovations are completed. We will all have more space to breathe downstairs. Lola will get a playroom, and me my own office. This means the twins will get back their den at the bottom of the garden – a large wooden structure they used to hang out in with their friends that I'm currently using to run my business. I can put my own stamp on it all. My thoughts drift to the décor I've already chosen for each room. The bright, light colours and furnishings which will bring the living space to life.

Samantha leads me into the kitchen, an extension of the minimalist hallway, where the only items on the white marble kitchen counter are a kettle and a vase adorned with red roses and stems of eucalyptus.

'Tell me more about Isabella.'

She raises her eyebrows. 'Where the hell did that come from?'

'I don't know. Max never wants to talk about her.'

'She was a lovely woman.' My sister pokes my shoulder and gives me a loving smile. 'But not as lovely as you, of course.'

'He never talks about her, or how she died.' When I fell pregnant, and Max invited me to move into his home, I didn't think it would bother me that he'd once shared it with another woman. Isabella had been dead eight years. But with her memories still very much alive through her children, it has troubled me more than I thought.

'I guess he finds it too difficult.'

'I'm wondering if, when the twins leave for uni, we should get a place of our own. With the sale of the business and the equity I have from my apartment, we could afford somewhere pretty decent. But Max isn't keen.'

'Why?'

'It's complicated. He says they'll be back during their holidays and is worried that if we move, they won't feel like it's their home and will never come back.'

'I guess that's reasonable. They're still so young. Max told me about the fire,' she says as if she wants to change the subject. It's great that my sister and husband are close, but it annoys me when they discuss me. They are so close that I've wondered a couple of times if they ever had a fling between his first wife dying and her meeting Ezra. Something she denied when I asked her after too many cocktails on one of our girlie weekends away. But it left me wondering.

'Nice roses. Ezra?' I ask, knowing the answer will be yes. Ezra adores her with every cell of his gym-loving body.

She nods as she places a capsule in the Nespresso machine. It lets out a low, steady hum as it heats up. 'What did you do?' she asks.

'Sorry?'

'The fire. What happened?'

I roll my eyes and relay the evening. 'Max came home and found us just as the flames started to get out of control.'

Lola giggles as Samantha blows raspberries into the crook of her neck. 'That must've been frightening.'

'It was. But what's more frightening is I have no recollection of putting the rice on. The other thing I don't remember is drinking nearly half a bottle of wine, which apparently I did because Max found the evidence in the fridge. I swear I didn't touch it.' I pause, wondering if it was Jasmine who drank it. But she never appeared even the slightest tipsy. I tell Samantha about the keys.

'You're exhausted, Annie. Exhaustion can play dreadful tricks on our minds.'

'How's Katerina?' I ask. Katerina is a friend of hers from school who also had a baby recently.

'All good,' she says. 'Poppy's sleeping through the night.'

See what I mean!

'So have you done it yet?' she asks.

I bite my lip. I should never have shared my deepest, darkest secret with my sister. I should've kept it to myself. 'I—'

We turn to the front door opening.

'I'm home.'

Ezra's broad frame enters the kitchen. He drops a sports bag by the door. He's a tall guy with striking eyes the colour of mint, and a well-defined jawline you see on men in the pictures of glossy magazines. Marry that with an incredibly kind heart, and my sister always said she'd won the jackpot when he decided she was the one for him. I've grown to love him as much as I love her.

'You're home early,' I say.

'Late, actually. I was on nights.'

'They work you far too hard,' I say.

'That's the price you pay for being a doctor.' He kisses Samantha on the lips before pecking me on the cheek. 'I'm off for a shower.'

I take our coffees, and Samantha takes Lola, to the living

room, a large, uncluttered room that overlooks the small garden and the woods beyond. I sink into the soft sofa, thinking back to the flat I owned before I met Max. Although smaller, it was similar to this one.

Samantha sits down. Her legs bounce rapidly. A sign something is bothering her. It's a habit she's had since we were kids. But Lola seems to enjoy it. 'You look troubled, sis.'

'I thought the same about you,' I say.

'I'm fine. What's up with you?'

'If I tell you something, will you promise not to tell Max?' I say.

'Sure.'

'I think it was one of the twins. They started the fire.'

NINE

Samantha stops bouncing Lola. 'Wow. That's a dreadful accusation.'

'You mustn't repeat that to anyone.'

Her faint eyebrows furrow. 'Of course not.'

'And I think they hid the keys so I couldn't get out.'

'Which one of them?'

I shrug. 'I don't know.' My voice trembles. I shouldn't have revealed my fears about them to her. As much as we love each other, she is Max's business partner. They've known each other for years. 'All I know is, I don't trust either of them.'

'Oh, Annie. I know they can be difficult. It's their age. And it's a challenging situation. But they're not evil. What makes you think they'd start a fire?'

'They hate me, that's for sure.'

She shakes her head. 'I don't think that's true.'

'You're wrong. I see it in the way Jasmine looks at me. Jacob, not so much. He scares me in different ways.' I scoff. 'He can't even look me in the eye.'

'He can't look many people in the eye. He's been that way for as long as I've known him.'

'But I've been living with them for a year now. And it's not like I broke up their parents' marriage.' I sigh heavily. 'I've tried so hard with them, but they treat me like crap when Max isn't around. Especially Jasmine.'

I fix my gaze onto the plant beside the sofa. Some of the leaves are withered. It's not like my sister to have neglected one of her many plants that adorn the place like jewels. Some of the leaves have turned brown. That's how I feel – wilted and weathered and thoroughly browned off.

Samantha continues. 'I'm not sticking up for them. Not at all. But, please, put yourself in their shoes. All they'd ever known was life with their mum and dad. And then their mum dies, and it's just the three of them for eight years. Then he meets a woman. Three months later, she's pregnant, and he's moved her in. And then a baby appears. Crikey, that's a lot for someone to take on. Especially a teenager.'

My sister. Forever the voice of reason.

'I hear you. And I feel for them at times, but... but... I'm concerned. They want me out of the way.' I rub my forehead. Now I'm saying it out loud, I sound like the crazy, delusional woman Jasmine told Max I was during a heated argument one night when they didn't know I was listening.

'Annie. That's not true. It's just been difficult for them. It's their age, too. All teenagers give their parents a hard time in one way or another. It comes as part of the package.'

Tears prick my eyes, but I refuse to let them fall. 'I think there's something physically wrong with me.'

'What?'

I shrug. 'I don't know. Most nights when I finally get some sleep, I keep having nightmares about the birth and... and about someone trying to kill me.' I tell her about the figure that regularly appears in my dreams lately, when I finally manage to get some sleep. It lurks in the shadows. Their face, an apparition of familiarity I can't place, is too fuzzy for me to see it clearly, blurring into the darkness like the light on a winter's afternoon.

'Annie!' She places my contented daughter in the crook of her arm and shuffles along the sofa closer to me. Her lips twist to the side. 'Do you think, perhaps it'd be a good idea to go and see someone?'

A swell of irritation surges through me. 'You know I spoke to the consultant about how I felt when I went back for my check-up. He ordered that extra scan. Everything has healed nicely. There's nothing wrong with me.'

Visions of the birth flash through my mind. The hell I went through when they couldn't get Lola out and the complications began. The signs of distress she was displaying. An irregular heart rate pattern, the midwife told me. Within half an hour, they'd whisked me into theatre, cut me open and ripped her out. I never knew anything about it until I woke up. And when the drugs wore off, the pain was so excruciating, I thought I was going to die. It was only when my temperature hit the high thirties that prompted a follow-up scan did they realise why. The surgical team had left part of the placenta in. They waited for it to pass naturally. It took four days.

It was my punishment, I told myself. Retribution for what I'd done. I cried for days.

'Annie, are you listening?' Samantha waves a hand in my face.

'Sorry?'

'You were miles away. I said, I was thinking you might see a therapist, perhaps?'

'You sound like Max. Have you two been discussing me?'

'He's worried about you, sis. So am I, especially after what you've just told me. Those dreams sound harrowing.'

She doesn't believe a word I've just told her.

And if she doesn't believe me, no one will.

TEN

I yawn, staring at my phone, frustrated because I can't remember why I picked it up. It was something to do with Lola, I think, but as much as I search my thoughts, I can't make sense of them. It has been like this constantly since Lola arrived as one day blurs into the next.

Max raises his voice. 'Annie! Did you hear me, darling? Bottle.'

I turn to where he's sitting at the breakfast bar, scrolling through his phone with one hand while holding a cranky Lola in the other. Jasmine is watching something on her iPad, while eating a bagel. Jacob is in the living room, thrashing out a tune on the piano. The noise is deafening, even from here in the kitchen.

Max's phone pings. He stops scrolling and glances from the screen to me as if he's checking I'm looking. 'I said if you get me her bottle I'll feed her.'

'Who's that?' I ask.

'Just work.' He locks the phone and turns his full attention to our daughter. 'I'll deal with it later.'

I open the fridge door. The smell of meat from last night's

pizza makes me gag. Every evening, I make up six bottles and store them on the top shelf at the back of the fridge for the following twenty-four hours. I made up six yesterday, I'm sure I did – just before I started cooking the chilli. There should still be one remaining. I shift the packaged items and dishes of leftover food around but can't find a bottle. I must have only made up five yesterday. But that's crazy. Perhaps I've already given her another bottle. But I can barely get her to finish the six I make. I search again. 'I haven't got one made up.'

'Why not? You always make enough to last until this feed.' Max tries to disguise the hint of irritation in his voice with a fake smile.

I recheck the fridge. Just to make sure the remaining bottle has not been moved to another shelf. Lola's irritability morphs to angry cries. 'I'll have to make up another one.'

'That'll take ages.' Max tries to console our daughter. 'She's hungry now.'

'I don't know what's happened.' A sense of unease passes through me. Exasperated, I check the steriliser. All six bottles are rinsed and waiting to go. It doesn't make sense. I turn the machine on.

'Be as quick as you can, darling.' Max rocks Lola and starts pacing the kitchen.

Flicking the kettle switch, I open the cupboard and grab a tin of formula. The crescendo of Lola's wailing reaches a new level, a fever pitch competing successfully with her brother playing the piano. It goes right through me.

There's a knock at the front door. Jacob stops playing the piano.

'That's probably Zoe.' Max repositions Lola, trying to comfort her, holding her back against his chest and wrapping his strong arms around her.

'Zoe?' I say.

Lola's face scrunches up into a ball of redness. She emits a shrill cry that shreds my nerves to pieces.

Max jigs her up and down as he heads to the kitchen door. 'The friend Cameron recommended. She's come to meet us.'

'Wait!' I stare at him, confused. 'Since when did I agree to this?'

'I told you yesterday that she's coming to talk to us today. I knew you weren't listening. She's looking for some part-time work until she goes travelling. I've checked her out. She has some fantastic references.'

'You're making decisions without me.'

'I'm not. I discussed it with you last night. Jeez, Annie. Give me a break. I'm just trying to do right by my family.'

I cringe as Lola lets out an ear-splitting mother of all screams.

He steps backwards until he's standing beside me. Lowering his voice, he rubs his thumb along my cheek. 'You need some help, darling.' He turns to the door. 'We all need some help,' he calls over his shoulder as he leaves the room with our shrieking baby.

Anger rages inside of me, reaching boiling point like the water in the kettle. Robotically, I make up a bottle of milk and rotate it under the cold water tap.

Max returns. 'Zoe, meet my wife, Annie.'

Forcing a smile, I turn to a fresh-faced, brown-eyed young woman, around mid-twenties, with blonde shoulder-length hair. She is casually dressed in leggings and an oversized shocking pink sweater. It could be a younger version of myself standing there. It's chilling yet comforting in a sombre kind of way.

'Hey there, Annie. Nice to meet you.' Raising a hand, Zoe gives a quick wave before turning to Max. 'Here, let me.' She tucks her hair behind her ears, and I notice a large mole by her left lobe. I've always wondered why they call them beauty spots, and now I understand. It adds to her attractiveness.

She takes Lola from Max as fluidly as if she were her own.

Lola immediately stops crying as this stranger carefully lays our baby over her forearm and lightly pats her back. A blanket of peace descends like I've been at a noisy party and walked outside for some fresh air.

Max and I exchange looks. He jolts his chin forward and grins.

'Here, I've got this. Let me feed her for you.' Zoe holds out her hand, as if it's a given I'll say yes. She speaks with a gentle American accent that has a calming effect. The voice of an angel in the chaos of our family life.

I hand over the bottle, momentarily entranced by this heavenly appearance.

She smiles sweetly. 'Have you checked it's the right temperature?'

'No. Not yet,' I say.

She repositions Lola over her shoulder, and, removing the lid from the bottle, shakes a few drops onto the inside of her wrist. 'Yikes. I think that's too hot.'

'Annie!' Max says. He takes the bottle from Zoe. 'Let me.' He runs it under the cold tap, making idle chit-chat while I stand looking on in silence.

He hands the bottle back to her. In a swift, smooth movement, Lola is lodged in the crook of her arm and hungrily imbibing her supper.

'Wow!' Max lets out a large breath. 'You're hired.'

ELEVEN

Zoe laughs.

I glare at Max. 'Why don't you tell us more about yourself?' I say to Zoe. 'Where have you worked before?'

'Did you manage to check out my résumé?' She glances from me to Max, competently feeding Lola as if my baby is her own.

'Annie hasn't had a chance to read it yet,' Max interrupts. 'But I have. Why don't we go into the living room, and we can chat.'

'I'll make some drinks,' I say. 'Tea?'

They both nod. Max leads her out of the room.

I prepare three cups, trying to disregard the deep sense of unease sloshing about in my stomach. Max doesn't get it. I don't want anyone else looking after my baby. As much as I'd like the chance to breathe, leaving Lola with a stranger doesn't sit comfortably with me. I'm never going to have another baby. The fear that still lives within me that she wasn't going to make it, and the complications afterwards when they left part of the placenta in me, put paid to that. The least I can do is rear the one I've been blessed with.

My sister would die to be in my position with a baby of her own.

When I take the drinks to the living room, Max and Zoe are casually chatting on the sofa with their backs to me as she feeds our baby. I stand at the door. It all looks so comfortable. As if she has been a feature in our lives forever. But that's Max all over. He has the charm and that rare ability to coerce the shyest of people to venture out of their shells.

'So you could potentially work with us for a few months,' Max says.

'Until March,' Zoe replies in her lyrical accent. A voice that would make you want to fall asleep if you were listening to an audiobook she was narrating.

'That could work until we find someone more permanent.'

More permanent. What is he on about? We haven't discussed anything temporary yet, let alone more permanent.

A fleeting thought passes through my mind. One I've been thinking a lot these past few weeks. That he thinks I'm not capable of looking after our daughter.

Or perhaps he has invited this young woman into our house to spy on me. It's irrational, but I can't help the thoughts passing through my mind.

'Let's wait until Annie is here.' Max turns as if he is about to call me. Those beautiful blue eyes smile lovingly at me. 'There you are, darling.'

Walking around the sofa, I set the tray onto the bevelled glass-topped coffee table. One of the few pieces of furniture I insisted on bringing with me when I moved here. I think about my old apartment. The always-tidy, large, two-bedroom apartment, overlooking the river I had all to myself. Now I share a house with four others. It's stifling.

'Give her to me while you have your drink.' I hold out my arms to take my baby.

'You're good. Just sit back and relax.' Zoe glances at Lola, feeding contently, and smiles. 'I'll grab my drink when this little one's done with hers.'

Seeing her with Lola heightens my unease. Maybe I'm just being paranoid because someone new is holding my baby, but I really don't like it. I sit on the edge of the sofa opposite her, one eye on my drink, the other on her. She is staring at the décor on top of the mini grand – a display of photos, mainly of the twins with their mum. There's one of the four of them on a beach, a perfect photo detailing an azure blue sky and radiant sunshine. When I moved in, Max asked me if I wanted him to take them all down, but it felt mean. I understood she was the twins' mother and how that would affect them.

'Say, you've a wonderful house here. You must love it. So much character!'

'So tell us about yourself,' I say, catching Max beaming.

'I live in Pasadena.'

'Who with?' I ask.

'Alone,' she replies, a glint of sadness in her eyes. 'My mother passed away earlier this year.'

'I'm sorry to hear that,' I say.

'It's been tough, which is why I decided to do some travelling.'

There's an awkward silence before Max swiftly moves the conversation forward. 'Why don't you tell Annie about some of the families you've worked for.'

I still don't like the way she looks so comfortable with my baby. She reels off a list detailing the names and ages of the children she has looked after, from newborns to teens. 'All of the families will give me a reference. I'm certain of that. The problem is' – she glances at Max – 'as I mentioned on the phone, I don't have a visa, so I can only be paid in cash.'

'Sure.' Max nods and smiles. 'That won't be a problem.'

I wring my hands. He's talking as if we've already hired her.

'And also' – she glances from Max to me – 'I explained to

Max on the phone, it would only be a part-time position as I want to travel around the UK while I'm here.'

'How part-time?' Max asks.

'Ideally, I only want to work three days a week. Monday to Wednesday. Or Tuesday to Thursday, perhaps, but I can be flexible if you need me more some weeks. And I can stay for a few hours' trial now if you like.' She turns to me. 'Max told me you've started back at work already. What do you do?'

As Lola happily drinks her milk, I tell her about my small online clothing business, selling timeless neutral clothing for women, and Max tells her about his much bigger software company that he is selling.

Zoe tells us more about the families she has worked for. I watch her. There's something comforting about the way she handles Lola, I must admit. Perhaps Max is right. Having an extra pair of hands could help me get my life back in some kind of order.

When Lola has finished feeding, Zoe places the empty bottle on the tray. 'Do you want to take her now?' she asks me.

I hold out my arms. But as soon as I take my baby, she screeches. Max gets up, taking control. He sweeps Lola from my arms. 'Zoe, would you look after her for five minutes while Annie and I have a chat?'

Before I have the chance to protest, Max is leading me along the hallway towards his office to the sound of Zoe singing to our daughter.

* * *

'Let's have a quick word about this.' Max closes the door. 'I don't think we'll get better than her. Do you like her? You must.'

'I don't know. I need time to think about it.'

I look around his perfectly tidy office. It's totally opposite to the pigsty the rest of the house resembles. It's a large room, painted a dark shade of grey, and it smells woody, like autumn leaves. His desk is situated in the turret facing the driveway. Our friend Nisha, who adopts the rules of feng shui, told him it's bad luck to have your back to the door in an office. It clogs the flow of energy. But he laughed and said he likes to overlook the driveway to monitor who is coming to the front door. In the middle of the room sits a large table, where he holds meetings with Samantha and Sean now that their offices are out of action.

'What's there to think about? She's perfect,' Max says.

'I just don't feel comfortable leaving our baby with a stranger.'

'We won't. You'll be here the whole time. And I can work from home when you want to go out. It'll give you the chance to rest and catch up on your work so you're not so stressed all the time.'

'I'm not stressed all the time.' I study the bookshelves built between the windows that hold mostly books on computers and programming that I'll never understand.

He reaches out to take my hand. He looks drained. 'We don't want to lose her. You heard her. She has another job offer, so we need to give her an answer now.'

'She never said that.'

'She did.' He squeezes my hand tenderly. 'You weren't listening. You were in your usual daydreaming daze.'

I raise my voice. 'Daydreaming daze? What's that meant to mean?'

He hesitates before saying, 'Ever since Lola was born, it's like you're not really with it. I really wish you'd go to the doctor's and talk to someone.'

I can feel the hairs on my arm rising. I shudder. For the first time, I wonder if he's trying to gaslight me.

His tone softens. 'Why don't you call some of the people she's previously worked for? You'll see what I mean. It'll reassure you that we're making the right decision. It's just a short-term fix until you get better.'

I glare at him. 'Better? I'm not ill, Max. I've had a baby.'

'I'm sorry. That came out wrong.' He rubs his forehead. 'But you've had a difficult time. I... I—'

A dreadful thought comes to me. Is he trying to replace me? 'You what, Max?'

'Just call the people!'

For the first time since we met, he's scaring me. He pulls his phone out of his pocket and scrolls through the screen. 'Here's her CV. Take a look for yourself.'

I take the phone and read through her credentials. 'You're right. She has a wealth of experience.'

'Indeed she does.' Max raises his eyebrows in hope.

'So why do I have an uneasy feeling that she's not as perfect as she appears on paper?'

'Oh, Annie. See it for what it is, can you?' Max runs his hands through his hair again. 'There's someone here who can help us.'

TWELVE

I'm sitting in the armchair by the patio doors feeding Lola, stifling one yawn after another, struggling to keep awake. She is being particularly fussy today, and it's taking me forever.

My head nods. I jolt awake. It's not even eight a.m. and I wish it were bedtime. To keep me awake, I watch the builders through the patio doors, toiling on the renovations. The hard winter frost is making their work tough. It's as much of a mess out there as it is in here. The ground is a dishevelment of rubble and discarded materials – offcuts of wood and fragments of pipes – scattered around a manmade path to protect the grass. Jigsaw and Cameron appear, their broad frames stomping across the boards.

Jasmine and Jacob sit at the breakfast bar eating bowls of cereal, their necks bent over their phones. They have polar opposite personalities. Both highly intelligent kids, they won scholarships to a local private school where they have spent their secondary education, but whereas Jacob is a hermit and, apart from attending school and the orchestra and bands he belongs to, rarely ventures out, Jasmine would never be here if she had her way. But to be fair, she has buckled down recently with mock exams fast approaching after Christmas. She wants to go to university in London next September to study fine art. Jacob wants to go to the same university to study astrophysics. If I'm honest, I can't wait for them to go. The next ten months loom ahead like a long, bumpy ride I dread having to take.

The builders' morning banter can be heard above the news filling the room from the radio. *A woman has been found not guilty of the murder of her ten-week-old daughter. The baby was discovered with fatal head injuries from being violently shaken. She later died in Alder Hey Children's Hospital in Liverpool,* the newsreader reports. *The mother was suffering from postnatal depression.*

My gaze lingers on my baby daughter clasping her bottle with her teeny hands, disturbed that anyone could harm such a defenceless human being.

'Some people don't belong in this world,' Jasmine comments. She looks at me. 'Do they?'

'Sorry?' I say.

'Did you hear what that woman did to her baby?' she says.

'She was found not guilty!' I say.

Jasmine gesticulates with her spoon. 'I don't believe—'

Max rushes into the kitchen dressed in jeans and a white polo shirt. I breathe in the refreshing scent of apple shampoo. 'The bloody downstairs toilet isn't flushing again. I asked Jigsaw last week if he'd take a look at it.'

He's got so friendly with the builders that they've gladly carried out extra jobs around the house, especially Cameron and Jigsaw. It began at the end of the first week they started here, when Max offered all the workmen a beer. He's a generous soul like that. He'd give a beggar his last penny. But one beer led to another as Cameron declared it was his twenty-third birthday, and he and Jigsaw ended up staying until late into the evening. They've mended the shelf that collapsed in Max's office and replaced a washer on the kitchen tap that had been leaking since I moved in. In return, he has handed beer money their way. Win-win. That's Max all round. He has the ability to get people working to his advantage.

'I guess they're here for the house renovations, not to sort out your internal issues, Dad,' Jasmine pipes up.

'I know. I know!' Max laughs at himself. 'I'll remind him again today.'

'Aren't you going into the office?' I ask. Usually, he wears a suit to the office or at least a shirt and tie.

He's direct and to the point. 'I'm working from home today.'

'You never said.'

'Sean and Samantha are coming over later for a meeting.'

I sigh. I know he can't help having to find alternative venues to hold meetings since their offices were flooded. Certain issues need to be discussed away from the main workforce. But why can't they go to Sean's or Samantha's place? They came here last week. It's a pain having even more extra bodies around. The house has become a thoroughfare of people. I don't know who's going to turn up from one minute to the other. It's driving me insane.

'We've got to plan for the meeting with the Americans on Wednesday.'

'Why are you meeting here? Can't you go to one of theirs?' I already know the answer to this question. He wants to keep an eye on me.

'It's just easier.' He turns to address the twins. 'If you two hurry up, I'll drop you at school.'

Jasmine drops her spoon into her bowl with a clang. 'We'll be five minutes, Dad.' She nudges her brother. 'Come on. I can't be late today. I've got to meet with my art teacher.'

I watch Jacob follow his sister out of the room like a puppy dog.

Max rolls his eyes as he picks up their dirty dishes and stacks them in the dishwasher.

I want to tell him he should make them clean up their own mess, but I keep quiet. It's not the time for another argument about the part he has played in their laziness. I don't actually know if laziness is the right word. It's more ignorance. But what I've slowly learned about my husband is that although he has most people eating out of his hand, that's not the case with his son and eldest daughter. He'll do anything for a quiet life as far as his kids are concerned. If they were my real children, I wouldn't hesitate in making them tidy up after themselves.

But there's one thing Jasmine has made abundantly clear to me.

I'm not their real mother.

And I never will be.

THIRTEEN

It's a struggle to get myself together again. It's happening every day now. Every hour is a struggle, each day a mountain to climb. I should go to the doctor's. But they will only say the same. They've done all the tests. There's nothing wrong with me. I'm a new mum. I need to rest. Rest! Who can rest with a new baby? I wanted to scream at the doctor during an appointment a few weeks ago.

I'm robotically sorting through the laundry, trying to find a clean muslin for Lola before I go out, when the doorbell goes. Max rushes out of his office to answer it. I peer over the banister. Nisha and Sean are standing in the hallway. Sean waves at me and wishes me good morning in his usual cheery manner. I've never met someone with such an infectious energy. I return his gesture as he follows Max into his office to join my sister, who arrived a quarter of an hour ago. The sound of the office door slamming shut resounds around the house.

Nisha waves up to me. Her long silky hair shines in the morning sunlight blazing through the windows. I wish I could get my hair to shine the way hers does. Since Lola came along, it's limp and lifeless. Flawless and glowing, Nisha's rich, earthy skin tone is to die for, as well. In fact, everything about Nisha is just perfect.

'I just dropped Sean off, so I thought I'd pop in and say hello. I've got something for you,' she calls up.

I head downstairs. 'Where's Sean's car?'

'In the garage having two new tyres.' She hands me a small pile of her health magazines. 'I thought you might like these.'

I smile. She has been on at me to try yoga ever since we met. I flick through the pages of the first magazine, looking absently at the impossible poses my body wasn't built to achieve. I'm far too uncoordinated.

'I must dash,' she says. 'I have a client coming at ten.'

Nisha is a psychologist and runs her own private practice from an office in her garden. She pecks my cheek. 'Catch you soon.'

After I've seen her out, I hear raised voices beating from Max's office. I consider offering them a cup of tea, but it sounds as if they are having more than a heated debate. Instead, I head to the kitchen, and I'm drinking the cold cup of tea I made earlier but hadn't got around to finishing when Samantha appears. I do a double-take. 'What happened to your face?'

She blinks as she touches the red mark on her jaw. 'I caught it on the car door yesterday. Does it look bad?'

There's something different about her. It's the same thought I had when I visited her at her apartment the other day. 'It's red. It looks painful.'

'How are you today?' she asks. 'You're looking a little—'

'Dishevelled?'

She grins. 'That's one way to put it. Where's Lola?'

'Having a nap.'

'I was hoping for a cuddle.'

'Please don't go up there. She's quiet. I need time to sort myself out.' I sweep an arm around the kitchen. 'Look at the state of it in here. And look at me. I haven't even had the chance to get dressed yet. What were you three arguing about?'

'What?'

'I heard you. You three were arguing. What about?'

She blinks repeatedly. 'Business.'

I watch her walk out of the door.

She has just lied to me. Ever since we were kids, she has always blinked excessively when she lies.

Just after noon, Max appears at the kitchen door. I follow his vision darting around the kitchen. Everywhere I look, disorder surrounds us like the thorns of the overgrown blackberry bushes in the garden. The ones Max keeps promising to cut back but never gets around to. He massages the crease between his eyebrows. 'What time's Lola's appointment, darling?'

I stare at him, not understanding.

'Hasn't she got her vaccinations today?'

I push my hand to my mouth. 'Oh, no! I forgot. I need to go.' Apart from putting a wash load on, I don't even know what I've been doing all morning. The heavy fog of exhaustion seems to make even the simplest of tasks take forever.

He approaches me. There's a tense silence. 'Annie, we need to get some help around here.'

We still haven't got back to Zoe to confirm if we want her or not. He keeps hounding me, but I'm still unsure. There was something about her I didn't trust, but Max insists we won't get someone as experienced or as flexible.

'Leave it, Max. I'm dealing with it. What were you three arguing about?'

'Just business.' He gently takes Lola from my arms. 'Why don't I stay with her while you go and get dressed.'

There's a coldness between us. A chill I haven't felt before.

. . .

I sit in the waiting room at the GP surgery scrolling on Instagram to keep myself awake, while Lola snoozes in her car seat.

It's surprising how your habits change when you have kids. I used to be on Instagram all the time. Looking for my next travel destination or another recipe to cook from my favourite pages was a bit of an obsession. I used to love following the fashion bloggers, too, but now my feed is full of all things baby-related. A photo of a woman sitting on the backstep of a house staring at the ground catches my eye. Her elbows are resting on her knees, her chin on her hands. I read the post. It talks about the mum-guilt we carry around like bags of heavy shopping that makes us continually doubt ourselves.

Lola awakes. Her cries attract attention from the patients sitting around us. Stifling a yawn, I release the buckle of her car seat and get her out to comfort her.

Thankfully, a recorded voice saves me. *Lola Carpenter. Nurse Porter in room six.*

I find room six, where a middle-aged nurse, with greying hair tied in a bun at the nape of her neck, tells me to take a seat.

'She won't stop crying.' I try to control my voice. This is an appointment for Lola, not for me.

'It's what babies do, I'm afraid.' The nurse places a hand on Lola's chest. Her smile curves graciously towards her kind eyes. 'Now, now. Calm down.' Her voice is so soft and soothing as if each word is wrapped in layers of soft cotton wool.

Lola immediately quietens. I look at the nurse with an expression that asks, why can't my baby react like that to me? It shouldn't hurt, but it does. It's deeply painful.

'Now let's get these jabs done.'

How can she handle my baby with such ease when I seem to be all fumbling fingers and klutzy thumbs? Even when she injects the needle into Lola's arm, my baby doesn't make a sound.

'Why won't she stop crying for me?' I try to hide the desperation in my voice. 'She never stops.'

The nurse delivers the spiel I've heard so many times about how hard it is being a new mum. 'She's had all the tests. There are no other identifiable causes.' She clicks the mouse around her computer screen. 'Some babies are like this. Try to stay calm. Babies feed off of our anxiety, you know.'

How do you stay calm when your baby is constantly crying? I want to ask her, but instead say, 'She's still suffering from dreadful colic.' I don't tell her she cried non-stop for two hours straight last night. I took her downstairs so as not to disturb the others, and I ended up crying with her.

'That's not unusual.'

'But I was told it'd end by the time she reached four months.'

The nurse's soft brow furrows. She slightly tilts her head and slowly nods. 'I know you won't want to hear this, but, in some babies, colic can last until they are six months old.'

I suck my lips into themselves, trapping words in my mouth. I can't tell her that what she has just told me makes me want to walk out of this room and leave my baby with her.

FOURTEEN

The afternoon light is fading as I arrive home. Samantha's car is still parked on the road. I love my sister to pieces, but my whole body aches and I've got a splitting headache. A relentless pounding accompanied by waves of nausea. My whole body is screaming exhaustion. All I want is some peace while Lola is still asleep.

I take my baby inside and transfer her to her cot, hoping she'll stay asleep while I get my act together. From experience, I know she'll wake up if I leave her in her car seat. And she'll just start crying. More tears. I couldn't stand it. Not now. Not while I feel so damn rotten.

As I hurry downstairs, raised voices beat through Max's office door. The tension has heated up a notch. I turn my ear to the door.

Max raises his voice to shouting level. 'If you two hadn't spent so much time messing around, we wouldn't be in this shambles. It's a complete shitshow.'

Sean barks back. 'I hardly think that's the case, Max. I resent you saying that. We're all doing our best.'

'Come on,' Samantha chimes in, as if she is trying to placate the situation. 'We need to pull together.'

Max says something I don't catch.

'Fuck off, Max. You're out of order.' I don't think I've ever heard Sean swear.

A fist bangs on the table.

'Me out of order?' Max is shouting now. It's so unlike him.

I know they've got their stresses, but I've never heard them argue like this. But then, I've never been party to their meetings before. It's hard to understand how they've managed to make the company so successful if this is how they operate. I knock and put my head around the door to offer them drinks. There's definitely an atmosphere. Even happy-go-lucky Sean isn't his cordial self.

'Drinks?' I offer, studying three stern faces.

'No, we're going out.' Max stands. 'Sean and I have got a meeting with the lawyers.'

Samantha kicks back her chair. 'I'm going home.'

Sean, using his hands as leverage on the tabletop, pulls himself up. There's an awkward silence.

I watch Max. He's busy packing his laptop into its bag. 'I'll see you later, then,' I say.

'I won't be long,' Max replies. But he still doesn't return eye contact.

In the kitchen, I boil the kettle. I'm getting the milk out of the fridge when the bottle of Chardonnay left from the night of the fire catches my eye. I hesitate. A strong longing overcomes me. I lean my head against the side of the fridge. How I could kill for a glass of wine right now. I glance at the kitchen clock. It's ten to four. The evening stretches long ahead with Lola having had an extended afternoon nap. I gaze at the bottle. It's as if the devil is whispering in my ear, 'Just one glass can't hurt.' But it will only make my headache worse. I fill the kettle and put it on to boil.

I turn to a knock on the utility room door. I head to answer it, noticing the overflowing washing basket and the dirty laundry towering towards the ceiling. 'It's only Cameron,' a voice calls out. I open the door. His light-hearted voice fills the room. 'Max asked us to check one of the catches on the patio doors. Is now a good time for us to come in?' He runs his hand through his blond curly hair that falls to his shoulders. It's hair that many women would die for. But his skin, not so. It's puckered and weathered from too many hours spent surfing in the Californian sun in his youth.

'Did you hear me put the kettle on?' I tease.

He laughs. He does that a lot, I've noticed. Laughs. Something lacking in this house recently. Recently? Who am I kidding? This house has lacked laughter since Lola was born. And if you asked the twins, they'd most likely say since I moved in. What a terrible thing to admit.

The smell of tobacco follows Cameron and Jigsaw into the room. Jigsaw is holding a toolbox. 'If you're offering. A cuppa would be great.' They slip their feet into blue plastic overshoes.

'Max said he mentioned to you that the toilet isn't working,' I say, making three cups of tea.

'Yes, ma'am.' Jigsaw feigns a salute, laughing. He's a large guy, nearly half as wide as he is tall, with a buzzcut and extraordinarily large hands. 'I'll get on with it as soon as we've had a look at that door. See what's up.'

I take a few gulps of tea before popping upstairs to check on Lola, relieved to see she's fast asleep still. As I'm coming back down, Max, Sean and Samantha are on their way out as Jigsaw enters the hallway. He has removed his sweatshirt, baring sleeves of tattoos that cover his muscly forearms. He ties the sweatshirt around his waist. 'We've fixed the door. It was just a screw that needed tightening.'

'Can you take a look at that toilet I asked you about last week?' Max barks at him. His tone is out of order.

'Max.' I shoot him a look. I can't work out what's got into him.

He slams the front door on his way out.

FIFTEEN

I return to the kitchen and find my iPad. Settling on one of the stools at the breakfast bar, I log in to my emails. As much as I'm not in the mood, I can't ignore the growing unanswered messages any more. My accountants have been chasing me to sign off on my year-end accounts and settle their invoice. I finish my cup of tea and log in to their system, yawning. My eyelids are heavy. I slap my cheeks. I can't fall asleep. I need to get this done before I get Lola up.

A voice startles me. Cameron marches into the room. 'That toilet needs a new valve.' He reaches into his pocket and removes his phone. 'I'll have Jigsaw grab one for you. He's heading to the warehouse in the morning. In the meantime, don't use it. I've set a chair against the door to keep it off-limits.' He pauses. 'Are you OK, Annie?'

'Fine. Why?' I straighten my spine, yawning again.

'You're looking pretty pale.'

'All good.'

He hops from foot to foot, removing the blue overshoes and frowning at me. 'We're all headed home now. We'll see you in the morning.'

'Yes. See you then.'

I stare at my screen blurring before me, getting nothing done. Lola awakes and lets out her signature wail.

As I'm halfway up the stairs, there's a knock at the door. I hurry back down to answer it. It's an Amazon delivery guy with a parcel: a baby carrier meant to help colicky babies that a mum from the mother and baby group recommended. It cost a fortune, but Max encouraged me to go for it. You can't put a price on her suffering, ours either, he'd said. Inside is also a new toy. Another recommendation.

I take them upstairs, each step a struggle. Billie Eilish is playing loudly from Jasmine's room. I head towards the noise to ask her to turn it down but stop. Fight your battles. That's what internet stepmothers say. She'll only turn my simple request into an argument.

When I get into our room, I gasp.

Jasmine is standing over Lola's cot.

'Jasmine?'

Her bobbed hair swings as she turns sharply. Something drops to the floor with a thud.

'What are you doing?' I whisper.

SIXTEEN

Jasmine bends to pick up the item from the floor. It's her phone. 'I was just snapping some shots.'

'Why?' My stomach cramps. Lola is crying.

Jasmine steps away from the cot. She holds up both hands as if she's defending herself. 'I have an assignment to do for my final portfolio.'

'What's that got to do with Lola?' I wince at the pain in my stomach. It's consuming me.

She hesitates before speaking. 'The project is titled *Sleep*.' She trips over the words leaving her mouth too fast. 'I th... I thought I'd paint Lo... my sister asleep. Don't worry, I won't show her face.'

'You could've asked.'

She brushes past me, her stride purposeful as she walks out of the room. She stops and turns to me. 'I didn't think it'd be a problem. She *is* my sister.' Her footsteps thump up the stairs to her bedroom.

Lola's face is bright red. I pick her up, trying to comfort her in my arms while fighting the overwhelming urge to sleep. 'It's OK, baby girl. Mumma's here.'

Jasmine's presence has unnerved me. The music from her room stops. She thumps back downstairs, and the front door slams shut. I shake my head. I should be used to her behaviour by now, but I still find it unsettling.

I need to have a shower. It's the only way I'll get through the long evening ahead. I strap Lola in her car seat and take her into the en suite. It's a large room that Max and his first wife had converted from a bedroom when they moved here. I detest the green tiles. My stomach cramps. I should've mentioned these pains to the nurse. I rock Lola's car seat with my foot while I slip out of my clothes. Stepping into the shower, I try to block out the sound of my baby's cries and the layer of guilt enshrouding me with the price of motherhood that's stifling me more every day.

When I step out, the room spins. I need to lie down. Grabbing my dressing gown, I slip into it, unstrap Lola and lie on the bed. It's a struggle to keep my eyes open. So tired. I'm always so damn tired.

Before I know it, I wake up, confused. My baby. Where is my baby? My stomach heaves. I'm going to be sick. I run to the en suite but stop as I step through the door. Am I still dreaming?

Fear overcomes the spasms of nausea tightly gripping my stomach. I scream, but nothing comes out. I'm fixed to the spot, staring at the lifeless body. This can't be right. I slap my face. I must be dreaming.

But I'm not.

She's dead.

And that's *my* belt from *my* dressing gown wrapped around her neck.

I reach out to take her hand. Should I even be touching her?

Help.

I need help.

Clutching the edges of my dressing gown, I run out of the bedroom screaming. My voice doesn't let me down this time. 'Max!'

My desperate roars echo around the silence of the house like a roll of thunder.

'Max! Help! She's dead.'

SEVENTEEN

No one comes.

Bolting down the stairs, I scream Max's name again and again, but there's no answer. I push open his office door. The room spins. It's empty in there.

Then I remember he said he was going out. I search my brain, trying to recall where to, but I can't. He said he wouldn't be long, though. I run to the window and look outside. Max's BMW is gone, but Samantha's car is still parked on the opposite side of the road. That doesn't make sense. Samantha said she was going.

Leaving his office, I dart around the rooms downstairs, but no one's there, either. I can't think. This is hell. The twins. They need to help me. I take off up the stairs, screaming their names. My legs are heavy and weak. I hurry to Jasmine's room. She's not there. Then I remember that she stormed out earlier.

I run back to my bedroom. As I swing around the top of the banister, my legs buckle. A car arrives in the driveway, the wheels scrunching over gravel. The front door opens. Max and Sean walk in. That's strange. They were going to that meeting with their lawyer. I glance at my watch. I've been asleep for over an hour. 'Help! Max. Help!'

Max bolts to the bottom of the stairs, looking up at me.

'Come up here. Quick. Quick,' I scream.

He takes the stairs two at a time. 'What the hell's going on?'

Sean momentarily hovers on the bottom stair before catching up with Max halfway up.

'She's dead. Come quickly.'

I barely whisper. 'She's dead,' I repeat.

'What the hell?' Max cries.

I look from him to Sean. They've reached the top of the stairs, staring at me as if I'm mad. I clutch my face, wondering if I'm dreaming – stuck in one of the many distressing nightmares that plague me night after disturbing night.

Max is shaking my shoulders. 'Who's dead, Annie?'

'My sister,' I manage to choke out.

EIGHTEEN

I hang over the banister and scream her name over and over again. I stare hopelessly at Max's office door, in a desperate chance she'll come running out of there. So much of my life has been unclear recently... But I didn't imagine this.

Max shakes me again. 'Annie, calm down. Samantha went home. We saw her leave. She drove off the same time as us.'

'But her car's outside.'

'It's not.'

'It is. It's parked on the other side of the road.' It's surreal. I feel as if I'm not here. As if I'm floating above my body like a ghost, watching this horror story unfold. 'I'm telling you.' I tear my body away from his oppressive hold. 'You've got to believe me.' I say a silent prayer. Please, God. Please, tell me it was just a bad dream.

But I know what I saw.

'Calm down, Annie.' Sean and Max exchange a look as if they are questioning my lucidity.

'She's in the en suite.' I turn and dart back to the bedroom, grasping at the edges of my dressing gown which is threatening to expose my naked body.

Max catches up with me with Sean on his tail.

I reach the en suite.

And there she is.

I'm not dreaming.

This is for real.

One end of my dressing gown belt is wrapped around my sister's neck, and the other is tied to the middle of the floor-to-ceiling chrome radiator that looks like a ladder. Her bottom is a few inches from the floor.

'Oh, God!' Sean pushes past Max, who is standing paralysed, the same as I was when first faced with this horror scene. 'Sam!' Sean straddles her lifeless body. His howls fill the room. 'No. No. No.'

They shout her name as if their demands can bring her back. Max pushes back her drooped head. It's a frightening sight. Her face has turned a putrid shade of purple, and her eyes, partially opened, are cloudy, her pupils fixed in a look of distress.

I heave.

Sean takes charge. 'We need to free her.' He lifts her body from under her armpits, releasing the tension of the belt.

'Should we be touching her?' Max says.

'She could still be alive. Quick.' Sean gives Max a beseeching look. 'Don't just stand there, untie the belt.' He shouts at my sister. 'Sam, Sam, come on, stay with us. Please, don't do this. Don't leave us.' He roars at Max, 'Do something!'

Time stands still in a blur of panic. My whole body is shaking involuntarily as if I've just had an electric shock.

Max attempts to undo the tight knot of the fabric tied to the radiator. My sister's head flops forwards.

I scream again, a shrill, piercing cry of pain.

This can't be real.

After all the confusion of the past few months, I hope that

I'm actually dreaming this time. That any minute, I'm going to wake up drenched in sweat.

'Annie, get some scissors,' Sean yells, struggling under my sister's weight. 'I can't hold her for much longer.'

'I don't have any up here,' I say.

'Go and get some from Jasmine or Jacob. Run,' Sean orders.

'I've got it.' Max releases the belt.

Sean lays her body flat. He cradles her head and lowers his ear to her mouth.

'Samantha, don't leave me. You can't leave me,' I wail.

Sean checks her pulse. His bottom lip quivers, his eyes transfixed on the body in disbelief. 'She's gone.' He collapses backwards.

I scream over and over. 'No. No. No.' All I want to do is wake up from this nightmare.

'We need to start CPR. Now!' Max yells. 'And we need to call an ambulance. And the police.'

'Which one?' I'm confused. I can't think straight.

'Both.' Max positions the palms of his hands on Samantha's chest. He looks up at me. Pain contorts his face into a ball of anguish. 'Go and call them. Quick.' He starts pumping. But deep down, we both know his efforts are futile. 'Hurry. Quick!'

NINETEEN

My head is pounding, my heart racing. I grab my phone from the bedside cabinet but I'm all fingers and thumbs and drop the bloody thing. It crashes to the floor. 'Do I ask for the police or an ambulance?' I shout as I grab the phone from the floor.

Max's breaths come short and sharp from the effort of administering CPR. 'Just tell the operator what's happened, and they'll put you through to the right person.'

'Where's Lola?' I mutter. I slam my hands on my head. She was asleep on the bed with me. I scurry through the crumpled duvet.

My baby's not there.

Max yells at Sean, telling him to pull himself together and help him.

Where's my baby?

'Annie, what are you doing?' Max's voice grows louder and louder. 'We can't waste time. Pull yourself together. Ambulance, now!' he cries.

I dial 999. In a panicked voice, I relay what's happened to the woman on the end of the line.

'They're sending help,' I tell Sean and my husband crouched over Samantha's body, as they try to revive her.

The voice of survival tells me this isn't real. This can't be happening. I've got it all wrong. A pain cuts across my stomach like a knife. I cling to the doorframe as I update the operator, relaying her advice to Max and Sean. 'Keep doing what you're doing until help arrives.'

Max pumps Samantha's chest, his face frozen into a look of horror. 'Whatever happened, Annie?' he says when Sean takes over. He rests on his heels, wiping a layer of sweat from his forehead.

'I don't know. I fell asleep on the bed. I didn't hear her come into the room. When I woke up, I found her like this.'

'What was she doing up here?' Sean asks.

Max glares at me. 'Annie, answer us.'

I feel like I'm in a court of law being cross-examined. 'I don't know. I was asleep,' I shout in desperation. 'Please do something. Please save her.'

Suddenly, I feel exposed, standing half-naked in only my dressing gown without the belt. I need to get dressed. And I need to find my baby.

I try to go through what happened before I found my sister, but my brain is a fog so dense it's impossible to see through. Everything around me has merged together, like a smudged piece of Jasmine's artwork. With my phone wedged between my shoulder and ear, I open my wardrobe door, fumbling for some clothes. A bitter taste fills my mouth. I feel like I'm going to be sick.

I summon all my strength to focus, but my head is pounding. Finding a pair of sweatpants and a hoodie, I quickly fumble into them, willing myself to ride the waves of nausea rushing through me. I need to find my baby.

A banging on the front door startles the three of us. 'Go!' Max shouts at me.

I run from the room and descend the stairs hurriedly, tripping on the bottom step and sending my phone flying. I scoop it up as I continue across the hallway to open the front door. A first responder is standing on the doorstep. He hurries in with a red bag slung over his shoulder.

'Help is here,' I say to the operator. She ends the call, and I lead the guy upstairs, appraising him of the situation, unable to stop myself from tripping over my words.

When he enters the en suite, I perch on the side of the bed and watch through the doorway, listening to the crisis unfold as I will them to save my sister.

TWENTY

'Where's Lola?' She was asleep on the bed with me. I need to find my daughter.

I dash to the en suite to tell Max Lola has disappeared, but it sounds absurd in the circumstances. This is a nightmare. I don't know what to do for the best. Help them with my sister, or find my baby.

Several thoughts rush through my mind. Maybe I left her in the car. I turn around. Her car seat is by her cot. I rub my brow. Perhaps I was mistaken and Jasmine took her after the photograph incident. But Jasmine left the room alone. She must've come back for her. But, no. She went out. I heard her slam the door.

My baby. I need to find my baby.

I must have left her in her bouncing cradle, but I don't remember doing that. My heart is pounding as I rush downstairs and into the kitchen. She's not there. I tear around the downstairs room crying out her name, desperately seeking a response from her. But she isn't down here.

I take the stairs two at a time and rush up to Jacob's room, stopping to see him sitting in his gaming chair wearing his coat and scarf, rocking Lola in his arms, while tapping on the keyboard of his computer. 'Jacob!' The relief in my voice is palpable. 'What are you doing?'

Brushing the curtain of curls from his face, his eyes lock onto mine. 'Has there been a murder?' The way he says it unnerves me even more.

I squint at him, reaching for my baby. 'No.' He's seventeen. He needs to hear the truth, but I can't bring myself to say my sister has taken her own life. 'It's my sister. Something terrible has happened.'

Jacob stops tapping on the computer and rocks Lola faster. Something about the way he serenely watches her chills me. It's impossible to act so calm with such drama playing out around us. His right leg jigs up and down.

'You were smothering her,' he says.

TWENTY-ONE

My breath catches in my throat. 'What?'

'I came home from school, and I heard Lola crying so I went into your room. Your arm was over her face. You were suffocating her.'

I stare at him aghast. The fear inside me intensifies.

'So I brought her in here with me.'

I take a deep sigh of relief. I thought he meant I was suffocating my sister. 'She was asleep on my chest,' I say.

'That's not where I found her. She was on the bed under your arm.'

The sudden need to hold my baby is overwhelming, but another knock at the front door startles me. I don't know what to do. I have to trust him. He wouldn't do anything to hurt Lola. Whatever the twins feel about me, they love their baby sister.

'Thank you, Jacob. Can you keep her here while I help your dad?' As the request leaves my mouth, I wonder if I'm doing the right thing.

'Sure,' he says.

I descend the two flights of stairs as fast as I can, but my legs are so heavy. It feels as if I'm wading across a muddy field in a winter storm.

When I open the door, two uniformed officers stand on the porch. They introduce themselves as PC Vickers and PC White. PC Vickers is mid-fifties, his eyes tired and heavy, as opposed to PC White, a fresh-faced guy who looks so young, just out of school. But, then again, everyone looks young to me lately.

The officers ask questions, establishing facts as they follow me up the stairs and back into the bedroom.

The paramedic waves a phone. 'I've called it in.'

I stare at him.

It's official.

My sister is dead.

I'm numb. It can't be true. This is simply another of the nightmares that plague me every night. I pinch myself. It's as true as I'm standing here. I'm never going to see my sister again.

'We'll take over from here,' PC Vickers addresses Max and Sean. 'A detective and scene of crime officer are on their way.'

That doesn't seem right. 'Why a detective?' I murmur, disorientated. They shouldn't be here. I want them out of this house.

PC Vickers turns to me. 'This is a sudden death. Unexplained.'

'She killed herself,' I say, speaking low. 'My sister killed herself.'

'It's par for the course, I'm afraid. Does she have a partner?'

'A husband.' Max's voice wavers.

'Have you told him?' the officer asks.

'No,' Max says.

'Can you give me his contact details?'

With trembling hands, I find Ezra's number on my phone. 'This is my brother-in-law's number. He's a doctor. He might be working.'

'Where does he work?'

'At King George's Hospital.'

'My colleagues will sort it.'

'I should tell him.' I can't bear the thought of Ezra hearing this news from someone else. But neither can I bear the thought of breaking it to him. Like me, he's going to be utterly devastated.

Max takes my arm. 'No, darling. Leave it to the police. We'll go and see him later.' He grabs Sean's arm. 'We need to get out of here.' His tone wavers. 'Come on, mate.' His voice is as soft as a whisper in the chaos escalating around us. 'She's gone.'

The paramedic echoes my husband's words.

'We can't leave her,' Sean whimpers.

'You must,' the paramedic says. 'We're here.'

Max tugs Sean's arm, pulling him up until he reluctantly succumbs.

My sister can't be gone. Our childhood flashes through my mind. Us taking it in turns to push each other on the swings at the park, playing with our Barbie dolls, baking ginger cookies at Christmas. And later getting ready together on a Friday evening for a night on the town.

Now I'll never hear her voice again.

And I'll never see her again.

PC Vickers addresses PC White. 'Stay here, can you, until Pitman arrives?' He follows Max and Sean out of the en suite. 'Let's go downstairs.'

Max grabs my hand and follows Sean and PC Vickers to the bedroom door. 'I need to go and see the kids. Where's Lola?' he asks me.

'With Jacob.'

'Who's Jacob?' PC Vickers asks.

'My son,' Max says.

'Where is he?'

'In his bedroom.'

'Bring him downstairs,' Vickers says in an authoritative tone. 'Anyone else in the house?'

'My other daughter,' Max says.

'No,' I say. 'Jasmine went out.'

Vickers points a finger forcefully towards the ground floor. 'Bring whoever's here downstairs. Everyone downstairs now, please.'

TWENTY-TWO

I lean against the kitchen sink, staring blankly at the floor. The image of Samantha's purple, lifeless face won't leave me. I can't believe she's gone. Other than Max and the kids she's the only family I have. I think back to when I saw her the other day at her apartment. Something wasn't right then. But this?

Tears blur my vision. My mind can't cope with the enormity of what's happened. Samantha is the constant in my life. It's insurmountable to think she's gone.

Sean is perched on one of the breakfast stools, his elbows on the kitchen counter. He massages his temples with his fingers. The light from the overhanging pendant shines on his bald head. He's usually a jovial person, the social spark of every gathering, but now he sits subdued, staring into space.

Jasmine arrived home when we all got downstairs, and now she and Jacob are wedged into the armchair by the patio doors. Lola is propped on Jasmine's lap, giggling as she bashes the coloured sections of the musical activity station Jacob is holding. A cow moos. A pig snorts. A horse neighs. Noises so out of kilter with the downpour of stress and grief drowning the room.

'What happens now?' My thoughts muddle as I anticipate the days ahead.

Max shrugs. 'I don't know, Annie. I've not exactly been in this situation before.' He tucks a strand of my hair behind my ear, his touch as soft as a feather. 'I'm sorry. That came out wrong. I didn't mean it sarcastically.'

'Lola needs a bottle.' I'm amazed my maternal instincts kick in despite my shock and grief.

Jasmine transfers Lola to Jacob's lap. 'I'll go get one.'

A knock at the front door makes me jump. Max goes to answer it.

A man walks in and introduces himself as Detective Inspector Pitman, a thickset man with an expression that comes with a warning. He is a person not to get on the wrong side of. He speaks, but I can't fully concentrate.

Sean offers him a seat at the breakfast bar next to him.

The DI walks over to the stool but doesn't sit down. His tall, sturdy frame is a commanding presence in the smallness of us all. He produces a notebook from his black satchel.

I compose a text to Ezra, telling him I need to see him urgently and to call me. 'I'll make some drinks,' I say because I need something to do. Anything other than face the tsunami of grief heading my way.

I fill the kettle with water, taking orders for seven cups of tea. I'd rather have something stronger. Something to calm my nerves. I'm sure Max and Sean would, as well, but I know it'd be inappropriate. As I pull a carton of milk from the fridge, there's an open bottle of Chardonnay sitting in the door. That's strange. I can't recall opening it. I rub my head. I'm confused. I didn't open it. I'm sure of it. Max usually drinks red wine. But Jasmine sometimes has a glass of white with dinner. She must have had a glass without asking. Or is it the bottle left over from the night of the fire? I blink several times. I can't remember.

I line up the cups and make the tea. When I take the teabags to the bin, I'm awash with disbelief to see an empty bottle of wine lying on top of the pile of discarded recycling. I observe the bottle, incredulous. A thought scares me. Did I drink the wine? Is that why I feel so awful?

I glance around the kitchen.

The DI is staring at me.

I drop the bin lid. It crashes closed, the noise reverberating around the room. My vision blurs. I stare around me. Faces are out of focus as if I'm having one of my nightmares. All their unblinking eyes are looking at me. It's unsettling, spooky, as if they are a bunch of zombies out to get me. I blink rapidly until my vision corrects itself and I apologise for the noise.

I hand out cups of tea while the DI fires questions like bullets from a gun, asking who found the body, timings and our relationship with Samantha. 'If she'd left for the day, why did she come back here?'

Sean shrugs. 'I haven't a clue.'

Max shrugs, too. 'Neither do I.'

'Perhaps she left something here,' Jasmine suggests. Her voice sounds different to usual, authoritative and heavy, suddenly too mature for a teenager.

The DI nods from Max to Sean before his attention turns to me. 'And why was she upstairs in your bedroom?'

Max butts in. 'The toilet downstairs isn't working. I can only guess she went up there to use the toilet.'

The DI frowns. 'But why the en suite? Isn't there another toilet she could've used? A family bathroom?'

'Yep. So that I can't answer,' Max says.

'Did she ever mention anything about being depressed?'

Max shrugs. The corners of his mouth drop as he shakes his head. He's holding back on something. I'm sure of it. He looks at Sean. Sean doesn't look at him.

'No. She never mentioned anything to me.' His voice trails off, a hint of uncertainty masking his usual confident tone.

The DI turns to me and repeats the question.

'She and her husband found out earlier this year that they couldn't have children. She was sad about that.' My voice trembles. 'But not enough to kill herself.'

'Some people are good at putting on a show. Have there been any similar incidents with her in the past?'

'What do you mean?' I ask.

'Did she ever make any previous attempts to take her own life?'

I shake my head. 'No. Never.' Maybe she did, and she never told me about it. The thought fills me with a harrowing sadness.

'What happens now?' Sean asks.

'My colleague who I arrived with is a scene of crime officer. He is assessing the scene.'

Crime? 'Why?' I ask. 'Suicide isn't a crime.'

'It's standard procedure whenever anyone takes their own life.'

My hands need something to do. I fiddle with the drawstrings of my hoodie, repeatedly slipping them through my fingers.

The DI continues. 'In these circumstances, we can never rule out any wrongdoing, so we have to approach our findings as a potential crime scene.'

Crime scene? 'I don't understand.'

'We need to rule out that this death wasn't the result of criminal action. And—'

'She killed herself.' I butt in. 'How can that be criminal action?'

'We don't know until we gather all the facts.' The DI softens his tone. 'I'm so dreadfully sorry for your loss. I can put you in touch with someone who can help you. I know this isn't easy. What you've witnessed today is traumatic, but we will need you to make a statement.'

A fresh wave of fear overcomes me.

I lean back against the wall.

It was the belt to *my* dressing gown that was found around Samantha's neck. And it was *me* who found her. I hope they don't think I somehow helped her to do this.

TWENTY-THREE

Max tells me he'll take me and the kids to Sean and Nisha's house. 'They don't need to see the body being taken away. Neither do you.' He pauses before adding, 'Unless you want to be here.' He draws me to him, enfolding me into his embrace, but I can't feel his touch. I'm empty, as if I've crawled into a vacuum so I can deal with the pain. 'Just tell me what you want to do, darling.'

I don't want to go, but I don't want to stay here either. It will be too difficult to see her body leave. 'I'll take them.'

'I'll stay here and deal with things. Are you sure you're OK to drive?'

I nod.

He squeezes my arm reassuringly. 'It's for the best.'

I head to the utility room in a daze. Lola needs some clean clothes, and I need to pack a bag for her. She hasn't even had a bath yet today. I rest my hand on the counter, shaking my head in disbelief. There will be no more texts. No more of the funny memes my sister shared in our family WhatsApp group that always made me laugh. No more of the one person who knew everything about me. No more of so much. My heart is broken.

I frown at the pile of dirty washing growing out of control above the washing machine, startled at my thoughts of putting a load on. It's strange how the mind can go into survival mode in a crisis. But when I look closer, the drum is already full of wet towels. I'm confused. I can't remember putting that load on.

Sighing heavily, I open the machine and drag out the wet items, muttering a long string of expletives to see Max's new white shirt among the wet towels. It has turned an ugly shade of pink and is missing the bottom button, too. He loves this shirt. The twins chipped in to buy it for his birthday. He's going to kill me. And so are they. I'll have to replace it before they find it. I quickly roll it into a small bundle and tuck it behind the bottles of laundry detergent and fabric softener at the back of the cupboard. There are more pressing items on my agenda at the moment.

With Lola's bag packed, I grab my handbag and keys, glancing around the kitchen, searching for something else I should take with me, but I can't think what else I need.

Max straps Lola in her car seat. 'The twins aren't coming with you.'

'Why not?'

He rolls his eyes and shrugs. 'Come on, let's get you in the car.'

'What was that all about earlier?' I say when I close the front door.

Max glances back towards the house and then at me. 'What do you mean?'

'What were you, Sean and Samantha arguing about earlier?' My voice trembles at the mention of my dead sister's name.

He touches the corner of his mouth. It's a habit of his when he's nervous. It was one of the first things I noticed when I met him at my sister's wedding. He was doing it constantly until the wine started flowing and he loosened up. 'Hell, Annie. This isn't the time.' He marches to the car.

'It is the time.' I lengthen my stride to keep up with him. 'There's something you're not telling me.'

He inhales a large breath and slowly releases it into the cold night air.

'Tell me, Max?'

He opens the car door and places Lola inside, feeding the seatbelt through the gaps in the back of her seat and tightening the slack before clicking it into place. 'We can talk later.'

Climbing into the front, I close the door and wind down the window. 'No. I want to know now.'

'Know what?'

'Why were you three arguing earlier?'

'I told you. It was just business related.' He dips his head through the window and kisses me. 'I'll come over as soon as I can. I love you.' He taps the top of the car.

I watch my husband break into a jog back to the house, wondering if he has just told me the truth or one big fat lie.

I fear it's the latter.

TWENTY-FOUR

I grip the steering wheel. My hands are violently shaking. I thought I'd be OK, but I'm in no fit state to drive, though I need to get away from here, away from the vision of my sister that won't leave me.

With my sister... gone, there's only one other person I feel I can trust right now.

I phone Nisha. 'I need your help.'

'I've been trying to call you. Whatever's happened? Sean rang and told me about Samantha.'

I brief her on the horror I've witnessed that has changed my life forever.

She expresses her shock. 'Sean said to stay away,' she says.

'I'll update you more when I see you. Max wanted me to bring the twins to yours, but they won't come.' My voice trembles. 'I don't want to be here when they take her away. But I daren't drive. I'm shaking too much. Can you come and pick me up?'

'Give me five.'

I turn on the radio to drown out Lola's whines and check my phone. Ezra hasn't replied to my text. He must still be at work. My heart aches for him for the irony. He's at work saving someone's life, when his wife has just taken her own.

Lola's whines intensify. I hop into the back seat, trying to comfort my baby while I wait for Nisha. I position my arm over the top of her car seat to shield her from the interior car light shining into her eyes. My sister's face when I found her flashes in my thoughts. An image that has set fire to my soul and will burn forever. There's an emptiness in me, something missing that nothing, no one, will ever be able to replace.

But it doesn't make sense. Samantha isn't the type to do this. Since we were little, she's always been so happy, so content with life. Until, that is, earlier this year when she discovered Ezra couldn't father children. She put on a brave face to those around her. Said it didn't matter – they would travel the world instead and enjoy a more orderly, relaxed life alone but together. But beneath the mask of bravery she wore every day, the news destroyed her soul. I've been so tightly wrapped up in my own troubles that I didn't make enough time for her. I let her down. I should've made sure she was OK.

Lola continues whining. I try to soothe her, my nerves stretched to snapping point. 'It's all going to be all right,' I repeat to my baby, if only to kid myself. I think about the repercussions of today's events. I've lost my best friend. Gone. And Lola's lost her only aunty. One who adored her. Gone. Nothing is ever going to be the same for any of us.

Lola scrunches up her face as her whining morphs into unrelenting, repetitive cries that echo incessantly around the car. I should be crying, too, but oddly, my eyes are dry and empty, as if I've locked my grief away until I can fully deal with it.

The noise grows unacceptably loud. 'Let's wait outside.' I unbuckle the seatbelt and lift the chair out of the car. A heavy gust of wind whips through me. I look up at the house that commands such a presence with its turrets reaching into the night sky. The wind warps the branches of a large oak tree in front of Jasmine's bedroom window. The light is on. The twins are standing at the window. The branches sway and their shadows dance around. From what I can tell, the twins are looking directly at me and talking to each other as if they are discussing me. I wave, but they don't wave back.

The wind picks up, howling in the darkness of the garden and bending the branches of the other surrounding trees. An empty bag of sand whirls into the air. I hurry to the end of the driveway where a heap of black bags full to bursting point is stacked beside the non-recycling bin. Cars swish past: people keen to get home after a day at work. Ordinary people with normal lives. How I crave the simplicity of how I once lived.

Within minutes, Nisha's Range Rover pulls up. She helps me secure Lola in the back seat. 'What the hell?' She jumps back into the car as I take the passenger seat. 'I texted Sean to say I was coming to pick you up, and he replied to say not to come in.'

'I think he's in shock. We all are.' I look up at Jasmine's bedroom window again. The twins are still standing there. I wave again. Jasmine draws the curtains.

Nisha squeezes my forearm. 'I'm so sorry, Annie. This is absolutely dreadful.'

'It's hell. I can't believe she did this.'

Her soft voice is comfort in the chaos. 'Come on. Let's get you back to mine.'

'Will you take me to her apartment? I need to see Ezra.'

'Sure.'

Lola settles as soon as Nisha pulls into the road and drives away. My phone rings. It's Max.

'The police can't get hold of Ezra. He's not at work. Apparently he's on annual leave, and he's not at the apartment. Do you know where he could be?'

'Samantha never mentioned anything about him going

away. I saw him on Friday, as well. He'd just come in from a shift. He never mentioned anything.'

A voice sounds in the background. I can't make out if it's one of the PCs or the DI. 'I'll be right with you,' Max calls, his voice muffled. 'Why's your car still here?' he asks me.

'I was shaking too much. It didn't feel safe to drive. Nisha picked me up.'

'We need to contact Ezra. Think hard, Annie. Did he or Samantha say anything about him going away?'

I recall the visit to my sister last week. 'I don't think they did.'

'Do you have contact details for any of Ezra's friends?'

'No.' They aren't people I've mixed with.

'I've got to go. The police want to speak to me. I love you, darling. I'll be with you as soon as I can.'

A sick feeling of dread torments me as he ends the call, and I think back to when I saw Samantha in the kitchen earlier. I wonder if the red mark on Samantha's face had something to do with Ezra, and that's why she's now lying in a bag ready to go to the morgue.

TWENTY-FIVE

'Forget going to Ezra's,' I say to Nisha. 'He's not there, apparently.' With a trembling hand, I try my brother-in-law's number again. 'He's not picking up.' I relay the conversation I've just had with Max.

Heavy drops of rain pound the car, bouncing off the bonnet. The windscreen wipers swipe streams of water into the gutter as Nisha drives us to her house. Lola has settled, so I expand on what happened as the late-afternoon drama rolled into the early evening tragedy, my voice fading to a mumble as I reach the point I found my sister.

Nisha's eyes stay focused on the road, taking it all in until she stops at a set of temporary traffic lights. 'Did she ever give any indication she was considering doing this?'

I shake my head. 'Never.'

'I saw her on Friday, when I dropped into the office.' Nisha's leather-gloved fingers tap the steering wheel. 'I remember thinking there was something not quite right about her.'

'In what way?'

'You know what she was like. Always so friendly, but she

seemed a little off with me. Then she had an argument with Max.'

I turn my head sharply. 'Did she? What about?'

She hesitates. 'I don't know, but it was pretty heated. One minute, she was there, and the next, she'd gone. When I mentioned it to Sean, he brushed it off – said it was probably to do with the business deal. It's been pretty stressful there, he said. But they all want this deal to go through, so they've been working through issues.'

'They were all arguing today, as well. I asked Samantha and Max what it was about, but they both said the same – it was business related.'

She indicates to turn into the driveway of her large detached house set back from the busy road. Half of the driveway is lawn, the other half paved with space for at least eight cars. They moved here last year after Sean's parents died and left him in excess of two million pounds. The house is lit up like a Christmas tree with a delicate display of icicle lights wrapped around the facia that feeds down to the two bay trees flanking the grand oak front door.

I get out and unstrap Lola, my hands still shaking. She immediately starts crying. I try to replace her dummy. She refuses it. Nisha reaches out an arm and hooks it through the handle of the car seat. 'Let me take her.' She manages to coax Lola to take the dummy and Lola settles. 'You've enough to deal with.'

She ushers me inside, the warmth of her house a comfort after the cold wind and rain. There's a smell of lavender in the air from the essential oils she always has burning. It usually gives the house an uplifting feeling. But nothing could lift the mood today.

'Come on, let's get you settled. The kids are all out or doing their homework, so they won't disturb us.'

The family golden retriever puppy jumps up, barking. Nisha lifts Lola's car seat into the air. 'Down, Bonnie. Down.'

I follow her carrying Lola into her interior-magazine-worthy kitchen with its top-of-the-range appliances and high-gloss finished units. Bonnie trots obediently by her side. Nisha places the car seat on the expansive wooden dining table. 'You wait here, little one, while I get your mum settled.'

Lola immediately starts crying. I drop down on the chair beside her, and I wipe her tear-streaked cheeks glistening in the light. Her beautiful blue eyes lock onto mine with a look of desperation as if she is trying to tell me something.

'Does she need a feed?' Nisha asks.

'Jasmine just gave her one.' I hold my head in my hands. 'It's the colic.'

Nisha swoops the car seat off the table. 'I'm going to get one of the kids to play with her.'

'No. No. Give her to me,' I say. 'I'll try and sing to her.'

'The change of scenery might help her,' Nisha insists. 'She's probably picking up on all the bad vibes. I'll be back in a tick.'

I succumb to her offer and try to call Max again. I'm over-ridden with guilt. I shouldn't have left my sister. He doesn't answer.

I puff out a large breath, staring at the floor. My mind is a maze of unanswered questions I'm going around in circles trying to answer. But the fact remains. My sister wouldn't have taken her own life.

But I'm obviously wrong.

I pick up one of Nisha's yoga magazines, trying to distract myself. I flick the page to a young woman with red hair, wavy like my sister's, and think of her now on the way to the morgue, cold and alone. But I still can't cry. It's as if my emotions tap has jammed in the off position, leaving my eyes bone-dry.

Nisha sweeps back into the room with Bonnie at her feet. 'Maisie's taken her to the playroom. You know what she's like.

She'll keep her entertained for a while.' Maisie is her eleven-year-old daughter, her youngest. She's the sweetest kid, as sweet as sugar.

She waves her phone at me. 'Sean just texted. The police are finishing up. They're coming back. Do you want a coffee, or something stronger?'

'Coffee, please. Double espresso.' I need something to wake me up.

She pops a capsule in the Nespresso machine. It gurgles and hisses before the espresso drips into the cup. She brings it to me, along with a bottle of water for herself.

'Did he give you any indication of how long they'd be?' I ask.

She shakes her head.

I take a sip of coffee. I can't taste anything; my senses are as raw as my nerves. 'I'm scared, Nisha. Really scared.'

'Scared of what?'

'Something isn't right.'

'In what way?'

'I can't put my finger on it. Samantha. The twins. Max.'

I take a deep breath, preparing to continue, but stop myself. Nisha is a close friend, but as much as I trust her, it's probably best not to express how I feel. After all, she is married to one of my husband's best friends.

I keep the thought to myself that I can't help but fear the worst. I've been so distracted by Lola that maybe I haven't seen what's been happening right under my nose – that something had been going on between Max and my sister, whom I found hanging in my en suite.

Maybe my husband and I both have secrets.

TWENTY-SIX

I shake my head, trying to dismiss my irrational fears. Shock can play funny games with your mind. I sip my coffee instead. 'I just can't believe she's gone. It's so... final.'

'It's a tragic situation.' Nisha rolls up the sleeves of her loose sweatshirt and whips an elastic band from her wrist, sweeping her long dark hair into a ponytail. 'You must talk about the situation. Not necessarily now, but in the coming days, weeks. I'm always here to listen if you want. You know that.'

The need to talk about Samantha is overwhelming. I ramble on about us growing up and going to live with our aunt and uncle when our mother died. We'd only known life with Mum as our father had walked out when I was born. Nisha listens intently as I tell her about when Mum died. I was twelve, and Samantha was fourteen. I talk about how she always looked out for me until Lola was born, and how things changed recently. My sister loved Lola. There's no doubt about that. But, although she never admitted it, my baby was a reminder of the child she'd never have, and the mother she'd never be.

'It must've been difficult for her. Do you think this is why she did this?'

I shrug. 'I didn't see any signs. Ezra might know more.' I pick up my phone and try him again. I call his number, only to reach his voicemail again. 'I don't understand where he could be.'

We turn to a beam of light from a car pulling into the driveway. I jump up. 'That's Max and Sean.'

They enter the kitchen in silence, both as white as the kitchen units. Max jingles his keys. 'Where's Lola? We need to go. I've left the twins.'

The thought of going back to his house fills me with dread.

'Maisie's playing with her,' Nisha says.

'I'll go and get her.' He marches out of the room before I have the chance to protest.

'Are the police still there?' I ask Sean.

'No, they've left,' he replies. 'We've all got to go down to the station in the morning and make a statement.'

I frown. 'A statement. Yes. Yes. The police officer mentioned that earlier. Why do you and Max have to go? You weren't there when it happened.'

'Standard procedure, apparently. We were there around the time she...' He hesitates and swallows hard. 'She... you know.' He walks to the dresser at the side of the room, an imposing piece of furniture that matches the high-gloss kitchen units. He yanks at one of the cupboard doors that opens to an array of alcoholic beverages like an Aladdin's cave. He pulls out a bottle of whisky and pours himself a drink.

'Why did she do this?' Nisha asks her husband. A question that seems unfitting at this precise moment in my presence.

'How am I meant to know?' His voice is harsh but hollow. So unlike the social spark we all know. It's like a different person is standing before us, drinking from the generous measure of whisky.

'You worked with her. Did she not give any clues that she had reached such a low point?' I say.

Max returns before Sean has the chance to answer. He is holding Lola's car seat in one hand and Lola facing us in the other. She kicks her legs and punches her arms out in front of her, giggling. A ray of sunshine in the darkness of the room. Max secures her into her car seat. 'You ready?'

I stand and sling my bag over my shoulder, confused at his abruptness. There's an atmosphere, a tension between the people standing before me, but I can't work out why.

'We need to talk.' I buckle my seatbelt.

Max glances at me. His eyes are bloodshot. 'We sure do.' He turns to focus on the road. 'Were you drinking, Annie? Is that why you were passed out and didn't hear Samantha come into the room?'

'No! How dare you say that.'

'I saw the empty bottle in the bin.'

'I was going to talk to you about that.' This isn't the time, but I can't help blurting out, 'I think it's Jasmine drinking the wine.'

He takes his eyes off the road to look at me. I can't make out if his expression is quizzical or disbelieving. 'The kids don't need to sneakily drink booze. I've always offered them a glass of wine if they want one.'

'You need to speak to her, because it wasn't me.' I pause. 'What just happened in there?' I ask to change the subject. I don't have the energy to argue.

'What do you mean?'

'I sensed an atmosphere between you and Sean.'

He lets out a long breath. 'My business partner – your sister and my sister-in-law – has just killed herself, Annie.' His voice cracks, breaking under the strain. 'I'm pretty cut up.'

'Nisha said Samantha was off when she popped into the office last week, and you were arguing with her then, as well. What about?'

His lips twist to the side. 'I can't remember. Business probably.'

'Max.' I lower my voice. 'What aren't you telling me?'

He takes his eyes off the road to look at me.

'Why are you lying to me?'

His silence fires a ball of anger within me.

'Why?' I repeat. This isn't making sense.

He raises his voice. 'Look, Annie. We're selling the company. Of course partners argue at a time like this. There are differences of opinion as to the best way to go about certain aspects. The fact is, I've fallen out of love with the company. You know how unhappy I've been. I just want out now. All three of us have disagreed at different points on how to do things. That's how it is.'

'Will the sale still go ahead?' Discussing this in the circumstances doesn't feel right, but I need to know.

He nods. 'The partnership agreement states that on the death of any of the partners, the voting rights of the deceased pass to the other two.'

'What about Ezra?'

'Her financial share will pass to him upon the sale, but not the voting rights.' He pauses before saying, 'I can't understand how you never heard her come into the room, Annie.'

I can't work out if there's a hint of accusation in his voice, or if it's a whisper in my imagination. 'I fell asleep.'

'How can you just fall asleep in the middle of the day?'

'Because I'm knackered,' I cry. 'Anyway, it wasn't the middle of the day. It was late afternoon.'

'And what about Lola? Jacob said you were smothering her.'

'That's not true.'

'I'm calling Zoe when we get home. Now this has happened, we need help with Lola.'

'I don't want you to.'

'I have to, Annie. It's my job to protect you all. Now this has happened to Samantha, we have to get some help. You can sleep on the sofa tonight if you want.'

'Why would I do that?'

'I thought you might find it too difficult being in our room after what's happened,' he says softly, taking my hand. 'If it wasn't for the bloody renovations, we could move into the spare room.'

'What about Lola?'

'She can stay with me in our room.'

'What about you?'

'I'd rather sleep somewhere else, but we can't move Lola's cot. It's up to you, darling. Whatever you feel comfortable with. We could go to a hotel if you'd prefer?'

'I'll be fine.' He's got a plane to catch in the morning. I can't leave him with Lola. And I don't want to go anywhere else. As odd as it sounds, I have an urge to be here, close to where my sister took her last breath. It's weirdly grotesque, yet strangely comforting.

As if reading my mind, he says, 'I'm going to phone the lawyers and see if we can postpone the meeting. I'll change the flights.'

'Is that wise? This is a crucial time. You don't want to lose this deal.'

'I can't leave you after what's happened. Besides, I need to be at the station in the morning. We all do.'

When we get home, I order pizzas and robotically throw together a salad while Max bathes Lola and puts her to bed. I should have ordered something different, but I couldn't face the wrath from the twins.

When he appears, Max says, 'I've changed my flight to Wednesday. Oh, and I had a word with Jasmine. She says she hasn't touched the wine.'

I pause laying the table, a knife in my hand. 'Well it wasn't me. Have you spoken to Jacob?'

'Jacob never touches alcohol. You know that.'

'Well it wasn't me,' I repeat, my voice raised. 'You can't blame me.'

'Calm down, darling. It's fine.'

'It's not fine, though, is it? I don't like the way you're looking at me. It's as if you don't believe me.'

The twins appear. 'I just want to say, I haven't touched your wine,' Jasmine says.

'Leave it,' Max says.

She shakes her head, defiantly, glaring at Max. 'You don't believe me, do you?'

'It must've been me,' Max shouts. It makes us all jump. 'I must've drunk it. Come on. It's been a hell of a day. Let's just sit down and have a meal.'

Few words are exchanged during the meal. Max switches on the TV to a programme about preparing your garden for summer. I turn to look out of the patio doors but it's too dark to see outside. Dark and dismal. That's exactly how I feel I'm going to spend the rest of my life. I force down a couple of mouthfuls of salad. It's all I can manage.

I glance around the table at the three of them. I catch the twins exchanging looks out of the corner of their eyes. Messages only each other can decode. Max picks at his food, and so does Jasmine, peeling the topping off the pizza and leaving the dough. Jacob makes up for it, clearing all three of their plates like a vacuum cleaner. Jasmine drops her fork on her plate.

'You don't even like white wine,' she says to Max.

Max glares at her. 'I said that's enough.'

I zone out as he asks them about school. I finish my glass of juice. The three of them blur into one as another headache begins. My stomach contracts in pain. Familiar feelings that have been coming and going for a while now.

I need to go and see a doctor.

TWENTY-SEVEN

With each passing hour, I regret not taking Max's suggestion to sleep on the sofa.

He drops off soon after we get into bed, but I toss and turn for hours. I glance at my phone. It's now three a.m., and I've hardly slept a wink, simply drifted in and out of nightmares between getting up to settle Lola.

Middle-of-the-night anxiety sets in as the wind rattles the window. I keep having to remove the duvet as I'm sweating, only to be shivering minutes later. I lie staring at the wall. Otherwise I have to face the door to the en suite, and every time I do, I'm gripped by an emotional pain that hurts like hell. A pain I've never felt before. It's a raw emptiness that cuts to the bone. I'm never going to see my sister again.

I finally fall asleep only to meet the figure that plagues my dreams night after disturbing night. Now and again, they emerge from the gloomy backdrop as if they're teasing me. It's those times I believe they're a man. But often, I catch an outline of their hair that glimmers in the light and flows down their back, and I'm sure they're a woman. I call after them. They respond, but I can't decipher what they're saying. I grasp at their arm, desperate to see who they are, but they start spinning, faster and faster, and their features distort until they disappear into the shadows...

The next thing I know, I awake to a loud noise. Bang. Bang. Bang. The builders have already started work for the day. I swear under my breath. For heaven's sake, Max! You could've cancelled them today. Disorientated, I sit up. Lola isn't in her cot. An irrational fear rips through me. Throwing back the covers, I rush to find my dressing gown, only to remember that the police took it away as evidence.

Evidence.

That word makes my sister's actions sound like a crime.

I grab Max's dressing gown from the bed and race for the stairs, my heart pounding. But it's OK. Rumblings of Max's voice and Lola giggling sound from the kitchen.

I return to the bedroom. My sister consumes my thoughts. I find my phone. It's five to eight. One of the builders outside shouts an order. It filters into the room. 'That lot needs moving. Get onto it now, can you?' There's a cup of tea on the bedside table. Max must have brought it up earlier. I take a sip. It's lukewarm and tastes disgusting, but I drink it as I read my messages. There's one from the police. They still can't get hold of Ezra and have requested contact details for his friends and family. Ezra is a single child, and his parents are travelling the world. I have no idea how to get hold of them. I call him again. He's still not answering.

I slip into a pair of leggings and an oversized sweater. The racket from outside is relentless. Bang. Bang. Bang. Clang. Clang. Clang. It's as if they're thrashing my head with a hammer.

I perch on the side of the bed, staring at my phone. As soon as it's eight o'clock, I call the doctor's. It's time to get some help.

I can see that. I can't carry on feeling so dreadfully ill all the time. The receptionist tells me they don't have any free appointments today. They never have. But if I go along at the end of the morning session, they will fit me in to see a GP.

Downstairs, I pause at the living room door. Jacob, dressed in his school uniform, sits upright at the piano as if he has waited for me to come down before thrashing out one of his heavy tunes. It's gloomy in there save a streak of daylight making its way through the window. It makes his appearance haunting, as if he's from another era, a century or more ago. He begins playing. The noise crashes like thunder, a torrent of deafening sound.

Max is in the kitchen, holding Lola while eating a slice of buttered toast. Dark circles ring his eyes. 'You OK?' he mouths. The top buttons of his shirt are open, and the sleeves rolled up to his elbows.

I nod to the garden. 'Couldn't you have cancelled them coming today?'

'I'm so sorry. I didn't even think. I'll ask them to leave early.'

'It's fine.' The sooner the builders are done and out of our hair, the better.

'She's here,' he says.

I take the stool at the breakfast bar next to him. 'Who?'

'Zoe.'

'What? Where?' I frown.

'She's just popped to the toilet. Why are you looking confused? We spoke about this last night.'

'Spoke about what?'

'Me calling her and arranging for her to work today.'

'No we didn't.'

He sighs. 'We did, darling. When we were washing up after dinner. Don't you remember?' He throws down the piece of toast he's eating and places an arm around me, holding me tightly. Lola starts crying. I pull away. 'You have to go to the police station later,' he says. 'I can stay here while you do that. But I need to work.' He nods to our baby. 'Zoe can look after her while you're out and I get some things done.'

I also need to go to the GP, but I don't tell him that. He's right. It will be easier with another pair of hands.

Jacob crashes the piano keys harder and harder. I grit my teeth. Max doesn't even seem to notice. He takes my hand while jigging Lola in his other arm. 'Don't worry. It's only temporary. Once the business is sold, I'll be free to help more. Everything is going to be OK. I promise you, darling.'

I wish I could believe him.

TWENTY-EIGHT

Zoe appears. At first I think she's sent a replacement. I'm taken aback. She's had her hair cut into a choppy pixie-cut style.

'I didn't recognise you,' I say.

She laughs, touching her head. 'It's a bit drastic, isn't it? I used to have my hair like this when I was younger. It's so much easier to manage.'

'It suits you,' I say. It shows off her large mole and accentuates the dimples that appear when she smiles.

She tells me how sorry she is to hear about my sister and about a friend of hers who took her own life in college. There's something comforting in the way she tells her story. Her eyes well up as we chat about it.

Lola starts fussing. 'I've given Zoe a tour of the downstairs. Why don't you show her around upstairs while I look after Lola?' Max suggests.

'Hey, no worries. Hand her over. You get on with what you need to.' Zoe whips our daughter from Max's arms. Lola immediately settles.

Despite my initial reluctance, I take Zoe up to the first floor, while talking through Lola's daily schedule. Not that she has one. Every time I've tried to settle her into a schedule, they've not only gone right out of the window, but landed splattered on the ground.

At the top of the stairs, I grab hold of the banister. I'm not wholly with it. I feel like I'm drifting, floating on a raft of uncertainty. 'I should type up some notes for you,' I say.

'It's all good. I remember things pretty well, but I'll jot down some notes just in case.' She pulls out her phone from the back pocket of her jeans. 'Tell me her daily routine.'

'To be honest. I've tried to get her into a routine, but I haven't been that successful.' I swallow the mother guilt that all the comparisons with other mums bring.

'I understand. It's really hard establishing a pattern, but that's where I can help.' She types notes on her phone with one hand while simultaneously keeping Lola amused on her hip with the other. 'Do you take her to any groups?'

'Groups?'

'Swimming, music, baby yoga.'

'Baby yoga? Does that even exist?' I laugh, imagining trying to stretch Lola into a downward dog. 'There's a baby and toddler group I drop into now and again.'

'I'll check out what else is going on locally.'

Another wallop of guilt slaps me across the face. I should have done that.

'What do you want me to do while she naps?' Zoe transfers Lola to her other hip. 'I'm happy to cook, clean, tidy, sort the washing.'

I'm still unsure how much I can trust this woman. But perhaps Max is right. Maybe she could be good for our family. 'There is something.' I'm not sure how far to go with this. 'I'm worried about the twins.'

She frowns. 'In what way?'

I hesitate, unsure how much to confide in this stranger.

'They have a lot going on. And sometimes I worry they may feel left out.' I reach out and stroke the silky soft skin of my daughter's face. 'This one has taken all the attention these past few months.'

'Naturally.'

'Things have been hectic since she was born.'

She nods her understanding.

'Anything you can do to help them feel more part of the family unit would help. Just something to be aware of, I guess.'

She bounces Lola on her hip. 'We can chat to your brother and sister, little one, can't we?' Her lips curve into a comforting smile. 'Leave it to me. I've worked with many teenagers before. There was a family kind of like yours – the Hiatts. The dad remarried four or five years after his wife died, and his kids made things pretty ugly for their stepmom, which is why they brought me in.' She rolls her eyes. 'Honestly, they were brats to start with. They gave her such a hard time. But they came around in the end.'

'How?'

'I became the go-between. Made them see things from the new wife's point of view.'

'How long did it take?'

Her face screws up in thought. 'A few weeks, a month, maybe.'

I let out a deep sigh. 'I'd love your help to do the same.'

She gives a collegial smile. 'Leave it with me.' She nods. 'I'd love to help. I'll see what I can do.'

A hammering at the front door interrupts our conversation. I leave Lola with Zoe and go to answer it. An Amazon delivery guy hands me a large parcel. I can't remember ordering anything. I study the label. It's for Max.

Lola giggles as Zoe descends the stairs. 'You get on with what you need to. I'll call you if I have any problems,' Zoe says as she meets me at the bottom. 'I'll take her to the living room and play with her until you're done.' She looks at Lola. 'Perhaps we can ask your brother to play some calmer tunes.' She winks at me.

Perhaps I read her wrong. Perhaps she could prove helpful round here. The glue that can help us stick together.

TWENTY-NINE

Having never stepped inside a police station before, the experience is intimidating. A female police officer sits opposite me on a matching plastic chair in the small interview room, trying to make me feel at ease, but the atmosphere is stifling. 'I know this must be hard for you, Annie. Can I call you Annie?'

I nod. 'I'll give you as much information as I can, but I'm not really sure how I can help.' I fidget in the chair. 'I'm as shocked as everyone else about what's happened.'

The police officer steeples her fingers and rests her chin on them. 'I understand you were asleep in the bedroom when the incident occurred.'

'That's right.'

'And you didn't hear anything?'

I shake my head. 'Nothing. If only I had.'

'And your sister gave no indication she was considering doing this?'

'When I saw her last week – I popped into her apartment with my daughter – she seemed a little distracted. And I thought she looked more tired than usual, but she never said anything. I've had a lot going on myself, so perhaps she didn't feel she could talk to me.'

'What's been going on with you?'

'I've got a four-month-old baby with dreadful colic.'

Her eyes shine with empathy. 'That's difficult. I hope she settles soon. We still can't get hold of your brother-in-law. Do you have any idea where he might be?'

I shake my head. 'I didn't know he'd taken annual leave. Neither of them mentioned it to me.'

'Would that have been the sort of thing she'd have generally told you?'

Her question confuses me. Should I have known? Perhaps Samantha did tell me, and I wasn't listening. Maybe I was in, what Max terms, one of my usual *daydreaming dazes*. 'I guess not.'

She frowns and asks further questions that I answer the best I can. I walk through my day yesterday and when I saw my sister. She asks me to sign a statement. The whole process doesn't take as long as I thought it would. So I can't understand why I leave the room thinking this woman believes I was somehow involved in my sister's death.

On the way to see the GP, I call Zoe. She's doing just fine, she tells me. Lola is napping, and she has just put a wash load on and tidied the kitchen.

Dr Evans is a character you can't help but take an immediate liking to. His round, jolly face and prune-coloured nose remind me of an off-duty Santa. All he needs is the mandatory bushy white beard and a sack of presents. He invites me to take a seat beside his organised desk. 'How can I help?'

I'm determined not to let the conversation degenerate into my woes of motherhood. 'I'm not really sure where to start.'

'At the beginning often helps.' His eyes scan the screen. 'You're a relatively new mum, I see. And you had a C-section.'

'And I haven't felt right since.'

'In what way?'

I take a deep breath. I think about the conversation I had with Nisha. 'I keep getting these stomach cramps, and my friend – she's a psychologist – believes I could have postnatal depression. My husband, too. They don't understand. I just need sleep. And... yesterday—' I pause to control the tears threatening to flood through the dam of protection I've built around myself. 'Yesterday, my sister took her own life. Please just give me something to help me sleep.'

'I'm so sorry for your loss.' He turns to his screen. 'We have a professional grief counsellor I can put you in contact with.' His voice is gentle and soothing. 'Can I suggest you talk to them?'

'But I can't sleep, and it's driving me insane.'

'Why don't you tell me how you're feeling. Give me your version of yourself.'

I pick at the handle of my handbag. 'I can't put a finger on it exactly, but I don't think I'm depressed. It's just... Oh, I don't know... not all the time, but a lot of the time, my head is so fuzzy.' I shrug. 'I don't know how to describe it... foggy. And I forget things. And there are these voices in my head. Sometimes, not always. But when they come I can't make them go away.' I shrug. 'I'm just constantly bushed.'

'You're a new mum. It's to be expected. And now you've had this added trauma.'

I spill my life. 'My daughter has got colic. She cries incessantly. My stepchildren are difficult. We're having part of our house renovated, living among mess and dust and builders constantly in and out.' I scoff. 'Our house is like Oxford Street on Christmas Eve.' I bite my lower lip. 'I feel nauseous all the time. And, I feel as if... as if...' I shrug. 'It's hard to find the right words, but sometimes I feel my body is full of poison.'

He carries out observations, taking my temperature before wrapping the cuff of a blood pressure monitor around my upper arm. 'Are you taking any medication at the moment?'

'Only vitamins following the birth. My friend, the psychologist, recommended them.'

'Nothing else?'

I shake my head.

'Mmn.' He frowns. 'Have you ever suffered from high blood pressure?'

I look into his eyes. They appear as tired as mine. 'No. Why, is it high?'

'One hundred and thirty-six over eighty-two, which is higher than I would expect for you. I'm going to send you to the nurse for a full set of bloods.'

'What's wrong with me?'

'I don't like second-guessing, Mrs Carpenter. Let's get your bloods done and take it from there. And in the meantime, I'm going to arrange for you to have a scan and an appointment for you to see our grief specialist.'

'What about my sleeping problem? Can't you give me something to help me sleep?'

'I'd rather get your bloods done first. In the meantime, is there someone who can help you? A family member, perhaps? It's important you get some help.'

I leave him, frustrated and annoyed. No one seems to understand that if I could just have a few good full nights of sleep, I'd feel so much better.

But maybe I'm wrong.

Perhaps there is something more sinister going on with my body. The anxiety that usually kicks in at night, but has started to rear its ugly head earlier in the day, storms through me.

I think of my baby.
I can't be ill. She needs me.

THIRTY

On the way home, I stop at Samantha and Ezra's apartment. When they moved here, they gave me a key for emergencies, and for the times they went on holiday and I watered their plants.

I place the key in the lock but pause. It seems wrong to let myself in now. But I need to find out what's happened to Ezra. I turn the key and step inside, scrunching my eyes tightly at the orangey signature smell of my sister. The smell is fading, probably because her essential oils haven't been burning for a few days. Soon, it will be gone, like the scent of her perfume, never to be rekindled again. The thought makes me let out a long, low howl. 'Why did you do this, Samantha? Why?' I cry out to the air heavy with her memories.

I shiver. It's colder in here than outside. I check the thermostat on the wall by the contemporary coat stand loaded with my sister's coats, bags and scarves. That's strange. The heating has been completely turned off. I turn to the coat stand and scrunch the smooth leather of her tan-coloured winter jacket, breathing in the musky smell. It reminds me of the day she bought it when we went shopping together in London. Ezra had given her the money to treat herself as it was her birthday. He'd meant to be going with her but had been called into work, so I went instead. We shopped for hours to find the right jacket.

I slowly shake my head. She always knew what she wanted, my sister.

And death wasn't it.

I head to the living room. Usually I'm OK being here alone, but today not so. I feel like an intruder about to be caught.

But I want clues, answers, as to why my sister took her own life.

Four empty beer cans on the coffee table confuse me. They are Heineken. The beer Ezra drinks, which he rarely does, so four seems an awful lot. I look around, but nothing else seems out of place. I walk around the apartment. It's eerie without the two of them. I end up in their bedroom. The bed is unmade. That's not right. Ever since we were young, my sister was a stickler for making her bed. I pick up her silk nightie from the floor. My pockets of sadness deepen as I rub the silk between my fingers. She's never going to wear this again.

I'm about the leave the room when I notice a book on her bedside cabinet. It's a Peter James. I do a double-take. It's the one Max is reading at the moment. What a coincidence. I pick it up, noticing the bookmark sticking out of the top. I quickly yank it out, confirming my suspicions. The bookmark is years old. It has pictures of the twins when they were young beneath a plastic coating.

My stomach turns.

I throw the book down.

I need to speak to Max.

When I arrive home, Max is making a cup of coffee in the kitchen. 'What's he doing?' I ask, pointing to Cameron, who is up a ladder in the garden. I put my bag down on the centre island.

'I bought a security camera and some security lights from Amazon. He's putting them up. We have no security around here. It's a concern. I thought while we're having all the renovations done, we might as well get that job done. I've asked him to show you how to set up an app on your phone that monitors when they go off.'

'I went to Samantha's apartment.'

Max takes a sip of coffee. 'What for?'

'To see if Ezra was there. I need to ask you something.'

He raises his eyebrows and bites into a shortbread biscuit from the packet on the centre island.

I take a deep breath. 'I found your Peter James book that you're reading at the moment on Samantha's bedside cabinet. What's it doing *there*?'

He chokes on his mouthful of biscuit as he tries to swallow it. He coughs. 'I finished it and lent it to her.'

'Oh.'

'Why? What were you thinking?' He laughs. 'Playing detective, were you?'

A rush of heat rises up my neck. 'Nothing. I just thought it was strange, that's all. Your bookmark was in there.'

'That's where it went. I've been looking for that.'

I'm stumped. I don't know what I expected him to say but it wasn't that. 'Where do you think Ezra has gone?'

'It's very odd,' he says.

'It's more than odd. I'm scared.'

'What of?'

'That he knows why Samantha did this. And that's why he's disappeared.'

'Don't jump to conclusions. Wait until he turns up.'

THIRTY-ONE

For once, a peacefulness spans this tense house. But, then, it is two thirty in the morning. There's something unnerving about it, like the calm before a violent storm.

I yawn. We went to bed at nine last night. Max managed to grab a few hours of sleep, but I didn't. There is something macabre about our bedroom now. Death hangs in the air like a bad smell.

I look around the kitchen. It's still relatively neat from where Zoe tidied up yesterday. I'm sipping a cup of tea, waiting for Max to stop farting around and leave for the airport. Despite my insistence, he decided against booking a hotel. He didn't want to leave us after everything that's happened, he told me again when I suggested it, even though it meant getting up at this ridiculous time. I can't help wondering if he meant me. He didn't want to leave *me* alone with Lola... and the twins. More than once, he has questioned how I didn't manage to hear Samantha come into the bedroom. And how could I have been so deeply asleep that I didn't know Jacob had taken Lola? Subtle questions, but questions all the same. And fair ones I simply can't answer.

His flight is not until six, but he doesn't want to risk getting caught in traffic. It happened once before, in the early days of our relationship. When we went on our first holiday as a blended family, way before Lola was born. Jasmine was being particularly difficult, resulting in us leaving late, sitting in a four-mile traffic jam and missing our flight. I was livid, but Max, as usual, couldn't find it in himself to criticise his daughter. I can't recall what I was most annoyed at – missing the flight or the futile way in which he handled the situation.

He enters the kitchen, shrugging into his black woollen overcoat. 'You didn't have to get up.'

'I wanted to see you off.' There's a longing inside of me. A longing for us to return to how we were before I fell pregnant. The evenings of lengthy dinners, sharing a bottle of wine and intelligent conversation; the visits to an art gallery or museums, or the quiet evenings, cuddling on the sofa and watching a movie. It was all so intoxicating.

'Here, I made you a coffee. It'll help with the journey.' I push the mug towards him. Coffee slops over the edge onto the breakfast bar. 'Damn.' I grab a kitchen cloth from the sink to wipe it up.

'Have you seen my best white shirt?' he asks.

I inwardly wince. I'd forgotten about that. The shirt I'd put in the wash with the towels by mistake that's tucked at the back of the laundry cupboard. I'll order him a new one when I get to my computer later. 'It's in the wash.' Another day, another lie.

'I wanted it for the meeting.'

'Shall I iron you another one?'

'It's fine. I've packed my grey one. You're not worried, are you? There's plenty of people around. You won't be lonely.' He gives a wry smile.

I breathe sharply and cradle my cup of tea, appreciating the warmth seeping into my hands. 'No, Max. I certainly won't be lonely.'

'I've had a word with the twins to help out while I'm gone.' He sips his coffee, his face contorting at the strength of the drink.

My sister enters my thoughts. I close my eyes, trying to rid the image of the putrid, purple shade of her face on the afternoon she left us. Her cloudy eyes, the distress in her pupils, it haunts me. My thoughts turn to words, blurting out before I can stop them. 'I can't get the image of Samantha hanging there out of my mind.'

'I hear you, darling. Perhaps when we get the room decorated, it'll help. You can choose how to have it. Once the money comes through from the business, we can rip it all out and start again. What do you say?'

'I want to move.' The words leave my mouth before I can stop them.

'What?' Max checks his watch as if what I've just announced is a major inconvenience. 'Where has this come from? I thought you were happy here. We're happy here. Lola will grow out of this difficult stage. Things will get better.'

He doesn't see it. He's been too busy these past few months, what with Lola coming along and dealing with his business.

'The truth is, Max, I've never been happy here. I just hadn't realised it.' This isn't the time for this conversation. He's about to leave for a flight. But I can't stop myself. 'This is your house. Yours, Jacob's and Jasmine's home. All the memories are yours, not mine. And now Samantha's. Why don't we get the company sold, finish the renovation work, and get it on the market when the twins go to university next year. Make a fresh start. What do you say?'

'Not now, darling.'

'But think about it at least. On the flight. You've got eleven hours to kill.'

'Eleven hours to get some sleep and prep for the most important business meeting of my life.'

There's a distance between us. An intolerable distance that's been growing daily since Lola was born. Or perhaps it started before that. I can't tell. The days have merged unnoticed into weeks since she exploded into our lives. There's too much strain on us – the builders, the twins, a new baby, and now Samantha. No relationship can survive this much pressure.

'There's been so much going on.' He stands and grabs the handle of his cabin bag. 'Things will settle down, you'll see.'

'What time is Sean picking you up?'

'He's not.'

'Why?'

'He's on a different flight.'

'Why?'

'He's flying out later on.'

That doesn't make sense. 'You always travel together when you go away on business. Why are you flying separately?'

He hesitates too much for my liking. 'I couldn't get us seats on the same flight. It was too last minute.'

That does kind of make sense. But, still, I don't think he's being wholly truthful. 'Is everything all right between the two of you?'

'Why wouldn't it be?'

'What are you not telling me, Max?'

He frowns. 'What do you mean?'

I don't like the look in his eye. It's at odds with the tone of his voice. I shrug.

'I couldn't even get a business class seat,' he says as if he wants to change the subject. 'When I used to travel for Digital Central, they always flew me business class. I hope I'll be able to grab some sleep.' He hasn't mentioned that company for a while. He began working for them when he finished uni and left to start his own business. He was highly successful there and he and his first wife even moved to LA for a year.

There's a gentle knock at the door. 'That'll be my taxi.' He places his empty coffee cup on the side before I have a chance to continue. 'I've got to go. Don't come to the door. It's cold. I love you.'

He kisses me quickly on the cheek before disappearing in a puff of my exasperation, leaving me confused and standing alone. All alone.

THIRTY-TWO

I return to our bedroom, casting my gaze around the gloomy interior. It's so dark in here. Shadows linger into each of the corners. And it's not from the lack of light. It's the large pieces of mahogany furniture – the wardrobe and lofty chest of drawers – and the walls papered a forest green. The teak panelling on the wall behind the bed doesn't help. Like the rest of this crumbling house, it feels planted in the early part of the previous century.

I peer into the cot. In the soft glow of moonlight I can see Lola thankfully sleeping peacefully. Her tiny hands are scrunched by her face, her breaths the faintest puffs of air. I watch her for a while, savouring the peace, until my peripheral vision catches the closed door to the en suite, and a wretched pain clutches at my heart.

On my way back from the police station yesterday, I decided I wasn't going to sleep in here while Max was away. I was going to dismantle the cot and take it downstairs, but Max said that wasn't a good idea. He had moaned and groaned while constructing it when I was eight months pregnant. I had tried to help, calling out the instructions, pointing to which piece was next in the process. But the tools that came with the cot were the wrong size, which delivered another explosion of expletives. After battling along for a good hour, he went out and bought a set of Allen keys from the hardware store. There's no way I could take it apart and rebuild it in the living room. It would take too long, and I simply don't have the energy.

I settle back in bed and try to call Ezra again, desperate more than ever to speak to him. There are things we need to discuss. But once again, there's no answer.

I stare at the ceiling, but, frustratingly, I can't stop my eyes being drawn time and time again to the en suite. When sleep finally comes, I'm plagued by the faceless person who haunts me in my sleep. But for the first time, my sister becomes part of the terror that torments me every night.

I awake in a cold sweat. In the shadows, I eye a wisp of cobwebs hanging from the lampshade hovering above the bed as suddenly the room ignites in an explosion of light. It's as if a silent bomb has exploded. It both startles and terrifies me in equal measure. I sit bolt upright. The new security light Cameron put up outside must have tripped. Throwing off the duvet, I jump up and rush to the window, to see what may have triggered the system.

I'm not mistaken.

A figure darts across the lawn and around the side of the house.

I may be tired, but my senses are on full alert. Was that Jacob? I make for the stairs, muttering, 'Enough of these games.' The hallway is in darkness. Halfway down the stairs, I freeze. The familiar sound of the patio doors opening filters up the stairs from the kitchen.

Someone is coming in.

Or going out.

The security light casts zigzagging shadows across the hallway before extinguishing. My hand grabs the banister. The moonlight darting in and out from behind the scant cloud cover now provides the only source of light. A draught blows through my nightie. I shiver. When I reach the bottom, I feel my way along the hallway and creep into the kitchen. Sure enough, the patio doors are open. Only a little but enough for someone to have entered or exited.

I scan the room, desperately trying to detect movement. I turn on the light. The silence of the night supports my thoughts that there's no one here.

My hands are clammy. 'Shit!' I drop to my haunches as once again the security light flashes into action.

There may be no one in here, but there's certainly someone outside.

I scoot across the living room like a cat about to pounce on its prey. All I need to do is get to the doors and lock them. A few more steps, and I'll be there.

The light goes out again, accentuating the darkness, save the moon casting an inadequate ray. I have to lock the door.

Slowly, I reach out.

I scream as a figure stands menacingly in front of me.

'Did you see anyone?' asks a familiar voice as the figure comes into view and pulls the door wide open.

'Jacob. You scared the life out of me.'

'Sorry. I didn't mean to.' He steps inside. His untamed hair hangs over his face. He closes the door. 'Did you see anyone?' he repeats.

He's playing games with me.

'I did,' I say hesitantly. 'From my bedroom window.'

'I thought I did too. I came down to get a drink of water and saw the light go on. But I went out to look and there was no one there.'

'You shouldn't have gone out there alone.'

'Why not?'

I secure the door, checking several times it's locked. 'Because you could've got yourself hurt, Jacob.'

He sweeps a clump of hair away from his face and tucks it behind his ear. 'It's probably a fault with the security lights, or just animals.'

'But I saw a figure, and I—' I turn to a noise.

'What's with all the racket?' Jasmine stands in her fleece pyjamas at the entrance to the living room.

'The security light went off, and I went to have a look. No big drama,' Jacob says.

'I have to disagree. I saw a figure in the garden. I think we should call the police,' I say.

The twins exchange a look. Jacob's gaze drops to the ground. Jasmine rolls her eyes and lets out a groan. 'The police won't be bothered.'

'But I saw someone.'

'Did you? Really, Annie? Are you absolutely sure?' Her words echo her father's, questioning my sanity.

I remain silent.

Jacob pipes up, 'Why don't you look at the footage?'

'How?' I ask.

He points to the security cameras that Cameron fitted. 'Those things record movements and enable you to play it back. Let's have a look. It'll put your mind at rest.'

'We can't,' I say.

'Why not?' Jacob asks.

'Your dad said Cameron was going to set up the app on my phone, but he never did.'

Jasmine yawns. 'It's probably nothing.'

'You're probably right. Come on, let's get to bed.'

I shepherd them upstairs, whispering words of encouragement for them to get some sleep. Not that there's any chance of me heeding my own words.

Someone was outside. I know it.

And I think it was one or both of them playing games with me.

But why? With everything that has gone on with my sister, it's just plain cruel.

I have so many questions.

And literally no answers.

But I'll get them.

I will.

THIRTY-THREE

Reluctantly, I open my eyes. It's getting more difficult to get up by the day. My eyes sting. I inwardly groan at the day stretching long and heavy ahead, counting the hours before I can come back to bed. After the incident with the security lights, it took me ages to fall back to sleep, and when I did, I drifted from nightmare to nightmare. This time they centred around the twins and Max taking Lola away from me.

And my sister wasn't dead.

She was very much alive, helping them.

Lola is awake, cooing. Through the slats of the cot sides, I see her swinging her arms and kicking her legs beneath her sleepsuit towards her cot mobile, a collection of colourful ocean creatures suspended in the air that the twins bought when she was born. For once, she isn't fussing for her morning feed but instead is making a serene gurgling sound. She reaches for her feet, tugging at the soft material of her sleepsuit. It's the first time I've seen her do that. She'll be rolling over soon, according to the posts I've read on Instagram.

Vehicles pull up outside the house. Van doors slam shut.

The garden gate squeaks open, banging against the adjoining wall. Jigsaw's familiar raucous laugh at banter from Cameron's American accent resounds in the distance. I get up and look out of the side window. Workmen bound across the garden below heading to work. Not long to go now. Yesterday, the roofers were on the top boards of the scaffolding laying new slates on the roof. The work they've carried out now looks out of place in relation to the rest of the house. A modern pristine structure extending from a dilapidated, neglected house.

After I get dressed, Lola is surprisingly still content, so I leave her and try Ezra again. The call goes to his voicemail. My hand thumps the bed. This is getting more frustrating by the hour. Apart from when he's working, his phone is always glued to his ear like a teenager's. The suspicion I have for his absence deepens. Something is amiss. I think about calling the police to raise my concerns, but it feels utterly disloyal, and besides, they must already be thinking the same as me. Where the hell is he?

The shower in the bathroom on the floor above turns on. The twins must be getting up.

I open the photos app on my phone and click on the album I share with Samantha, titled *Sisters*. It's a collection of photos of, mainly, the two of us having fun that she set up about ten years ago. I start scrolling through but have to stop. The memories are too painful to visit. It's still all too raw.

I turn to my emails and scan the unopened ones. A tide of orders has come in since I caught up at the end of last week. They need actioning. I sigh heavily. What once filled me with great pleasure now seems like an insurmountable chore.

When I get Lola up, she is still happy. For once, it's a joy to enfold her into my arms. I kiss the top of her head. As I breathe in the fruity smell of baby shampoo, I catch a wisp of her dark hair in my mouth. She giggles as she reaches her hand to me, her eyes wide and trusting. My heart aches. Butterflies flutter in my stomach. There's a silent connection. A taste of how I imagined life to be with my baby when she was still a seed growing in my belly. Then the door to the en suite catches my eye, and I'm brought back to earth by a different almighty pain in my heart.

A knock at the front door disturbs the moment.

Lola immediately starts screaming.

I hurry downstairs with her bouncing on my hip to the sound of a truck arriving outside the front of the house. I open the door to find Zoe on the doorstep. She hit the ground running at full speed yesterday, and by the end of the day had a plan for establishing a successful daily routine that I knew I could never achieve on my own, so, following the advice from the doctor that I need some help, I agreed with Max to give her a week's trial. It's a start.

'Morning, you two.' She drops her rucksack inside the door and throws off her coat. 'Come here, little one.' She takes a crying Lola from me. 'What's wrong with you this morning? Come on, let's get you some breakfast.' Efficiently, she whisks my baby off to the kitchen before I have a chance to speak. I'm about to shut the door when a man in a black cap and a high-vis vest appears, asking me where I want him to dump the order of sand piled high on his dumper truck.

'I'm not sure,' I say. 'Can you go around the side and ask the builders.'

The kitchen is already a hive of activity. It's exhausting. Cameron is up a ladder, sponging the kitchen ceiling.

'What are you doing?' I ask.

'Hi, Mrs C. Max asked me to repair the stain damage left by the fire.' He rinses the sponge in a bucket resting on the platform of the ladder. 'I'll be finished real quick,' he says in his casual Californian tone. 'And I'll be out of your hair.' He squirts liquid from a spray bottle onto the ceiling.

That doesn't make sense. We're meant to be ripping the

kitchen out and starting again when the current renovations are completed. Phase II, that's what Max called it. The second lot of renovations to make the rest of the house a home that I'll feel comfortable in. So I can't understand why he has now asked Cameron to patch up the fire damage.

THIRTY-FOUR

Nothing is making sense. Every direction I turn, confusion awaits. A drilling noise starts. It goes right through me. The constant banging and crashing adds to the chaos we're living in, and the heavy weight of grief is playing with my emotions. I boil the kettle to make some tea.

Zoe follows the instructions I gave her yesterday for making up the bottles with one hand while comforting Lola in the other with tunes from her angelic voice. She and Cameron exchange banter. If I'm not mistaken, there appears to be a chemistry between them.

She tells him about the places she plans to visit. But I have to stop listening. It's too damn hard hearing someone talk about their life plans when they are so similar to what my sister wanted to achieve. Climbing Mount Kilimanjaro was top of Samantha's bucket list. As soon as the business was sold, she was going to book flights to go.

The same thought returns like a pesky friend who won't take no for an answer.

My sister would never have taken her own life.

Jasmine and Jacob are sitting at the centre island, adopting their usual morning poses – legs dangling and heads dropped over bowls of cereal while they scroll on their phones.

'Where do you keep the formula, did you say?' Zoe asks.

Jasmine answers for me. 'In the cupboard above the toaster.'

A cupboard door bangs shut. 'I figured that's what you said. But there's none here.'

'There must be. I got some just the other day,' I say.

Jasmine smirks, thinking I don't notice.

'Oh, man. Am I missing something?' Zoe says.

'The bottles for today should be in the fridge.' I open the fridge door and search the shelves.

Zoe points to the steriliser. 'Are they in there?'

I rip the lid off of the steriliser. She's right. All six bottles are standing to attention on the bottom shelf, the nipples, tops and one of Lola's dummies on the rack above.

I clutch my head. But I remember making up the bottles yesterday. Not this again. Perhaps I'm getting my days mixed up. I can't remember exactly.

'It happens. Don't worry. I can make up some more.' Zoe pulls a puzzled face. 'When we find the formula.'

I look in the cupboard where I keep the formula, now a vacant space. 'This is where it should be. I bought two tins last week.'

Jasmine nudges Jacob's elbow. They both turn to observe me as I methodically open the other cupboard doors, banging them shut in frustration. 'Perhaps it was the week before last I got them?' I'm doubting myself now. I must've misplaced them. Left them at the supermarket, perhaps.

Zoe lays a hand on my shoulder. 'Well, it's not like you haven't had a lot going on. I'll take Lola to the shops and get some more.'

I glance at the empty cupboard. 'She needs a feed now. Hang on.' I search her bag for the single use bottle I bought the other day for emergencies after the mishap I made with thinking I had another bottle ready and didn't. 'Here. Warm this up for her.'

'Great. And I'll replace it when I go to the shops.'

Fumbling in my purse, I find a twenty-pound note. 'This should cover it.'

'I'll get her sorted and go. You carry on with what you're doing.'

From the corner of my eye, I catch Jasmine glance at Jacob. A stranger wouldn't notice the roll of her eyes.

The ladder groans and creaks under Cameron's six foot stocky frame as he steps down. 'All done for now. Once it dries out, I think it'll be fine.' He digs in his pocket and pulls out a piece of metal. 'The new valve for the toilet. I'll fit it now.'

'I forgot about that,' I say. 'While you're here, can I ask you about the security cameras you guys fitted?'

'Fire away.'

I fumble to take my phone from my back pocket. The issue with the formula and bottles has dumped another load of unease on my shoulders. 'I need to set up the app on my phone so I can look at the footage.'

'No problem. Sorry, Max did ask me to show you yesterday, but I got called to another job. It's easy. I'll show you how.'

I hand my phone to him.

He doesn't take it. 'I'll give you instructions, then you'll know how to work it in future.'

I'd rather just give it to him. I'm too tired and irritated to deal with technology. But I take his point.

It doesn't take long before we have the app up and running on my phone. 'What time did you say it happened?' he asks.

'Three thirty-six,' Jacob pipes up.

'How precise,' Cameron says with a laugh.

Jacob blushes. He gets up from his stool and joins us.

I edge the footage along to three thirty-five a.m. to catch the minute before and press play. The three of us watch the video footage.

'See, that's where the light first comes on.' Jacob points to the screen. 'There's no one there. But wait for it. There we go. That's the second time. When I go out.'

There's silence, all three of us immersed in a video that reveals nothing.

'But I swear I saw someone outside.'

I'm determined to make them believe me.

Otherwise, I won't be able to believe myself.

'Perhaps you thought you saw something but didn't,' Cameron says. 'It was the middle of the night. It happens.'

'Maybe it was a shadow,' Jasmine says. There's no mistaking the mockery in her voice. 'Or a spirit of the night.' She throws her arms out in exaggeration, mimicking a ghost.

'I don't understand. They went around the side of the house. Perhaps they were out of camera shot.'

'I went out there, though. You saw me. There was no one there, Annie,' Jacob says in a matter-of-fact tone.

I back down. Even I think I'm sounding like a lunatic now. 'Is there any chance you could give the system a once-over?' I say to Cameron. 'When it went off, our whole bedroom lit up like the bloody Blackpool Tower.'

'Sure thing. I'll check the camera angles and see if I can get a wider shot to take in more of the garden. I can always put up another camera around the side if you order one. I'll catch you later.'

Jacob returns to his stool.

I replay the video three times.

There was no one there.

THIRTY-FIVE

I'm slowly going mad. My life is spiralling out of control.

All I want is to see my sister again. I miss her so much. Her death has left a raw, unremitting pain that hounds me day and night. It no longer feels right without her in my life.

It's a slog to get my act together, but I finally make it to my makeshift office in the large shed at the bottom of the garden, shivering while the heating kicks in. It's cram-packed in here, scarcely enough room for my small desk. Boxes of stock surround me, taking up half of the space, along with an old folding table I use to prepare orders. A wide old sofa lines the back wall, the focal point of the room when the twins used it as a den. They weren't happy when I took over this space. I suggested using one of the small attic rooms, but Max was insistent that I couldn't be lugging boxes up and down the stairs that far along my pregnancy. I couldn't blame their feelings, but Max did set up another den in the attic for them.

Switching on my computer, my gaze turns to the small window while I wait for the screen to come to life. I take a sharp breath as our bedroom window comes into view. I replay Monday in my mind like I have a thousand times. Samantha and Sean arrived. I couldn't pull myself together. Lola was being particularly tricky. I finally managed to get her to her vaccination appointment. I prepared dinner. Then came the terrible nausea and tiredness that drove me to bed. I fell asleep with Lola on my chest and awoke to find my sister dead.

I will myself not to think about it. Keep busy: that's the only way I'm going to get through the days ahead. I turn to my screen. My inbox is out of control, and all those orders need filling. I set to work, but I can't concentrate. The thought of letting Lola's feed get so low is frustrating me. I'm usually so well organised, it's hard to believe I've made such a fundamental mistake. Picking up my phone, I sign in to my banking app, furiously scrolling through the entries. I stop. There it is. The entry for the supermarket shopping last week when I'd bet the contents of my savings account that I bought two cans of formula.

I jump up, backing the chair into a pile of boxes. They topple. One falls on my foot. I swear as I kick it out of the way. It bursts open from the force, and the contents tumble onto the floor. 'Damn you!' I shout and kick it again.

Outside, the cold air hits me. I hurry along the path to the house, heading for the cellar accessed via a door in the hallway, where I store spare shopping bags. It's an unused space that Max plans to turn into a stylish cinema room one day. But that's a job for another time. The whole cellar needs digging out to increase the space to ceiling height, and it needs electricity and pipework for heating.

I open the door, dismayed to see the hook has broken; and the IKEA bag holding all the reusable bags that I was looking for has fallen down the makeshift staircase composed of a ladder and a wooden pole fixed to the wall with old brackets. I switch on the bulb. Carefully, I step down, dodging the cobwebs spanning the space. It's dark down there, void of any natural light. The old window that was once there has been removed, and the space bricked up. And ventilation is poor. I cough on what feels like over one hundred years of stale air trapped in the space. As I pick up the IKEA bag, I look upwards, sure I heard a noise coming from the doorway. Spooked, I scurry back up the ladder, but there's no one there.

I rummage through the IKEA bag. Got it! The reusable bag I purchased with my shopping from the supermarket last week. I hurry to the kitchen to prise it open. A scrunched-up receipt lies at the bottom. I straighten out the crinkles and run my finger down the items I purchased: a four-pint carton of milk, a bunch of bananas, a loaf of bread and a tube of toothpaste. And there it is. At the bottom of the list – an entry for two tubs of formula. I did buy them. And I'm ninety-nine per cent sure I put them in the cupboard.

My phone rings. I remove it from my pocket. Ezra's number flashes on the screen. At last. I answer it as I drop the receipt. It floats in a whisper as I bend to catch it before it lands on the floor. 'Where the hell have you been, Ezra?' I struggle to hide my exasperation. 'I've been trying to get hold of you.'

'I went away for a few days.' The flat tone of his voice tells me that the police, or someone, has got to him before me.

'You've heard, haven't you?' My voice cracks.

'I got back to twenty-six missed calls.' The confident man so full of life squeaks like a tiny mouse. 'The police told me.'

'Oh, Ezra. Give me five minutes, and I'll be there.'

THIRTY-SIX

I snatch my keys but think of Lola. Zoe has already left with her. My gut tells me not to leave her but my head and heart agree I need to see my brother-in-law. I find Zoe's number and tell her I need to pop out urgently and will be back within the hour.

'Don't sweat it,' she says. 'We're in the park. Lola's having fun. But we'll be back way before then.'

I end the call. She never told me she was taking Lola to the park. She should have asked me. I'll have to have a word with her. She needs to tell me if plans change. I consider calling her, but I have more pressing things on my mind. Besides, it's a discussion better to have face to face. I don't want to come across as confrontational. I'll talk to her later.

I dash out the front door, colliding with Cameron as I turn the corner to where my car is parked. We bump heads. Stars flash before my eyes.

'Sorry!' He steps backwards, rubbing his forehead. 'Did I hurt you?'

'It's fine,' I lie. We struck each other pretty sharply. We play a game of dodge, each darting to the same side, politely attempting to allow each other to pass. It's unsettling as if he's doing it on purpose. 'Just stop!' I shout.

He steps backwards, clearly offended. 'I'm so sorry, Annie.'

'No. I'm sorry.' I swallow hard. 'I've just got a lot going on.'

His features tighten into a pained expression as he holds up his calloused hands. 'Can I do anything to help you?' His kindness stabs me with guilt. Something else for me to carry around in the heavy bags of emotions that are weighing me down.

'I'm fine, thank you.'

I hurry to my car and rush to Ezra's apartment, grateful that he's finally back in contact but fearing what he's going to reveal. Because there must be something he can tell me to explain my sister's actions.

He answers the door dressed in jogging bottoms and a stained T-shirt. He reeks of alcohol, and the unusual smell of tobacco hangs in the air. His blood-red eyes bore into me. I want to cuddle him, hold him, share my grief with his, but as I reach out my arms, his hand drops from the door, and he turns away from me.

He doesn't speak, just leads me into the living room, where melancholy music plays from speakers on the sideboard. The floor is littered with clothes spilling from a sports bag. Empty cups and cans of beer sit around an ashtray full of discarded joint butts in the middle of the glass coffee table. This isn't right. Ezra is a doctor, a medical professional whose body is his temple. He goes to the gym four times a week and enjoys a drink or two, as did my sister. But I've never known him to smoke.

'Where have you been?' I catch sight of his phone by the ashtray. I point to it. 'I've tried countless times to get hold of you.'

'She never told you, did she?' He drops onto the sofa. His face is deathly pale, so unlike his usual rosy glow.

'Told me what?' I fold my arms. My heart is racing. 'What's going on, Ezra?'

His usual loving tone is lost somewhere in his billowing grief. 'She was having an affair.'

My eyes lock onto his intently. I laugh. I must have misheard him. 'What?'

His bottom lip quivers. 'Your sister was having an affair.'

THIRTY-SEVEN

My jaw drops. And so does my stomach. He's got that wrong. This man was my sister's world.

'No way! Samantha would never have done that to you.'

'She did.' He puffs out a large breath. 'She told me on Sunday evening that she was planning to leave me. I had to get away.' His watery eyes open wide. 'I took a train up to Scotland on Sunday night and left my phone here. I couldn't face speaking to anyone.' The pain on his face is excruciating. 'But she never gave any clue she was contemplating taking her own life.'

I quietly walk over to the sofa and sit beside him, lost for words.

He pulls a can of beer from a pack of four and offers it to me. I decline. Pulling the tab off the can, he tosses it among the rubbish on the table and takes a long sip of beer. 'Did you know about the affair?'

'No!' I reply. 'She never said anything to me. I promise you, Ezra. Nothing. I'm totally shocked.' I pause. Because that's not quite true, is it? 'Do you know who with?' My thoughts are racing, my suspicions way too close to home.

He hesitates, rubbing the stubble flecked with morsels of grey on his chin. His voice breaks, but he doesn't answer my question. 'I hit her.'

I think back to when I saw her on Monday when she came into the kitchen for a glass of water, shortly before she died. It was the last time I saw her alive. 'On the jaw?'

He nods.

'She told me it was the car door.'

'Well, it was me.' He places the can of beer on the coffee table and runs his fingers through his hair. 'I'm so ashamed.'

My phone rings. Hesitantly, I take it out of my pocket. I don't recognise the number. I'm unsure whether to accept it but wonder if it could be Max, so I press the green answer button.

'Hello, Annie.'

The voice is familiar, but I can't place it.

'DI Pitman, here.'

My heart skips a beat. 'What's happened?' Max enters my thoughts. 'Is it my husband? Has something happened to him?' I calculate where Max would be at this moment, and it's around thirty-nine thousand feet in the air.

'No, but I have been trying to get hold of your husband, but there's no answer.'

'He's not here. He's on a plane to California.'

'Yes. I'm aware of that. I thought perhaps he'd already landed. There's been some development in your sister's death, and I need to come and speak to you as a matter of urgency.'

THIRTY-EIGHT

All kinds of thoughts flash through my head. 'What development?'

'I can tell you more when I see you. Will you be in if I come to your house in fifteen minutes?'

'Sure. Can you—'

The line goes dead.

My eyes linger on my phone. 'That was the police.'

Ezra picks up another can of beer. 'What did they want?'

I relay the conversation.

'What does that mean?'

I shrug. 'I should get going. Do you want to come with me? You can stay with us for a while.'

'No offence, but I just want to be alone.'

'I'd better go.' Not giving him the opportunity to turn away, I peck him on the cheek and hug him, turning my head away from the smell of stale sweat. 'Let's speak later. We'll need to make arrangements at some point.'

His head drops towards his shoulder. 'Arrangements?'

'The funeral.'

The music changes track to Michael Bublé's 'Everything'. His eyes well up. So do mine. This was their first dance song at their wedding. How ironic. It's as if the tenacity of his grief is working with the devil. 'She's broken me, Annie.'

My heart goes out to him. This news is so unexpected. I reach out to hug him again, but he bats me away with his hand. 'Please come and stay with us.' I can't bring myself to leave him.

'No. Just go.'

His phone rings. He picks it up from the table and answers it. By the look on his face, I can tell it's the police having the same conversation with him that they've just had with me. 'The police are on their way here, as well,' he says.

'I'll speak to you later.' I let myself out, scared to leave him, but I need to get back before the police arrive.

I call Max when I get back into my car, but, unsurprisingly, I get his voicemail. I accidently call Nisha as I place the phone in the holder attached to the dashboard.

She answers before I have the chance to end the call.

'Is Sean there?' I ask.

'No, he's on his way to the airport. Why?'

'I've just seen Ezra, and he told me something dreadful.'

'What?'

'Samantha was having an affair. She told him on Sunday night she was leaving him.'

'No way!' Nisha cries.

'I can't believe it either.'

'Where has he been all this time?'

'He took himself off to Scotland. I've just had this strange call from the policeman who came on Monday. He's on his way over. He said there's been some development in Samantha's case. What could that mean?'

'I don't know. Hang on. I've got a call coming in.' There's a pause before she says, 'Sean's trying to get hold of me. I'll call you straight back.'

I drive home, shocked to the core at Ezra's revelation. Samantha never gave any clue that she was planning to leave him. And she certainly gave no hints she was having an affair. As far as I knew, they were happy.

It seems I never knew my sister at all.

THIRTY-NINE

Zoe hasn't returned with Lola by the time I get back. The chance to have a break has been a blessing in the circumstances, but now I'm missing the little fusspot. I call Zoe's number, but she doesn't answer. An uncomfortable sensation passes through me. I should never have left Lola with her. I call her again. She isn't answering. Damn her.

I stand at the centre island, my fingers vigorously tapping the edge, as I wait for them to come home and for the police to arrive. A low rumbling sound draws my attention to the garden. Cameron and Jigsaw are standing in front of a cement mixer, both smoking cigarettes.

Jigsaw catches me looking. In the fading sunlight as he waves, his large hand appears even larger. Cameron turns and nods at me, rubbing his head, referring to our collision earlier. I nod back and give him a thumbs up. They take one last drag of their cigarettes, flick the butts into the muddy ground and busy themselves filling the machine's rotating drum with shovels full of cement. The mixture slops like porridge into a waiting wheelbarrow.

There's a knock at the front door. I glance at the kitchen

clock. Fifteen minutes haven't even passed since the police called. I dash to answer it, only to find Zoe standing on the porch with a happy Lola wrapped snug and secure in her all-in-one snowsuit like a budding rose waiting to blossom.

I exhale a long breath. 'I was getting worried.'

'Sorry. She was loving the park so much. We fed the ducks at the pond.'

'Please let me know if you're going to take her somewhere. I just thought you were going to the shops.'

'I'm sorry, Annie. I didn't think. I will do next time.'

I help her with the buggy. 'The police are due here soon,' I say.

She stops pushing the buggy. The wheel balances on the raised threshold of the door. 'The police,' she says. 'Why?'

'Come in. Come in, and I'll tell you.' When we've manoeuvred the buggy inside, I shut the door and relay the news from the DI.

'Oh, man!' Her eyes flick from Lola to me. 'I should go.' A heavy note of concern darkens the melody of her languid accent.

'Why?' I ask. 'I could do with your help while I speak to the police.'

'I'm not meant to be working, remember, Annie. I told you and Max at the interview. I haven't got a work permit. I could be in big trouble if the police question what I'm doing here.' She hands me a bag of shopping with the items I asked her to get.

My phone rings. It's Nisha. 'Of course, of course.' I nod my head furiously at Zoe. 'I need to take this call.'

'Will you be all right if I just slip out? I'm worried about getting into bad trouble if they find out I'm working illegally.'

'Sure. You go. I'll call you later.' I answer the phone.

'I don't believe it,' Nisha says. 'The police have called Sean. He's had to forget his flight and go straight to the police station.'

'Why?'

The front door opens. Zoe waves at me and silently slips out.

Nisha's voice falters. 'From what I can make out, the autopsy has revealed some inconsistencies with the ligature marks on Samantha's neck.'

'What does that mean?' I ask.

'She didn't take her own life,' Nisha says.

She pauses.

'She was murdered.'

FORTY

I widen my eyes in disbelief as I struggle to grasp Nisha's words. Thoughts whirl around my mind wondering what this means for us all. There's a pulling and twisting sensation in my stomach as if the knots of anxiety that have been there for months have significantly tightened their hold.

A murder took place in the room next door to where I was asleep.

The murder of my sister.

And I never heard a thing.

'How come you've found that out before me?'

'I guess they wanted to stop Sean flying out to LA.' Nisha's voice is faint. 'Sean's on his way to the station now. They were going to come here, but he said he might as well go to the station.'

'They don't think Sean did it?' I quickly replay the scene from Monday afternoon in my mind. Sean wasn't even here. He didn't turn up with Max from the meeting with the lawyers until after I found Samantha's body. They'd gone for a meeting. 'That's absurd.'

'Of course they don't, but they want to speak again to everyone who was at your house that day.'

Lola starts fussing. Two red splodges rouge her cheeks. 'I've got to go.' I need to get my baby out of that all-in-one snowsuit before she starts screaming the place down. I couldn't cope. Not now.

Unstrapping Lola from the buggy, I take her into the kitchen and lay her on the centre island to remove her snowsuit. My hands are shaking as I digest Nisha's news. The receipt for the formula catches my attention. I grab it, searching for the entry for the tins of formula again. I need reassurance I'm not going mad. It's definitely there. I must have left the tins at the supermarket. That can be the only reason. I can't remember. But, then again, I haven't done a great job of remembering much lately.

Lola wriggles and squirms like a worm, resisting my touch yet seeming to crave it all the same. She raises her balled fist. 'Please don't cry, baby girl. Not now.' I look at the clock. It's two o'clock. The police will want to speak to the twins again, as well. I pick up Lola and place her on my shoulder. Patting her back, I slowly spin three-sixty on the spot, taking in the gravity of the situation. Because I still can't believe it.

On Monday, someone murdered my sister in this house.

A knock at the door disturbs my thoughts. I rush to answer it. DI Pitman's broad frame stands on the doorstep with another officer who I've never seen before.

'Hello, Annie.' He gestures to his colleague, a woman around my age dressed in a smart trouser suit. How I used to dress when I worked in the prestigious offices of an exclusive clothes chain before I set up my own business. 'This is Detective Sergeant Pinewood.'

A car hoots. I look beyond them. A police van stops outside the house on the opposite side of the road. Two men and a woman file out. One of them pulls open the side door. It roars along its rails and thuds to a stop.

I pat Lola's back harder, trying to control her incessant crying.

A police car pulls up next to the police van. More people climb out.

I wonder if I should confess that I already know about the bombshell they've come here to drop on me. 'What's happening?' I nod to the police, scurrying like ants towards my front door.

'Let's chat inside,' the DI says.

'I know why you're here. Sean's wife told me.' I step aside to let them in, trying to control my voice. One of the people from the van approaches the house now dressed in a forensic suit, mask and gloves, carrying a large, black case.

'OK. We need to allow my colleagues to come in and do their job.'

I've never felt so helpless.

They follow me into the kitchen, where I prop myself up against the centre island. Are they going to arrest me? Is this how it works? I don't know. It's not every day a murder takes place in your home, less than two feet from where you're sleeping. But that's an absurd thought. I've done nothing wrong.

'Are you two the only ones here, Annie?' He points to Lola. 'You and your baby?'

I nod.

He points towards the garden. 'And the builders?'

It's all I can do but nod again.

'Were they here the other day when you found Samantha?'

I think back. 'No, they'd gone home for the day.'

'Can you say that for sure?'

'Yes, I remember them leaving.'

'OK.' There's an urgency in his voice. He doesn't mince his

words. 'This house, and the garden, are now a crime scene, and I need you to accompany me down to the station.'

FORTY-ONE

The DI raises his voice above Lola's wails and the rotating cement mixer in the back garden, where a man dressed in a white oversuit is talking to Cameron and Jigsaw. Cameron lights a cigarette and passes the lighter to Jigsaw.

My voice wobbles. A jumble of thoughts races through my head. They can't think it was me, can they? Apart from Lola, I *was*, it seems, the only person here when the murder took place. The murder that happened only metres from where I was asleep. 'Am I under arrest?' As soon as I say this, I regret it. It's an absurd question.

'Absolutely not.' The DI frowns. 'We need to interview you as a witness. But since we're now dealing with a murder, you do need – as does everyone else – to leave the house so we can secure what's left of this crime scene.'

Our home, a crime scene? That's absurd. And my sister, murdered? It's a horrific reality, but all this time, I've known deep down that she'd never have taken her own life.

'So someone faked the suicide.'

'It appears so,' the DI says.

'Why would they do that?'

'That's what we will find out.'

Jigsaw turns his head to face the house, his face etched with disbelief. He catches my eye.

'My colleagues will deal with the people outside.'

'How do you know—' The same urgency in his voice is now apparent in mine. 'Know that she was murdered?'

'The pathologist who carried out the post-mortem found two sets of ligature marks around her neck. One from the dressing gown belt.' He holds my helpless gaze. 'And one made by some other type of ligature.'

Lola's shrill cries pierce through me. I remove her from my shoulder and place her in the crook of my arm, rocking her. 'What about my work?' I point to the garden. 'That's my home office. I need to get in there for my business.' It's bizarre the things you think about when faced with adversity. The DI frowns again. I can tell what he's thinking. What does work matter at a time like this?

'We can assist you to gather some items, but after that, I'm afraid you won't be able to return here until we've finished doing our work.'

'It's OK,' I say, reflecting. 'I wasn't thinking straight. Of course work doesn't matter.'

'The older children, where are they?'

'At school.' I glance at the wall clock. 'They finish in an hour.'

'We'll need to find you all somewhere else to stay.'

'How long for?'

'A few days at least while we search the house for any evidence not picked up on Monday. Do you have family you can stay with?'

I shake my head.

Lola is squirming in my arms. She's becoming unmanageable, her cries heightening the intensity of the situation.

'We can arrange a hotel for you. I'll have my colleague call the school and arrange for the older children to be picked up.'

'Not in a police car... please. That will freak my stepson out. He... he can be... sensitive.' Whatever my feelings about the twins, this latest news will disturb them. And then the thought occurs to me. In essence, everyone who was here on Monday is now a suspect, including Jacob. But he said he returned home after her death. That's why he was still in his coat and scarf when I found him with Lola. He took her from me because he said I was suffocating her. He could've murdered Samantha before he took Lola. But there's no reason why he'd want Samantha dead.

My thoughts turn to Jasmine, who left in a strop when I caught her photographing Lola. She said she went to a friend's house. But she could've slipped back in to commit the crime. A dark thought enters my head. Perhaps one of them, or both of them, did it to get to me. Or maybe they mistook her for me. That's crazy. I'm being irrational. I push the thought aside. 'Can't I pick them up and bring them to the station?'

He shakes his head. 'We'll arrange for an unmarked car to fetch them.'

'What about my husband?' I glance at the clock again, calculating where Max is on his journey. 'He's soon to land in Los Angeles for an important business meeting.'

The DI pauses, squinting as if he's in deep thought. 'That's fine. We can speak to him when he gets back.'

'I'm going to ask our friends if we can stay with them.'

Two members of the forensics team enter the kitchen. One of them places a black case on the floor by the patio doors and kneels beside it.

The DI's eyebrows draw together. He nods at Lola. 'Is your baby OK?'

I try to control how fast I'm patting her back, aware I'm

bordering on looking like a crazed woman. 'She suffers from bad colic. A bottle might help. Is that allowed? Do I have time?'

He nods. 'Perhaps DS Pinewood could hold her while you fetch the bottle.'

DS Pinewood steps forward. She opens her arms. 'Let me. I have a two-year-old, and I remember these days. My daughter didn't stop crying for a whole month.' She reaches out to take my baby. 'A total nightmare.' She takes Lola from me. Reluctantly, I let her go. 'Let's try to get you settled.' She holds Lola along the length of her forearm and firmly rubs the palm of her hand along Lola's back.

Lola immediately stops crying, which makes me want to start. But there are no tears. My eyes are like a dried-up old well. I couldn't cry when I found out Samantha had died, and I can't cry now. What's wrong with me?

The DS must sense my despondency. 'Don't feel bad. My daughter used to do the same – stop crying when someone else took over. I think they often feel our anxiety.'

The DI continues. 'Perhaps you could consider what you're going to need while you're away from the house, and DS Pinewood could escort you to gather your things. Is there anyone you could leave your baby with while you're at the station?'

Nisha is the only person. 'My friend Nisha. She's Sean's wife. She knows Lola well.' I look at him questioningly as if to ask if that's allowed.

'Do you want to give her a call and make arrangements?'

There's no missing the sternness in his voice that conveys this is a demand rather than a question.

FORTY-TWO

My car screeches to a halt on Nisha and Sean's driveway.

DI Pitman and DS Pinewood are behind me in an unmarked car.

I've spent the whole journey trying to determine who could've committed this heinous crime. Someone must have slipped into the house. There's no other explanation. I think back. There was an Amazon delivery on Monday. But my thoughts are irrational. I have no logical explanation as to why a delivery person would have wanted to murder my sister.

Lola wailed when the DS gave her back to me, but she has settled on the drive. I unclip the belt from around the car seat and get her out. The wind howls around me. I grab her bag from the footwell. It's heavy with all the paraphernalia I packed with DS Pinewood watching me, so closely at times she made me feel as if I was trying to hide the murder weapon.

Nisha flings open the door before I've even knocked. Her usually calm face is a canvas of worry. Even her brown skin has a pale tinge. 'What the hell?' She shakes her head in earnest.

'When is all this going to end?' I hand over my baby. At

least she's not crying for once. I slip Lola's bag off my shoulder and place it on the floor inside the door. 'There are two bottles in there. And a couple of changes of clothes, just in case. Everything she'll need for the rest of the day. I've packed the rest of her stuff in a suitcase in the back of the car that I'll bring in later.' A sudden thought enters my head: what if I don't get to come home tonight?

'I've put the travel cot up in our room so I can keep her with us if you want,' she says.

'Do you think I'll be there all night?' It's unthinkable.

'That wasn't what I was implying. I'm more thinking of giving you a break. You look exhausted.' Her eyes dart to the car parked behind mine. 'Who's that?'

'The police. They've been watching me like a hawk packing my stuff.'

She swings the car seat, smiling at Lola. But it's not her usual happy smile, but a forced curve of her full lips. 'What happens now?'

'They've shut down the house,' I say. 'No one is allowed in there.'

'When can you go back?'

I look up to the sky and let out a loud moan. 'How long is a piece of string? When they're done. Two days at the minimum, they reckon. Everyone who was at the house that day has to be interviewed as a witness. I don't understand.' I shrug. 'This is a nightmare.'

'Who do they think did it?'

Another shrug. Another look to the sky. 'I'm scared,' I whisper.

She looks at me questioningly.

'Because it was *my* belt, Nish, that was used to disguise the murder, which happened while *I* was asleep in the next room. And I was the only other person in the house when the murder took place.'

'Don't be so stupid. They can't think it was you.'
'It doesn't look good, though, does it?'

FORTY-THREE

The DI speaks loudly and clearly, his words echoing around the emptiness of the room. 'Can I get you anything, Annie?'

I shake my head. 'Are my stepchildren here yet?'

He nods. 'My colleague picked them up from school and brought them here.'

'Can I see them?'

'Not at the moment.'

'But they're not yet eighteen. They need someone to be with them.'

'We're arranging for a social worker to accompany them. Don't worry. We'll make sure they're well looked after.'

Fear surges through me. 'Am I under arrest?' I ask for the second time. The unease I've felt since talking to him at the house hasn't worn off.

'I've already said, no.' The DI runs his tongue along his top row of teeth. 'You're here as a witness, as I told you. You may leave at any time, but I would strongly advise against it. I need your full co-operation.'

He opens a plain manilla file from the desk and pulls out a document. 'Now, this is your witness statement.' He slides it across the table and pats the front page. 'I'd like you to read it again and think back to what happened at your house on Monday. Retrace your steps and tell me if there's anything you missed out. There's no rush. We have plenty of time.' He takes a sip of water from the paper cup he brought in with him. 'A lot was going on. It's easy to forget small things. Don't be afraid to add anything, however small. Sometimes, stepping away from the situation can trigger a memory and bring new evidence to light.'

'Do I need a solicitor?'

'You're not under arrest, Annie. But if you decide you want one, you can call one. Or I can arrange for a duty solicitor to come and sit in this session. But as I've already said, you're here as a witness.' I detect the faintest frustration from him for having to repeat himself.

I swallow the ball of panic growing in my throat since he arrived at Max's house earlier. I consider what Max would advise me to do. He's always in control of every situation. 'How long will it take to get a solicitor?'

He shrugs. 'It depends if there's one available.'

'Should I get one?'

'That's not for me to advise, but, as I said, you're only giving a witness statement. Please understand. Everyone who was at your house on Monday is a witness. One of you may have seen something. Even the tiniest of things you don't consider relevant could lead us to finding out who did this to your sister.'

The sick feeling of dread whirling around my body intensifies as I think of my poor sister. I can't understand who would want to hurt her, let alone murder her. With a trembling hand, I pick up the piece of paper and reread the statement I made on Monday. I never mentioned the raised voices coming from Max's office that afternoon. I wonder if I should. It could be relevant.

The DI stretches out his arms above his head and cracks his knuckles. 'Anything else you can think of?'

If the twins heard the arguments and tell the police about them, it will look odd if I don't mention them. But they were at school. But the builders were there, in and out. They could've mentioned it.

'Think carefully,' the DI says.

'There was a heated exchange between the three business partners.'

He shifts in his seat. 'What about?'

'I don't know exactly, but they're going through a stressful time selling their business, and Max said it isn't unusual for business partners to have disagreements.'

The DI asks further questions relating to the argument, but there's nothing else I can tell him.

'I know this is a difficult question to answer, but is there anyone who would want to harm Samantha? Anyone she argued with recently?'

'No! There was only that argument with Sean and Max. Everyone loved my sister. She was that kind of person. She never did a thing wrong.'

But that's not true.

She was having an affair.

I open my mouth to tell the DI, but he speaks first.

And what he says next shocks me to the core.

FORTY-FOUR

'Did you know your sister was pregnant?' DI Pitman says.

My hand flies to my chest as if to block the shock of his words. I recoil in the chair, turning my head from side to side.

'From speaking to her husband, it appears the baby wasn't his.'

'No,' I whisper. 'It can't be. Ezra can't father children.'

'He also told us that she had admitted to him that she was having an affair. Did you know about this?'

I shake my head. 'She never mentioned it to me.'

'When we last spoke, you said you and your sister were close.'

'That's right, we were, but I can assure you, she never told me about any affair.'

'But you don't seem surprised.'

This is torture. I feel like he's trying to trip me up. I need to keep calm. 'About the pregnancy, yes. I'm totally shocked. About the affair, no, because Ezra told me about it earlier today.' I vigorously shake my head. 'It wasn't him if that's what you think.'

'Him?' the detective asks, confused.

'Ezra. He never murdered my sister.'

'What makes you say that?'

'He wouldn't hurt a fly,' I say adamantly. I pause.

But he hit her.

'Ezra has a solid alibi. We have CCTV footage showing him at a hotel in Scotland on the afternoon of the murder. Do you have any idea who she was having an affair with?'

'No.' I shake my head vigorously again. 'Certainly no one I know.' But I can't be sure of that.

'That's often what people think, Annie. Think carefully. If we find out who she was having this affair with, it could help us considerably with our enquiries.'

'I don't know.' I bite my lip, drawing blood. The warm taste of metal fills my mouth as if I've chewed a penny coin. 'If I did, I'd tell you,' I lie.

He asks me about Samantha and Ezra's marriage.

'They were close. They had a great relationship.' I sigh as I realise I can't say that word any more. 'Had. Had a great relationship, I should say.' My words sound pathetic after what he has just revealed. They couldn't have been that close. This is breaking my heart. I thought I knew my sister so well. 'Or so I thought. But he'd never have harmed her.'

This isn't true, either! I'm lying left, right and centre.

I saw the red mark myself.

'He loved her,' I say. 'Besides, he's a doctor.'

'From my experience, this means nothing.' The DI asks about her friends and, again, if she had any enemies.

I squint at the absurdity of his insinuation. 'No, my sister didn't have enemies.' I pause before asking, 'Who could've done this?'

'I don't like to speculate, Annie. That's not the way I work. I like tangible evidence to lead me to an arrest. I must say, I'm perplexed that you were asleep when it happened – and it was late afternoon – and you didn't hear a thing.'

My heart thumps. 'I can't explain it either.'

'And neither were you aware of your stepson taking your baby from you.'

'What are you implying, Inspector?'

'I'm just pointing out that, apart from your baby, you were the only person in the house at the time of your sister's murder.'

'My stepson was there.'

'No.' The DI shakes his head. 'He wasn't. Our enquiries have proved that Jacob was still at school when the murder took place. Samantha was already dead by the time he arrived home. Your husband and his other business partner' – the DI checks his notes – 'Sean, had left the house, and so had your step-daughter.'

Another charge of tiredness overcomes me, but I haven't got time to be tired. I need to watch my back here. I can't stop the darkness racing through my mind. I gulp as a thought enters my head. What if whoever did this tried to set me up? I mean, it'd be easy for the guilty party to blame the sleep-deprived, crazed woman who fell asleep at an odd time of day.

But the only person I can think of who would do such a thing is one of the twins.

But surely they don't hate me enough to frame me for murder?

FORTY-FIVE

The twins are waiting in the reception area of the station, where a stomach-churning mix of old sweat and wrongfulness wafts in the air.

They are dressed in their school uniforms. Although they're nearly adults, they look so young, sitting in a police station, having been questioned about a murder. The murder of their stepmother's sister that took place in their home.

Jacob is slumped in a plastic chair, scrolling through his phone. Jasmine is next to him, bent over a low table, flicking through a magazine. Opposite them, a drunk in a tattered coat and a discoloured beret calls out advice to a middle-aged man sitting two seats away who is wearing a high-vis vest and a deep frown. The twins look up when I walk towards them, calling their names.

Jasmine closes the magazine and jumps up. Her pale face is drawn. 'Where's Lola?'

'With Nisha.'

'Can we go now?' she says.

Jacob stops scrolling. 'Is Dad going to come home?'

'No. They've said he doesn't need to.' I hold out my arms, beckoning them to follow me. 'Come on. Let's get out of here.'

'I want him to come back now.' Jacob speaks louder than he intends to.

The drunk asks Jacob what's wrong. The guy in the high-vis vest tells the drunk to shut the fuck up and mind his own business. They engage in an unhealthy exchange of expletives as we head to the automatic doors out of the station.

The twins follow me into a gust of wind, asking questions I don't have the answers to. 'I'm sorry,' Jasmine says, her tone soft. 'For the loss of your sister like this.' I can't tell if she means it or not. She has never spoken to me with such empathy. 'I need to go home to get stuff,' she says.

'So do I,' says Jacob, his hands in his pockets. The wind thrashes his curtain of hair around his face. 'I want my computer.'

'We can't go back there,' I say as calmly as I can manage. I don't want to start an argument with either of them. 'The police are there. It's a crime scene.'

'A crime scene,' Jacob repeats. 'Wow.'

'I packed you both some clothes, books and bits and pieces I thought you might need.'

Jasmine stops walking and grabs my arm. 'You went through my stuff?'

'It wasn't like that, Jasmine. I had no choice. I couldn't leave without packing some things for you both. The police officer told me we're not allowed back until the forensics team finishes everything they need to do.'

'How long will that take?' she asks.

I shrug. 'A few days at least. I didn't know what to do for the best. I didn't have long and had to think for all five of us. It was stressful.'

'This is so embarrassing.' She emits a large puff of air. 'It's going to be on the news, isn't it?' Her voice grows louder. 'Everyone is going to know our business.'

I don't know what to say to placate the situation. She's right. Everyone is going to find out what happened. For me, it's not so much of a problem. I don't know that many people around here, and I have nothing to hide. But I can see it being a travesty for a young woman her age.

'I can't go back there,' she says.

'Where?'

'To school.'

'You have to, Jasmine. You have exams after Christmas.' I squeeze her shoulder. It's the most physical contact we've had since Lola was born, when she found it in herself to kiss me in the hospital to congratulate me. 'Let's not worry about it at the moment. You don't have to go to school tomorrow if you don't want to.' I know Max would say the same.

We arrive at my car parked on a side road adjacent to the station. They both climb in the back because the front seat is loaded with bags. 'So, we had a murderer in our home,' Jacob says.

Before I start the engine, I ask, 'Did you see anyone else come in the house that day? Someone must've seen something.' I see them exchange a look in the rearview mirror. It's not until I fasten my seatbelt and take a deep breath do I realise how much I'm shivering. Switching on the heating, I turn the dial to maximum, rubbing my hands together to create some warmth.

'See, I told you.' Jasmine shoves her phone between the front seats. I go to take it, but she swipes it from my reach. She shoves it again, closer to me. I grasp her arm, guiding the screen into focus. Jacob tries to see but gives up and turns to his phone.

My heart skips a beat. A picture of Samantha fills the screen below the heading, *Local Woman Found Dead at Sister's House.* I bat her hand away and fish my phone out of my bag to read the story.

It's there in black and white. The police are investigating the murder of thirty-six-year-old local businesswoman Samantha Levin, wife to Ezra Levin, who they initially thought had taken her own life, but now appears was murdered in the home of her business partner and brother-in-law, Max Carpenter, in Branford Road on Monday afternoon.

'They've mentioned Dad's name.' Jasmine's breathing quickens, her breaths short and shallow. 'Now people know where we live.'

'It doesn't say which number,' Jacob says.

'It won't take a genius to work out which house is ours.' Jasmine is sobbing now. 'There'll be police cars outside and that yellow tape all over it. Everyone will know where we live. This is hell.'

I couldn't agree more.

But I can't let the hamster wheel of local gossip worry me. I have much more pressing thoughts to deal with. A deep shiver runs along my spine. More than ever, I need to keep a clear head.

Because I fear the police could well believe, if anyone is a suspect in my sister's murder, it's me.

FORTY-SIX

Jasmine continues her meltdown for the whole fifteen minutes it takes to journey back to Nisha and Sean's house. Despite the dark thoughts I have about her and her brother, I'm trying to be strong for them. It's an arduous task. At the end of the day, they're still children, but I can't help thinking I should be the one losing my mind. Maybe I already have?

The security lights flash on when I pull up. Jasmine doesn't wait for me to stop the car before opening the door. It's a habit of hers I hate; she does it all the time. 'Steady on,' I say, but she isn't listening. She's already pacing towards the front door, waving her hands wildly.

'Jasmine,' I call out. 'I need you to help me with the bags.'

Turning around, she skulks back to the car, her feet dragging over the stones. Opening the boot, she heaves out her green backpack. She hauls it over her left shoulder, her right one already holding the leather satchel I bought for her last Christmas. It cost me a fortune. I wasn't trying to buy her affection, but she'd had her eye on it for a while and had put it at the top of her Santa list. It seemed the right thing to do... at the time. But come Christmas morning when she opened it, she didn't seem impressed. More disappointed that I'd bought it for her and not Max.

She returns to the house, stooping under the weight of the bags. Nisha opens the door and steps outside onto the porch, hugging Jasmine with one hand and waving at me with the other.

Jacob is more helpful. He lifts the suitcase and his black backpack out of the boot. He doesn't say a word, simply hooks the backpack over his neck along with his school bag and drags the suitcase to the front door, leaving me with the bags on the front seat.

Nisha reaches out an arm to take a bag from me. Worry is etched in every line of my friend's troubled face.

'You moving in?' she says, attempting a joke, but no one is laughing. 'Sorry,' she adds. 'Lola's fine. Maisie is playing with her.' She hugs me. 'This is so shocking. I'm so sorry.'

She addresses the twins. 'I've put you in Will's room, Jacob. He's going to stay at his girlfriend's house. And you can share with Priti, Jasmine. I've put out the air mattress.' She lets go of me. 'And I've put you in the spare room. I've left fresh towels on the bed. I'll help you take your bags up. But first, I've just boiled the kettle. I think you could all do with a cuppa.'

It's going to take more than a cup of tea to calm everyone down.

'We can manage the bags.' Jacob heads to the stairs with his sister.

Every bone in my body aches. It's as if I've taken back-to-back spinning classes for the past twelve hours. I'm so frazzled I'm beginning to think something must be seriously wrong with me. I follow Nisha to the kitchen and fall into one of the chairs. I haven't even got the energy to go upstairs. 'Is Sean back?'

Nisha hands me a cup of tea. She shakes her pretty head. Even in the troubled circumstances, her beauty radiates through the lines of her worry that have appeared since I last saw her. 'I haven't heard a thing. I'd have thought he'd be back by now, though.'

The same thought had occurred to me. 'Max will probably get the same grilling when he gets back.' My phone rings as she takes a tray of drinks upstairs to the kids. I glance at the phone, relieved to see my husband's number scroll across the screen.

'Whatever's happened? The police have left a message asking me to call them urgently, and I've got six missed calls from Sean.'

'Where are you?' There's silence in the background. I was expecting the hustle and bustle of a busy airport.

'I've just checked in. I'm in the room.'

'Why didn't you call as soon as you landed?'

'My phone ran out of battery.' He sounds harassed.

'I don't know how to tell you this.'

'Tell me what?'

'Samantha didn't take her own life.' My voice trails off to a whisper. 'She was murdered.'

Anger surpasses my grief the more I think about it. Although it was tragic, she had the right to take her own life. No one else did.

Max is stunned into silence.

'Say something.'

He eventually speaks. 'I don't know what to say.' The silence is as uncomfortable as the distance between us. 'I'm glad I spoke to you before the police got hold of me. Do they have any idea who did it?'

'No. Not that they've admitted to me.'

'I'll come straight home.'

'The DI said you don't have to. They'll speak to you when you get back.'

'I'll do whatever you want, Annie. Just tell me.'

I really want him to change his flight and get back here straight away. I have so many questions for him, but I know how important it is that he sees this deal through. It will give us the break we need. The break to start again with our marriage and the chance of a future together. But then I wonder if that's now just a pipe dream. 'No. Do what you have to do. I guess it'll be good to get it all tied up now for Ezra's sake.'

'I'll call the police and let you know what they say. If you change your mind at any time, I'll get on the next available flight.' He asks about the kids before ending the call.

Nisha sits down with a cup of herbal tea.

I'm numb as if I've built up a dam of defence around myself to hold the tears waiting to flow. 'I can't cry. I loved my sister dearly. You know that. So why can't I cry? It doesn't feel normal.'

'People react in different ways to trauma. Sometimes it's emotional overwhelm, or situations paralyse our emotional responses. Don't feel bad. People grieve in different ways. Just allow yourself to feel what you feel and process your emotions.'

'Who did this?' I shake my head. 'I just don't get it.' I take a sip of tea. 'It's all online, you know. Jasmine showed me.'

'Don't read it.'

'What do you mean?'

She hesitates. 'Some people can be really mean. Vile, disgusting people.' This is a first. Nisha never has a bad word to say about anyone. She's one of the nicest people I've ever met: kind and generous, and always putting others first.

'I don't like the sound of that.' I grasp my phone.

She reaches out to stop me, encasing my hand in hers. 'Don't do it.'

'I have to know what people are saying.' I rip my hand away from her touch. 'Do people think it's me? That I murdered my sister?'

FORTY-SEVEN

'No.' Nisha tries to grab my hand again. She doesn't succeed. 'I haven't seen your name mentioned.' She pauses. 'It's Max and Sean.' Her tone of voice is different. As if, somehow, this latest news has planted a seed of doubt in her spiralling thoughts and time has given it a chance to grow.

'People think it was one of them?' I smack my hand on the table. The sound reverberates around the vastness of the beautiful kitchen. 'That's insane. They've known Samantha for years.'

'Which is why you mustn't read it all. There are nasty people out there.'

I can't help thinking she's trying to convince herself rather than me. 'And what's their motive meant to be?'

'So they get a bigger share of the business when it's sold.'

'But that's not the case,' I say.

'We know that, but you know what these kind of people are like, Annie.'

I tell her about seeing Ezra and what he told me about Samantha having an affair. 'She was pregnant.'

Nisha's hand shoots over her mouth. 'How do you know?'

'The police told me.'

She stares at her cup of tea. 'I'm totally shocked.'

'Not as much as I am. Please don't share this information with anyone,' I say. 'I want to protect her memory, and Ezra.'

'But you know it'll all come out at some point. How's he coping?'

'I haven't spoken to him since the police turned up.' I slowly shake my head. 'I just don't get it. The police told me I was the only one there when she was murdered – apart from Lola, of course.'

'But Jacob was there.'

I take a sip of tea, shaking my head. 'Apparently not. The police said they have evidence proving he was at school at the time of the murder. And Jasmine was at her friend's house. They are in the clear.'

'What about the builders?'

'The police asked about them, but they had all left for the day. Anyway, what would their motive have been? They didn't know Samantha.' I hesitate, but I have to ask, 'I know this may sound crazy, but you don't think one of the twins could be involved somehow, do you?'

Her eyebrows shoot upwards. 'Wow!'

I shrug.

'Annie! I've known the twins for years. There is no way they're capable of hurting someone like this. Causing trouble, yes, a little spoilt, definitely, but you've said so yourself, they are in the clear.'

I drop my head in my hands. 'I'm so totally drained.' I tell her about the recurring nightmares. The figure that appears from the shadows, that sometimes I think it's a male, and other times a female. My phone rings again, cutting our conversation short. *No Caller ID* flashes on the screen. The knot in my stomach tugs. 'I hope this isn't the police again.' I answer it.

'Mrs Carpenter. Dr Evans here. I've got your blood test

results back. Your liver function is showing some abnormal readings.'

This is all I need right now.

The doctor continues. 'Just to confirm, other than vitamin supplements, you're definitely not taking anything else?'

'No. Of course there were painkillers and a bunch of other things after the birth, but they've all stopped. Why?'

'I'd like to run some further tests to get to the bottom of what's happening here. Could you drop into the surgery tomorrow morning so we can take another set of bloods?'

'Sure. What does this mean?'

'It could be down to several reasons. So don't worry yourself for now. I've slotted you in for eleven thirty if that suits you. I won't be available, but the nurse will see you. I'll contact you once I have the results. These are more detailed tests, so don't expect to hear from me quickly.'

'What's wrong with me?'

'As I said, we need to run further tests before I can diagnose.' He ends the call, and I relay the conversation to Nisha, joggling my phone in my hands.

'Did you speak to him about your nightmares?' she asks.

'No, but I mentioned that you said I could be depressed. I told him I didn't agree. Hence, the first set of blood tests. What does an abnormal liver function mean?'

'It could mean several things.'

I turn to my phone and type the question into the search bar. Google throws back a number of common causes. 'Alcohol-related liver disease is at the top of the list!' That can't be the cause. I rarely drink these days. 'Non-alcohol-related fatty liver disease, gallstones, viral hepatitis, certain medications and herbal supplements. None of these apply to me. I'd be in pain if I had gallstones.' I search for viral hepatitis. 'And I'd have other symptoms if I had hepatitis.' I bounce my finger along each listed symptom. 'It says here: fever, jaundice and pain in the upper right part of the stomach. Do I look yellow?'

'No. Don't worry about it until you've had further tests. It could've just been a bad reading.'

'Don't tell Max. He's got enough to worry about. That reminds me. I need to call Zoe to tell her what's happened.' I realise she doesn't know about Zoe yet. I explain who she is. 'Jeez, poor girl. She's certainly landed herself right in it.'

'I'm glad you've got some help at last.'

'I didn't have a choice. Max took charge and was pretty insistent.'

'It was the right thing to do.'

'I know.' I finish my drink and stand. 'I'm going to unpack and have a lie-down before Lola needs me.' I give her a tight-lipped smile. 'Thanks for putting us all up. I don't know where else we would've gone. The police suggested a hotel. But this is better for the kids. And for me.'

'No problem. Anything you need, just shout. And don't worry about Lola tonight. We'll have her in our room. You get a good night's sleep.'

'I don't know what I would've done without you these past few months.'

'That's what friends are for. You'd do the same for me.'

She's right. I would.

My phone rings.

I grunt to see DI Pitman's number flash across the screen.

I could do without speaking to him, but I'll have to at some point. I answer the call.

'Annie,' he says. 'I have some more questions for you. Could you come down to the station in the morning, please. It shouldn't take too long.'

FORTY-EIGHT

The DI plays on my mind as I peer through the gap of the playroom door to check on Lola. It's crammed with toys and games in there. A massive doll's house commands the far right-hand corner, and a train track bends and curves around the floor. Various baby toys from when Nisha's tribe were young are scattered across the carpet that she must've unpacked: a baby playmat, rattles, sensory balls, teething toys and textured books. All these interesting toys, but Lola is sitting between Maisie's splayed legs biting on a baby teether in front of the TV. Maisie is babbling away to her.

Maisie notices me and smiles. She looks much younger than her eleven years with her dark plaited hair and skinny frame. She's such a cute kid. As are all of Sean and Nisha's kids. And so is their dog. I wonder what it must feel like to live in such a perfect family unit.

I wave at her as my phone rings again. I wish everyone would just leave me alone. It's Zoe. 'How are things?' she asks.

I update her on what has happened.

'That's insane. Would you still like me to come tomorrow?'

It feels rude to invite her here when the house is so busy,

but it would be good to have her help in the morning. 'I need to run some errands tomorrow. Perhaps you could come and help me for a few hours?' We arrange to meet.

'Sure. I'll be there,' she says in her comforting American tone.

I haul my bag upstairs, yawning. When I reach the top, voices drift from the bedroom to the left of the landing. The door is slightly ajar. Jasmine is talking to Priti. They are close friends. But on the occasions I've met her, I've always thought Priti was much more mature than my stepdaughter. And there's a calmness about her. She's a listener, unlike her younger sister, Maisie, who is a chatterbox.

'I'm convinced she's got something to do with it,' Jasmine says.

My heart jolts. I grip the banister.

'That's a pretty strong statement.' Priti is the voice of reason. She is a studious young woman, on the path to a career in medicine, and she is like her mum in so many ways, both in looks and temperament, it's uncanny. 'What makes you say that?'

'She's an alcoholic.'

My jaw drops. She's talking about me.

'I've never seen her drunk,' Priti says.

'You don't live with her. She says she doesn't drink, but she's always acting pissed. She even tried to blame missing wine on me. But at least Dad's started to notice it.'

'That doesn't make her a murderer, Jas.'

'She started a fire in our kitchen. Did you hear about that?'

'No!'

'She left a saucepan on the stove and fell asleep with Lola on the armchair.'

'She must've been really tired.'

'Dad found a half-empty bottle of wine in the fridge. She

drank all that while looking after a baby, then denied it. That's bloody irresponsible if you ask me.'

I stifle a gasp. Max has been discussing me with her. The thought slices through me, cutting me up. It's such a betrayal.

'Poor woman. You've always been down on her, you know.'

'We never invited her into our lives. It just happened.'

'She was pregnant. What did you expect your dad to do?'

Jasmine's voice momentarily softens. 'I know. I just wish Dad had consulted me and Jacob. We had no say in the matter. One day, we came home from school, and he just announced she was pregnant and their plans to move her in.' Sadness filters through her voice. 'It was our home for seventeen years, and we were expected to just put up and shut up. And then Lola came along, and it's been miserable ever since.'

'She's your sister, Jas,' Priti says with such compassion. She is going to make the most wonderful doctor one day.

'Half-sister.' Jasmine corrects her friend. 'I know, but she doesn't stop crying. I love her, but honestly, Prit, it's twenty-four-bloody-seven.'

'I guess they didn't go about it the right way.'

There is such maturity in Priti's voice that it's hard to believe these two young women are the same age. It's like a mother talking to her daughter, not two friends having a conversation.

'The thing is, though, Jas, you and Jacob will be leaving home in less than a year. I know how much you loved your mum, but you wouldn't want your dad to be on his own for the rest of his life. That'd be kinda sad. He's still so young. And he's such a good person. He deserves to be happy. Have you told him how you feel?' Priti sounds more like Nisha every time I meet her.

'What's the point? He'd only side with her. She's truly mad, though. Honestly, she worries me. She worries Dad, as well.

She's spaced out half the time. She needs help. Dad's tried to get her to see someone, but she won't have it.'

'I feel sorry for her,' Priti says. 'She's always seemed like a lovely woman to me.'

'She was,' Jasmine continues. 'Until Lola was born, and then she changed.'

I drop my head.

'What does Jacob think?' Priti asks.

'He agrees with me.' Jasmine continues. 'I know this sounds like a dreadful thing to say, and you won't like me for saying it, but isn't it strange that she was there, asleep in the next room, when her sister died?'

I can't have her saying these things about me. I step towards the bedroom door but stop. This isn't the time to have a blazing row with my stepdaughter. It's not fair on Priti, and I need to calm down first. I don't have the bandwidth for a showdown at this moment.

'What are you suggesting?' Priti asks.

If I were in the room with them now, I'd be able to see Jasmine give one of her shrugs where her shoulders reach her ears and stay there for a few seconds. 'I don't know. But something's not adding up.'

FORTY-NINE

I wake up with a jolt. The morning sunlight floods through the gaps in the bedroom blinds as brightly as yesterday's memories come flooding back. I sit up. I'm at Nisha and Sean's house. Nisha agreed to look after Lola for the night. My sister has been murdered, and my stepdaughter thinks I played a part in her demise. And I fear the police could well agree with her.

I grab my phone. It's eight thirty. It's the first time since Lola was born that I've slept this late. Or for this long. I don't understand how I could've done that with everything going on. And, strangely, I didn't have any nightmares. For once, I feel alive, not at death's door begging to be let in.

I check my texts, hoping Ezra has answered the messages I sent asking him to call me. There's nothing from him, but DI Pitman has left a message. I bite my bottom lip. Perhaps he has news about Samantha. I dial his number but am directed to his voicemail. I leave a message.

Discarding the duvet, I swing my legs over the side of the bed. I'm spaced out as if I've been drugged, but it's entirely different to how I usually feel. I feel pleasurably drunk on sleep. My suitcase lies open on the floor with a jumble of our clothes that I threw in yesterday. It seems so long ago. But it's not. It's only eighteen hours since the police officer, who supervised me as I grabbed everything I could think of for the five of us, said, 'I need to hurry you along.'

I scramble around for a pair of clean knickers and put them on. I can wear the same clothes as yesterday. Desperate measures for desperate times.

Lola is sitting in one of Nisha's kids' old highchairs when I get downstairs, smacking the tray with her tiny fists. The kitchen is alive with light. It makes me realise how dark Max's kitchen is.

'Morning,' Nisha says. 'Sleep all right?'

I yawn, stretching my arms above my head. 'That was the best night's sleep I've had since Lola was born. I forgot what it feels like to have uninterrupted sleep. Thanks for taking her for the night.'

'She was no problem. She only woke up once in the night. Help yourself to whatever. I'll put some fresh bread in the toaster if you fancy it.' She sweeps her hand around the table with the remains of a continental breakfast – croissants, toast, butter and jam, and a pot of freshly brewed coffee. 'This here' – she taps the top of a plastic tub – 'is my homemade granola. Try some. It's sugar free, but you wouldn't think so. Even Sean likes it.'

I pour some coffee, glancing around the large room. It's at least three times as big as Max's kitchen. The three large dome pendants hanging above a beautiful display of winter flowers on the large centre island catch my eye.

'Lola had a bottle at six,' Nisha says. 'I've made up six more for her. They're in the fridge.'

'Thanks. I don't know what I'd do without you.'

'Don't be silly. The twins got off to school OK. Jasmine said to tell you to look at your texts. She has sent you a message reminding you about her dental appointment today.'

I stare at her blankly.

'She has to have her braces tightened. She said you agreed to give her a lift. She needs picking up from school at two fifteen.'

'I can't remember her telling me that.' She never did. I'm sure of it. I take a deep breath. After overhearing what Jasmine was saying to Priti about me last night, and feeling energised, this will be a good opportunity to get her on her own and have a serious discussion with her. I can't have her saying what she was saying about me last night to other people.

'I guess we can all be forgiven for not remembering anything from yesterday.' Nisha stands up. 'I don't want to hand over this gorgeous one, but I'm afraid I have to.' She glances at her watch. 'I have a client due soon.'

'Thanks for everything. How's Sean?'

'Not good.' Deep lines crease her forehead. 'He didn't get home until midnight.'

'Midnight! Why did they keep him so long?'

'They grilled him about Samantha and the business. He spoke to Max this morning. The meeting went to plan. We should expect the first tranche of money to be transferred tomorrow.'

I feel my shoulders drop. 'It's finally happened, then. The business is sold.'

'It's a shame it's in such dire circumstances, but yes, it's all underway. What are your plans for today?' she asks. 'I'm working, I'm afraid, otherwise I'd spend some time with you.'

'Don't worry about me. I need to go and get my bloods done, and I've got a ton of errands to run.'

She picks up a pile of dirty dishes.

'Leave that to me. I'll clear up.'

Placing the dishes back on the table, she speaks, but stops.

'What?'

She looks troubled. 'Nothing.' She glances at her watch

again. 'I've got to go. Would you do me favour? Let Bonnie out for a wee before you go out.'

Lola starts crying. 'Are you bored, darling?' I say, lifting her out of the highchair. She screams, struggling to free herself from my arms. I pace up and down the kitchen, singing 'The Happy Song' thinking how ironic. I've never been so bloody sad in my life.

Lola won't settle. I go to the fridge, grab one of the bottles Nisha made and heat it while Lola struggles and screams in my arms. After a full night's sleep, it doesn't disturb me as much as it usually does. I stroll the length of the kitchen, while I wait for the microwave to warm the bottle, thinking about what I need to do today. I've agreed to meet Zoe this morning so she can look after Lola. I'm not so sure it's a good idea any more. Now I feel more refreshed I want to keep my baby with me.

The microwave pings. I grab the bottle and give it to Lola. The silence is comforting as she guzzles her milk contentedly, gazing lovingly into my eyes.

My heart bursts.

It's a surreal moment.

An unfamiliar feeling stirs in the pit of my stomach. I've never experienced such a fierce, overwhelming sense of love and pain before. I've always loved my baby, but I've never felt this divine connection to her. Holding her feels as natural as every breath I take. This is the biological drive of unconditional love I've been waiting for – what it feels like to truly bond with your baby I've read so much about. It's just come at such an odd time. But it's a relief to the troubles racing around my mind at one hundred miles per hour.

Tears of happiness prick my eyes. Or are they tears of sadness for my sister, who I'll never see again?

FIFTY

Sean appears. Dishevelled, he looks worse than I've ever seen him, despite being dressed in a suit and tie. Bonnie races to say good morning with a bark and a jump. Bending down, he strokes her head before pouring himself a cup of coffee and asking how I am and how sorry he is to hear about the turn my sister's case has taken. 'It's all done. The business is officially not ours any more.'

'Nisha told me.' I pause. 'Sean, tell me, what were you, my sister and Max arguing about the day she died?'

He grabs a half slice of buttered toast one of the kids has left and bites into it. 'What do you mean?'

'I heard the three of you. It turned ugly. What was it about?'

He shrugs. 'Business.' He takes another bite of the toast before discarding the remainder of the slice on the plate.

'It was more than that. What aren't you telling me?'

A glint of sweat on his forehead catches the light. 'Nothing, Annie. It was purely business related.'

'You told Max to fuck off.'

He runs his forefinger around the collar of his white shirt. 'Did I?'

'You never swear, Sean.'

'I can't remember.'

Lola finishes her bottle of milk. She's drowsy. I settle her in my arms and rock her, hoping she'll fall asleep. It will give me time to get myself sorted. I ask Sean more about the argument, but he's already rushing for the door. 'I'll catch you later,' he says.

The front door slams shut. I walk towards the window and watch him get into his car. A chill runs through me. Sean has always been the life and soul of the party. Now he's like the wallflower who doesn't want to be noticed. He appears to call someone and presses his phone to his ear. But he doesn't speak for long as if he's leaving someone a message. He starts the engine and drives off.

I pace the kitchen, with Bonnie at my feet, staring around this perfect hub and Nisha and Sean's perfect life and their perfect dog, wondering what, if anything, Sean is hiding from me.

Lola drifts off to sleep. I kiss her forehead as I head for the stairs to lay her down her for a nap. I'll clear away the breakfast stuff while she sleeps. I pass Sean's office door and stop. It's ajar. I take two steps backwards. It's wrong, I know, but I step inside.

It's as modern as the rest of the house. The desk is positioned in the far corner, diagonally opposite and facing the door. Nisha would have insisted on this. According to feng shui, it's the *power position* where you can maximise control while minimising surprises. The walls are painted white but several prints hung here and there add a pop of colour.

It's quiet. In fact, the whole house is quiet. With four kids, usually, it's a bomb of energy waiting to explode. I've never been here alone. Now you could hear a pin drop.

On Sean's desk is a picture of him, Max and my sister at an awards ceremony a few years back, before my time, when they won an industry award for a piece of software they'd developed

– the first of many. I've seen it before. My sister has the same picture somewhere in her apartment. But it looks different here. I can't work out why. I take a closer look. It's definitely the same photo. They are all dressed up, Samantha in an emerald green strapless ball gown and the men in black tie. Samantha is sitting in the middle, Sean to her left, Max to her right, and she has her arms around both of them, her hands on their shoulders. But there's something I've never noticed before.

It's the way that Max is looking at Samantha. The glint in his eye.

It's as if he's in love with her.

FIFTY-ONE

I can't get the photo out of my mind as I head out with Lola. My thoughts switch with each step I take as I wonder if my marriage is built on a bed of lies.

For once, Lola is all smiles. The weather is cold but dry, the sky a vivid winter blue. Despite the dark clouds hanging over my life, there's a lightness in my step. It's as if being away from Max's house has somehow freed me.

And then a sinister thought occurs to me: or perhaps it's being away from my husband. The notion brings the darkest of clouds: Max was poisoning me, and that's why I've been feeling so rotten for so long. Or perhaps it was the twins. I disregard the far-out thoughts toying with me.

But seeing the photo in Sean's office has disturbed me even more. I have to get away. But with the police investigation, there's no way I can disappear at the moment. But I need to find a way out of the trap I'm caught in.

Full of unease, I meet Zoe in town. It surprises me how good it feels to see someone unconnected to the drama playing out in my life. She's snugly wrapped in a coat and woolly hat.

'Hey, Annie. Good to see you.' She tickles Lola's chin. 'And you, little one. I've missed you.'

Lola appears equally as happy to see her. She waves her hands and kicks her legs tucked under her blanket. Zoe takes over pushing the buggy. Lola squeals in delight. A pang of guilt hits me for the mistrust I had for her when we first met. She's so good with my baby.

We stop at the GP's for the nurse to take another set of bloods. The same nurse with the kind smile and calming voice who administered Lola's vaccinations last week appears in the waiting room. She points to Lola, who is sitting on Zoe's lap babbling as Zoe bounces her up and down on her knee. The nurse beams. 'Someone's in a better mood today. Who's this? Big sister?'

'No,' I say, grinning thankfully at Zoe. 'She's helping me for a few months.'

'That's good to hear.' The nurse nods emphatically. 'Come into my room.'

Zoe stays with Lola while I follow the nurse to room two.

'And how are you?' the nurse asks.

I fake a smile. 'I've had better times.' It's too painful to talk about my sister. The nurse won't comment, but I test her all the same. 'The doctor said my last set of bloods showed I had abnormal liver function. What could that mean?' I try not to express my deep concern that something more sinister is going on with me.

The nurse squints at her computer screen. She frowns. 'A number of things.' She tightens the tourniquet around my upper arm. 'It's best not to hypothesise. Just wait for the results.'

I sigh.

The results are going to take too long.

I need to know now.

'Why don't I take her for a walk, while you run your

errands?' Zoe offers when we leave the surgery. 'I'll take her to the café in the park and give her a bottle to give you a bit more time. You can meet us there in an hour or so if you want. Or we could meet back at the car?'

I hesitate. I don't want to leave Lola, but it will be much quicker if I run my errands alone. 'If you're sure.'

She smiles. 'Absolutely.'

'Call me with any problems, and I'll be straight there.'

I watch Zoe walk off with my baby, suddenly overwhelmed by my sister's fate. I head to the pharmacy, but when I get there, I can't remember what I came for. I leave and wander around in a daze, numb from the cold and the pain that I'll never see my sister again. It's suffocating me, as if she took all the air from my lungs when she left this earth. Life is unbearable without her. It's the loneliest I've ever felt.

Before I know it, I'm walking to Ezra's apartment. The need to speak to someone about my sister – someone who knew her as well as I did – is overwhelming. Samantha's blue Audi TT that Sean drove back from Max's house occupies one of the apartment's two dedicated parking bays. I'll never see her drive that car again. I swallow the lump permanently grating the back of my throat for the firsts and lasts I'll have to face in the coming year.

I press the buzzer to Samantha's apartment. But it's not her apartment any more. It's Ezra's. The thought sends another surge of sadness crashing through me. It's crushing. There's no answer. I press the buzzer again. Ezra must be out.

I let myself in, shivering. It's wrong. I should call him. But I'm past caring. It's colder inside than it is outside. Taking off my coat, I drop it with my bag by the doormat and walk down the hallway, dodging the pair of trainers, a sports bag and the discarded clothes scattered here and there. It's not so minimalist any more. And it no longer smells like my sister in here. The scent of orange blossom potpourri has been replaced with the smell of male testosterone and burnt toast.

I pass the giant mirror Samantha bought at an antiques fair we went to together last year before I met Max. I thought it would look out of place in a modern apartment, but she was insistent. She was right. I catch a glimpse of myself. I look a mess. Strands of lank hair that the hood of my coat didn't protect from the rain are stuck to the side of my face and dark shadows from sleepless nights circle my eyes.

I walk from room to room, overwhelmed by the quietness, talking to my sister as if she can hear me. 'Who did this to you, Samantha? Who?'

I need answers.

I step to her study area in the corner of the living room. It looks bare without her computer, which the police must've taken. I open the drawers of the desk, searching for clues. The police must've done the same when they took her computer. Samantha would turn in her grave if she could see the mess they left it in. I open the bottom drawer and comb through the items, stopping suddenly when I come across a small button. I gasp. It's a mother-of-pearl button. The same button of Max's white shirt that I accidently turned pink when I put it in the wash with the red towels. A wash I swear I never put on.

The front door slams shut. I shove the button in my pocket and close the drawer. 'That you, Ezra,' I call out.

Ezra appears. He looks better than he did the last time I saw him, but his face is still a picture of grief splattered with shades of pale grey and blotches of angry red. 'What on earth are you doing here?'

'You never answered my question the other day,' I say.

'What question?'

'Who was Samantha having an affair with?'

He spins around and walks along the narrow passage towards the kitchen. I follow him. He empties a bottle of wine into a used glass. 'Want some? I've got another bottle.'

'Answer me,' I shout, stamping towards him. 'Who was my sister having an affair with?'

FIFTY-TWO

'It was Max, wasn't it?'

'You knew!' Ezra says.

Rain splatters the window. The bitter taste of betrayal reaches my throat as I think about the suspicions that have been tormenting me. Suspicions I couldn't find it in myself to face. The times I've seen Max and Samantha together in conversation. There was a closeness between them. And about all the nights he has worked late since Lola was born. Nights he could easily have spent with her. How I heard her talk about him with such fondness over the years before I met him.

It doesn't add up, though. They had ten years to get together before I came along. It doesn't make sense that he waited until he married me and we'd had a child.

I lower my voice as I pinch my fingers around the button in my pocket. 'I never thought Max would cheat on me.'

'Neither did I think Samantha would me.' There's an unusual coolness about him. It's as if he's taken control of his emotions. 'Who would've thought they would've done that to either of us? But they did.'

My chest tightens. 'What proof do you have? Did she actually tell you that?'

He shakes his head.

'Then what makes you say it was him?'

He sighs deeply. 'I found a message she sent to him the day before she was murdered.' He reaches for his phone. The rain outside intensifies, pelting the glass. He taps the screen.

I watch him in confusion, a dreaded sense of unease pulsing through me for what he's about to show me.

Slowly, he turns the screen to face me. 'Samantha sent this to Max early on Monday morning.' It was a message that Ezra has forwarded onto his own phone.

> I've done it. I can't wait until the sale goes through. Only a few more days and we can be together. I hope all has gone OK your end. I love you more than you'll ever know. S x

I step backwards and recoil as if someone has kicked me in the guts. It can't be true. But it's there in black and white. 'Do the police know about this?' Each breath I take sticks in my throat.

'I had to show them. Thank heavens they have CCTV footage showing me in Scotland on Monday. Otherwise, I'm sure they'd have me in the slammer by now.'

I grab the phone from him. My eyes dart nervously from him to the screen as I reread the message. 'You seriously don't think Max killed her?' I think back to Monday afternoon. 'He was out with Sean when it happened. Anyway, even if they had been having an affair, he had no reason to kill her.'

'Perhaps he'd decided not to go ahead with it and wanted her out of the way.'

'That's weak.'

'I don't know anything any more.' He throws his hands in

the air and drops them with a thud on his lap. 'Other than my life is over.'

I need to speak to Max. But the thought of facing him with all this is incomprehensible. 'When did you find this?'

'Yesterday. Just before the police came and took away Samantha's stuff.' His voice wavers. 'I was thinking about the funeral. Do you remember when Tanya died, and her parents arranged that rotating display of photos for the service?'

I nod. Tanya was Samantha's childhood friend. She died in a boating accident last year. Samantha was traumatised.

'I want the same for Samantha's funeral.' He pauses to control his emotions. 'So I logged on to her computer to download some photos. I wasn't even looking for anything incriminating.'

'What did the police say?'

'They'll investigate it.'

'I need to go.'

'I'm sorry, Annie.'

'Me too.' I gasp.

Each breath is a struggle, every thought twisted with deception. If Ezra tells the police that I thought it was Max all along who my sister was having an affair with, they could think I killed her in a fit of rage and tried to fake it as suicide.

Coupled with Jasmine backing up their theories, I could be in trouble.

Very big trouble.

FIFTY-THREE

I have to get away from here. When the police have finished sifting through what they call their crime scene, I can't go back.

The walk to meet Zoe and Lola gives me time to consider my and my daughter's future. Perhaps Lola and I could stay with Nisha and Sean until I find us somewhere else to live. But I'm scared Max might try to fight me for her. Proclaim I'm unfit to be a mother, as he has clearly expressed with all his suggestions I attend therapy to deal with my issues and his persistence in hiring extra help.

It's what he could've been planning all this time. He's been gaslighting me – preparing to take Lola away from me and run off with my sister. The thought floods me with a wave of intense disgust. But as I turn each corner to meet Zoe and Lola, the more I can't believe my sister would've done that to me.

'We've had a great time. I gave her a bottle,' Zoe says when I reach my car where she is already waiting. Lola is cooing contently in her buggy. She unclips Lola's car seat from the buggy frame. 'Let me help you in the car with her.' She buckles Lola in. 'Are you OK, Annie?' She looks at me uneasily.

I want to open up, but I hardly know her. 'I'm fine. And I'm grateful for your help.'

She smiles. She has such a kind smile. 'I'll see you on Monday, then.'

I head to the police station. DI Pitman frowns when he sees Lola's buggy. 'I didn't have anyone I could leave her with,' I lie. Frustratingly, Lola has fallen asleep. For once, I need her screaming the place down so that I have an excuse not to go through this.

'Perhaps I can find someone to mind her while we have a chat. I'm not comfortable having a baby in an interview. Besides, it'll be a distraction if she wakes up.'

'Who?'

'You've met DS Pinewood. Let me see if she's free.' He leaves me, only to return a minute later with the DS. At least it's someone I've met before. I reluctantly let the police officer take my baby away, with reassurances she'll come and get me if there are problems. I head up the corridor, echoing with doors opening and closing and commands from other officers.

It feels like Groundhog Day as I sit opposite DI Pitman. It's a different room to the last time I was here, windowless and airless, but the bland furniture and recording equipment are the same. Again, I'm only here as a witness, the DI tells me, although I sense a change in the tone of his voice. I try to stay calm, pushing the conversation with Ezra from my thoughts to deal with later. The last thing I need is for the DI to detect something else is playing on my mind.

As the meeting progresses, the DI grills me like a piece of meat. 'The thing is, Annie, if we're going to catch who did this to your sister, we need to know everything. I'd like to focus on the relationship you and Max had with your sister, and Samantha's affair.'

'I've nothing to add to what I've already told you.' My leg bounces incessantly. 'Samantha and I were close, but I didn't know about the affair.'

The DI clasps his hands together and cracks his knuckles. 'We've seen a message she sent to Max on the morning before her death.'

I bite my lip. 'I've just heard about that,' I say to buy some time. My heart beats hard. Part of me wants to throw Max to the dogs and let them tear him apart. But there's also still a part of me that can't believe he was having an affair, especially not with my sister. 'It must be a mistake.'

'Why do you say that?'

'There must be an explanation. Neither of them would've done that to me.'

He eyes me nonchalantly. 'But it's there, as plain as day. There's no denying it,' he says.

'I haven't had the opportunity to speak to him about it,' I say unconvincingly.

'Come on, Annie, who are you trying to kid? Me, or yourself?' He's trying to unsettle me.

'What do you mean by that?'

'Here's where I'm at. You claim you were asleep in the room next to where your sister was murdered. The sister who was having an affair with your husband.'

'Allegedly having an affair,' I say. 'You don't know that for sure.' I question why I'm defending Max when there is so much evidence to the contrary.

'We have very good reason to suspect they were.'

His words put the fear of the devil in me. I place my hands on the table. The time has come. 'I'm not answering any more of your questions until I've spoken to a lawyer.'

FIFTY-FOUR

My mind is in a whirl as I drive back to Nisha and Sean's place.

'I've prepared a vat of spagbol for supper,' Nisha says when I arrive back in her toasty kitchen. She's wearing a floaty dress, the hem to the floor, and leather slippers. Bonnie is on her hind legs, begging for a morsel. The warmth of the room makes me realise how cold Max's kitchen is. 'Everyone can help themselves as and when.' She places a lid on a giant cooking pot on the stove. She squints at me. 'Has something else happened?'

I fight the tears that are at bursting point. 'The police grilled me. Fortunately, Lola started having one of her screaming fits and saved me.'

'What did they grill you about?'

I'm close to tears. 'I think Max and Samantha might have been having an affair.'

She drops the wooden spoon she is holding onto a ceramic holder. 'That's ridiculous. Max is one hundred per cent in love with you.'

'Is he?' I cock my head, raising my eyebrows. 'Is he really?'

'Yes!'

I tell her about the button and my sister's text message to

Max. 'And that photo of the three of them. The one at the awards ceremony.'

'The one in Sean's office?'

'Samantha had the same photo,' I say. 'I've only just realised. The way Max is looking at her. It's like he was in love with her.'

She looks at me as if I'm mad. 'Don't be so ridiculous. They were close. I don't doubt that. But they'd been friends for years before you came along. Don't you think they'd have got together before if there was something... sexual... there? There must be an explanation for the button and the text.' She continues defending him. 'Don't do anything rash until you've spoken to him.'

'Do you know a good lawyer?'

'Why?'

'I told the police I wouldn't speak to them any more until I had a lawyer. I felt they were insinuating that Max and Samantha were having an affair. They find it odd that I was asleep in the room next to where she was murdered.'

'That's absurd.'

'I could've seen a duty solicitor, but there wasn't one free, and then Lola started.'

'They would've arrested you if they thought you were in any way involved.'

'I need a lawyer. Do you know one?'

'Only corporate ones that Sean and Max use. Let me ask one of my clients. Her husband is a lawyer, but I don't know if they're a criminal lawyer.'

'I need to find one.' I nod at my baby. 'I'm going to go and get her sorted.'

'Why don't you go and have a lie-down?' She points at Lola, fussing in her car seat. 'I'll look after this bundle of fun for an hour.'

An overwhelming feeling to keep my daughter close overcomes me. 'Thanks for the offer, but she needs a change, and I'm going to give her a bath.'

'Want me to do it? I'll ask Maisie to help. She'd love that.'

'It's fine. Thanks, anyway.'

She calls after me as I walk out of the door. 'I've put the kids' old baby gym in your room. I've checked everything still works. The music and movement should keep her entertained for a while.'

'You're an angel,' I say. 'I mean it. Thank you.'

The bedroom is large and clinical. An arrangement of colourful designer cushions decorate the white duvet and pillows of the king-sized bed. Large fitted wardrobes run the length of one wall, and a dressing table and two giant chests of drawers the other. So light compared to our dark bedroom.

Being here is making me notice all the faults in Max's house. Have I been a fool? Should I have noticed what was going on around me?

Shaking, I unbuckle Lola from her car seat and change her on the bed before placing her on her belly under the baby gym. She immediately rolls on her back fretting, until I press the big green button, which initiates gentle rainforest music. The stuffed animals hovering above her head immediately mesmerise her. 'Enjoy, baby girl.' I blow her a kiss as I dig my phone out of my pocket.

I can't wait until I pick Max up from the airport tomorrow. I have to ask him now.

But the call goes to voicemail. I glance at my watch, making a quick calculation. He's probably on his way to the airport or already there. The thought of seeing him repulses me, yet at the same time, I need to hear him say it – confirm what Ezra told me about him and my sister. But there'd be no point in him admitting it now. As far as he's aware, no one knows about the affair; he could keep quiet, and no one would ever be any the wiser.

I google local law firms and make a few enquiries. Time is not on my side, I tell them. I need to speak to someone urgently. They take my details and tell me someone will soon be in touch.

I chuck the phone on the bedside cabinet. Turning to the open suitcase beside the bed, I separate the hodgepodge of clothes into three piles – one for Lola, one for Max and the other for me. A dress of mine and a pair of Max's chinos need hanging up. The rest can remain in the suitcase.

Lola squeals as she takes a swipe at a colourful toucan.

'Are you having fun, darling?'

She giggles, swiping her hands and kicking her feet.

I open the wardrobe door. It's full of brightly coloured ski clothes of different sizes. Skiing is one of Sean's favourite pastimes. The whole family goes on a skiing holiday at least once a year. Two if they can. Usually, Max and the twins join them before they return to school after Christmas. But they didn't this year.

I try the next wardrobe door and the next. They are both full, but the end one has some space. I hang up my dress, but when I pick up Max's chinos, I think about what Ezra told me and throw them across the room in a fit of rage.

A glint of gold, which I first think is a coin, falls from a pocket and lands on the lush cream carpet.

I bend down to pick it up, and gasp.

On closer inspection it's a necklace.

With an 'S' shaped golden charm.

FIFTY-FIVE

My stomach convulses. It's Samantha's necklace. Ezra bought it for her birthday a few years ago. She used to absently fiddle with the charm when trying to emphasise a point. But I can't understand what it's doing in Max's pocket.

Again, questions. So many questions.

But this time, there can only be a simple answer.

Repulsion rips through me. Finding this has turned the screw of deceit even tighter. I take one end of the chain in each hand and yank. It snaps in two. The 'S' spins in the air and lands on the bed on the side Max would sleep if he were here. I hold the two ends in the palm of my hand. But despite the evidence staring me in the face, I still can't believe my sister would've done this to me.

But people surprise you. I've experienced that throughout my life. My father, who left my mum when I was born and ran off with her sister. My best friend at school, who I discovered was seeing my first true love behind my back. The guy who abruptly ended our five-year relationship when he finally decided to come running and shouting out of the closet.

I chuck the broken chain and charm next to the lamp on the

bedside cabinet and drop down on the edge of the bed, unable take my eyes off it. I turn to a knock at the bedroom door.

Jasmine appears, a look of thunder on her face. 'You were meant to pick me up to take me to the dentist. Why didn't you?' Her slender frame is lost in the enormity of the doorway.

I invite her in. I need to face her with what I heard her say about me to Priti. 'I'm so sorry.' I thump my forehead with the palm of my hand. 'I totally forgot.' Perhaps this isn't a good time to discuss last night.

She heads to Lola on the floor hitting out at a stuffed giraffe and tickles her tummy. Her voice softens. It's at odds with her fiery nature. Her head turns. Her eyes lock with mine. 'You forget a lot of things, Annie.'

'I'm sorry. I've had another dreadful day. Did it all go OK?'

'They feel tight.' She touches her mouth. 'It's painful.'

'I remember when I had braces. It takes some getting used to after they've been tightened. Ask Nisha if she's got any paracetamol.'

She stands up. 'Have you been online lately?'

I frown. 'No, why?'

'I think you should.' With that she marches off.

I close the door and turn to my phone, typing my sister's name into Google. Several newspaper articles relating to her death that I've already read appear. I scroll down and come across another one titled, *Sister Blamed for Businesswoman's Death.*

Confused, I think it must be related to another murder in another family but a picture of my sister fronts the article. I click on the story. My mouth drops open. I can't believe what I'm reading. Comments on social media are pointing the unfair finger of blame directly at me. I click on a link. It directs me to Facebook, and there it is in black and white. I whisper the comments as I scroll through them.

The sister was apparently asleep in the bedroom next door to where she was murdered.

Why haven't they thrown the book at the sister yet?

Bloody police! They don't move quickly enough in cases like this. So frickin' obvious it's the sister.

This can't go on.

I call another lawyer, but it's too late in the day. I send emails to two more via their contacts form.

I will not take the blame for this.

·

FIFTY-SIX

I grab Lola and run downstairs, clutching her against my hip. The smell of spagbol hits me as I'm halfway down. It's nauseating.

Nisha is sitting at the table, typing on her laptop. Bonnie is lying on her floaty dress. She stops typing. 'What's happened?' She must be able to tell what a state I'm in as she jumps up. Bonnie startles. Hurrying to me with her dog by her side, she takes Lola from me.

Hot tears burn my eyes. My hands slam against my chest, trying to control my erratic breaths. Sensing the panic, Lola lets out a cry. It penetrates through me. I shudder. I can't take it.

Nisha guides me to the table, trying to comfort Lola. She cradles her against her chest. 'Sit down. Come on, take some deep breaths.' She perches on the chair to the right of me, rocking Lola.

'Have you seen online? People are trying to blame me. And I found this.' With a trembling hand, I drop the necklace on the table.

'What's that?' she asks, jigging Lola up and down, trying to console her.

'It's my sister's necklace,' I say.

She frowns.

'I found it in Max's trouser pocket. The trousers he was wearing on Monday.'

'OK.'

'What's it doing in there?'

She breathes deeply. 'Woah! Hang tight. I'm going to get one of the girls to look after Lola for a while.' She scuttles from the room with my baby, her dog in tow. It's for the best. Lola can't understand what we're saying, but she can pick up on the vibes.

I stare at the necklace as I continuously pick up the two pieces of broken chain and drop them on the table.

I deserve this.

I deserve everything that is coming to me.

Nisha returns. 'Shall we have a glass of wine?'

I nod.

She goes to the fridge, pours two glasses and returns to sit beside me.

I take a gulp. The oaky taste catches in my throat. I take another gulp and drop my head to my chest.

She puts an arm across my shoulders. 'I know this is hard for you,' she says, 'but you need to speak to Max before jumping to any conclusions. As I said earlier, there could be many reasons why he has that necklace.'

'This is all my fault.'

Nisha grabs my hand. 'Don't be silly. No, it's not.'

My guard comes crashing down with a force I can't control. With my sister gone, I need to confide in someone. 'It is. It's my punishment,' I cry.

'Punishment for what?'

'Oh, Nisha. I've done something bad. Something utterly wicked.'

She squints at me, her bemused eyes searching for more.

'Samantha knew about it.'

'I'm sorry, Annie. But I'm really confused. Knew about what?'

'If I tell you something, you must promise you'll never tell another soul.'

She places both hands on her heart, one on the other. 'Of course.'

I look behind me and around the room, double checking we are alone. 'I don't know if Max is Lola's father.'

FIFTY-SEVEN

Perhaps she is adopting her professional stance, but her deadpan expression surprises me. I was expecting a look of horror. She slowly nods. 'OK. Do you want to talk about it?'

'I didn't cheat on Max.' I scoff at my words. I roll my eyes. 'Yes, of course, I've cheated on him, but not in the sense of sleeping with someone while we were together. After Samantha and Ezra's wedding, Max didn't call me until the following weekend. But on the Friday night, I went to a party and bumped into an ex. I was deeply disappointed that Max hadn't called me.' I shrug. 'Need I say more? You know where I'm going with this.'

'You slept with him and then with Max, and you don't know which one is the father.'

I drop my head; the shame of hearing someone else say it is too much.

'Didn't you use protection?'

I lift my head to answer her. 'Yes! Both times. But on one of the occasions, the condom obviously let me down.'

She rubs the crease between her eyes. 'And you've kept this all to yourself?'

'Samantha knew. She was on and on at me to get a DNA test done. She said if it showed Max was the father, then I could keep quiet about it. If not, then she thought I needed to tell him. I promised her I would do it.' I run my shaking hands down the sides of my face. 'It's killing me, Nisha. It's killing me.'

'It's illegal to get a DNA test without someone's knowledge.'

I nod. 'That's what's stopped me. I could shoot myself. I should've just come clean from the start. But we fell so helplessly in love that by the time I discovered I was pregnant, I couldn't bear the thought of telling him. I didn't want to lose him. Please don't judge me.'

She gives me a wry smile. 'I never judge people.'

'Naively, I thought I'd be able to tell once she was born. She's got the same colour eyes as Max, but everyone tells me she looks like me, not him.'

Nisha nods. 'I'll be honest with you. I thought the same. She's the spitting image of you. But look at my kids. The girls look very much like me, but not the boys.' She pauses as if deep in thought, before saying, 'So what are you going to do about it?'

'I was going to order a DNA test and get it sent to Samantha's place. But of course, I can't do that any more.'

'Do you want to get one sent here?'

'I feel like I'm putting you in an awkward position. It's not fair on you.'

'It's fine. Let me know when it's due to arrive. I'll look out for it. I think it's the right thing to do.'

'If she is Max's, I don't need to worry.'

'And if she's not?' she asks.

I shrug. 'Then I've got to tell him.'

FIFTY-EIGHT

My stomach is in knots, threads of anxiety tightly tied that are making me constantly nauseous. Earlier, I lay awake, debating whether to collect Max today. He has to go straight to the police station, and I can't let him do that until I've spoken to him first. I have to know the truth about him and my sister.

And about him and my daughter.

So when I got up this morning, I ordered the DNA test kit. I have to do the right thing. And I have to honour the promise I made to my sister. But I didn't get the kit sent to Nisha's house. It's not fair to involve her. I'm already regretting discussing the matter with her. I got it sent to Max's house. It will arrive in plain packaging, and I paid extra for a morning delivery slot.

From behind the retractable barrier, I scan the wave of passengers emerging through the arrivals door. Families rolling trolleys loaded with suitcases, couples hand-in-hand – or not – people rushing to greet loved ones or taxi drivers holding plaques with names for private transfers.

Lola is playing with a soft elephant toy that Maisie gave to her, crinkling its ear between her fingers and biting the corner. I recheck the arrivals board. The digital display shows Max's plane landed forty minutes ago. Passengers are now in baggage claim. He didn't take any checked-in luggage, so he should be out by now. I can't understand what's taking him so long. I'm edgy, in my mind replaying the inevitable conversation I can't escape.

My phone rings. I ignore the call but listen to the short message DS Pinewood leaves. The forensics are finishing at the house; their job is nearly complete. We can go back there tomorrow morning. The thought fills me with dread.

Max's face, long, drawn and incredibly pale, comes into view. His eyes are bloodshot and seem to have sunk into his face. He looks as if he hasn't slept since he kissed me goodbye before he caught the taxi to the airport.

For a moment, a strong yearning overcomes me. A longing for how we were together when we first met before I knew I was pregnant. The loved-up couple that was a source of envy to all my friends. I'd never known anything like it. It was a love I'd have done anything to keep... anything! I can't believe we've ended up here.

'Here he is,' I say, releasing the straps of Lola's car seat and scooping her into my arms. I turn her to face her daddy, who is walking towards us, wearing jeans and a five o'clock shadow, pulling a cabin bag. A rucksack is hanging from his stooped shoulder. He stops in front of us, releases the handle of his cabin bag and opens his arms.

I might be mistaken, but I think his bottom lip is quivering. I push Lola towards him before he can touch me.

He is overcome with emotion, kissing our squealing daughter before grabbing me into his embrace. He senses my reluctance. 'What's wrong?' His sea-blue eyes search mine for an answer.

I nod to a café across the way. My voice wobbles. 'Let's grab a drink. I could do with some caffeine before the drive back.'

'Good idea,' he says. 'I could murder a coffee, too.'

Murder.

'The coffee on the flight was dire.'

I try to reclaim Lola, but he dodges my grasp.

'I'll take her.' He flies her in the air like an aeroplane before holding her tightly against his chest. 'I've missed you all so much.' He snuggles his nose into the soft, hollow spot at the side of Lola's neck, breathing in her smell and smiling. She giggles. When I see them together like this, I can't believe he is not her real father.

I grab his cabin bag and Lola's car seat and lead the way to the café, settling us at a small table to the side of the counter. 'Could you get me a double espresso and a can of Coke, please.' He holds Lola up to his face and kisses her forehead. 'Daddy needs something to keep him awake as well.'

When I return with our drinks, I sit opposite him.

'You look different,' he says.

'How?'

'I don't know.' He cocks his head to the side. 'Your eyes... they look brighter, somehow.' He asks about Samantha and the developments in the case. 'I can't believe what's happened. Someone else must've come into the house. That can be the only explanation. What about the Amazon guy?'

I wipe the dribble from Lola's chin with a paper napkin. 'The police have checked him out. His work log shows him eight miles away. Anyway, what would his motive have been?'

He shrugs.

I condense the last few days into a two-minute synopsis, delaying the inevitable.

'Pregnant! But—'

'I know. It can't be Ezra's, so it must be who she was having an affair with.'

His eyes widen, but he changes the subject. 'How have the twins been?'

'Fine.'

He briefs me on his trip, filling in what he didn't manage to tell me during our short conversations. 'It's over, Annie. The business is sold. We can start moving on with our lives. Let's go on holiday. I was flicking through a brochure on the plane. Dubai. I'll arrange it. We could even take Zoe to give you a proper break.'

He doesn't get it.

I tell him I need a lawyer.

'I know someone, but is it really necessary? I'll speak to the police.'

He really doesn't get it.

'You're looking well, given everything that's been going on.' He balances our gurgling daughter on his knee and reaches to touch my face.

I flinch.

He's taken aback. 'What's wrong?'

I was going to wait until we got in the car before facing him. A crowded airport café isn't the place to have this kind of conversation. But it can't wait. Gingerly, I open my purse to find the white button I found in Samantha's drawer. I hold it up.

'That's from my white shirt!' He takes it. 'Where did you find it?'

'In Samatha's desk drawer.'

'She must've found it at work.'

'And what excuse do you have for this, hey, Max?' I pinch Samantha's necklace between my forefinger and thumb, edging it out of the zipped section of the purse. I jangle it in front of his weary face before dropping it on the paper napkin in front of him.

He gasps. 'That's Samantha's.'

'I know it is. The question is, Max, what are you doing with it?'

'Where did you get it from?'

'It fell out of the pocket of your chinos.'

He rolls his eyes and lets out a noisy puff of air. 'Jeez! Don't let the police see it.'

My spine straightens. 'Why?'

'It won't look good.' He edges Lola's car seat towards him and bends down to place her inside. If I'm not mistaken, his hands are shaking.

'What won't look good?' I shout above the drone of conversation from other customers around us. Heads turn.

He scans the café from his bent position as he buckles the straps of Lola's car set. His forefinger taps his lips. 'Ssh.' There's a look of desperation in his eyes.

'Don't ssh me.'

'Just calm down. We don't need other people listening to this conversation,' he whispers.

'Calm down? My sister was murdered in our house, right next to where I was sleeping, and you have her necklace in the pocket of the trousers you were wearing at the time,' I hiss.

'It's not what it looks like.'

'Why do I always feel you're telling me one thing, but you mean another?'

He sits up and cups his face in his hands. His head shakes as he massages his eyes with the palms of his hands.

I lean closer to him. 'Tell me straight. Why have you got this necklace? And why did my sister send you a message on the morning she was murdered, saying she couldn't wait for you to be together?'

He lifts his head. 'How do you know about that?'

'Ezra found it on her phone and showed it to me.'

His eyes fix on mine.

My stomach turns. That dreadful lurch that tells me whatever he says next, I'm not going to like. 'What, Max? You're scaring me.'

His lips twitch as if he is trying to find the right words to say.

My breath quickens. 'Spit it out.'

'I need to tell you something.'

FIFTY-NINE

'Were you and Samantha having an affair? Tell me.'

The dark skin beneath his blue eyes crinkles. 'Annie! What kind of question is that?' He appears genuinely hurt. 'For a moment, I thought you were going to ask me if I killed her.' He scoffs. Even now, when I feel such anger towards him, his eyes move me. 'What the hell is wrong with you, Annie? How could you even think I'd do that to you?'

My hackles rise in defence. 'What then?'

He hesitates. 'What I'm going to tell you has to stay between the two of us.'

The knots in my stomach tighten, each tug a pull on my shattered emotions.

'It was Sean. Samantha and Sean were having an affair.'

I lean back, my hands clutching the table. 'No way.'

He slowly nods, his bottom lip protruding slightly. But it's the profound look of compassion in those beautiful eyes that confirms he's telling me the truth. 'That text message was meant for him. Samantha sent it to me by mistake. She told Ezra on Sunday night that she was leaving him. The plan was for Sean to tell Nisha he was leaving her at the same time. But he backed down. Decided it wasn't what he wanted.'

'Sean and Samantha!' I say, still stunned. I thought Nisha and Sean's relationship was as solid as a concrete wall.

'Does Ezra know she was pregnant?' Max asks.

I nod. 'He thinks it was you.'

'Me?' he says too loudly. He flings his hand to his chest. The woman beside him turns her head to look.

At first, I wonder if he's lying. But there's no way he could get away with it. 'That's what he said.'

He lowers his voice. 'Has he told the police that?'

I shrug, staring at my drink, overcome with relief, yet still filled with dread, and I don't know why. 'How long had they been seeing each other?'

'A few months, apparently.' He gently rocks Lola's car seat. 'I don't know that for sure. It could be longer. Who knows if they were telling the truth on that front.'

'I can't believe you've kept this to yourself all this time. Why didn't you tell me?'

'For various reasons. I was desperate to keep the sale of the business moving forward. The last thing we all needed was that blowing up in our faces. And then I told Samantha I'd tell you if she didn't. But she was as worried about you as I've been. And I know how close you are to Nisha. I didn't want to add to your stress by putting you in a situation where you felt you had to tell her. I only had your best interests at heart. Honestly, darling.'

My heart sinks. I bite my lip, scared of what I might say. He has only been looking out for me. He raises Lola and kisses her forehead. 'I've missed you all so much.'

'Poor Nisha.'

'I know. That's why I was so angry with them.'

'How did you find out?'

'I caught them kissing in the office one night. I'd left for the day but forgot to take some papers that I needed to drop off at the solicitor's, so I went back for them.' The corners of his lips arch downwards. 'The final straw was seeing that message that was meant for Sean.'

'Is that what you were arguing about on Monday? I heard you, you know.'

He shakes his head. 'No. We were arguing about the sale. Samantha was being difficult. In essence, she'd given Sean an ultimatum – that he had until the end of last weekend to leave Nisha. If not, they were over. They made a pact. Like I said, they were both going to do it on Sunday evening. But he bottled out and told Samantha on Monday morning it was over between them. He wasn't going to leave Nisha. But she'd already told Ezra.'

I shake my head in disbelief.

'We had to carry on with the meeting, though. There were so many things still to finalise for the meeting in LA. It's another reason I've been so anxious for the sale to go through. I knew I couldn't carry on working with either of them. She had started being difficult.'

'How?'

'Threatening to put a stop to the sale.'

'Why?'

'To be difficult. She was so angry with Sean. And heartbroken. And pregnant, I guess.'

'Could she have done that – stopped the sale?'

'Hell, yes.'

I vocalise the thought that springs into my mind. 'You don't think it could've been Sean that murdered her?' As soon as I say it, I realise how absurd this sounds. Sean, the bubbly joker loved by all.

'Sean? No way. But who knows? I'd never have put him down as the type to cheat. But you never really know anyone, do you? Silly guy. Fool. Total fool. But that wasn't a reason to murder her. Besides, I was with him the whole time that day.'

He jigs Lola faster on his knee. 'Drop the idea. Sean might have cheated on his wife, but he's not a murderer.'

'The police questioned him for ages.'

'I know. He told me.'

'How are things between the two of you?'

'They'll never be the same.' He gives a thin-lipped smile. 'I thought she took her own life because Sean had finished their affair. But now this turn of events.'

'It makes sense now. Why Sean was so upset.'

His eyes well up. 'We're both gutted. I knew Samantha for years. We were close.' His eyes fix on the necklace as he passes it through his fingers.

'And the necklace?'

'I found it on the floor in my office. You know how she always played with it; she must've broken the clasp unknowingly while the three of us were arguing.'

Guilt hits me for doubting him. He's my husband, and I should've had more faith.

I reach out and take his hand in mine.

He shakes his head, fixing his eyes on mine. 'How could you have doubted me?'

'I'm sorry. I don't know what's got into me these past few weeks, months, even.' I want to confess, tell him everything. But now is not the time. I need to find out if he is Lola's father or not first. Because if he is, I don't need to tell him anything. We can draw a big fat line in the sand and move on.

'Did you tell the police about the affair?' I ask.

'No.'

'Isn't that lying?'

'To be honest, I didn't know what to do. It wasn't my news to share. Sean and I had a massive argument about it on Monday when I came to pick you and Lola up from their house. I told him he had to tell the police.'

'Will they tell Nisha?' I ask.

'I don't think so. They'll leave it up to him to do that. He has to. I can't have Ezra thinking it was me she was having an affair with.'

I tell him about what I overheard Jasmine say to Priti.

He rolls his eyes. 'She has no right to say such things. I'll have a word with her.'

'Will you, Max? Will you, though?'

'Yes!' He looks hurt. 'I promise you. I know you think I'm weak where the twins are concerned, but Jasmine's right. I should've talked to them more. Involved them in you moving in. Made them think they were part of the decision. I wasn't fair to them. But that doesn't excuse her for saying those things about you. She always was an outspoken little miss. Leave it with me.'

'I need to tell Nisha.'

'You can't.'

'I can't not tell her, Max. It'll come out eventually. And how will she feel if she's the last one to find out?'

'It has to come from him.' He draws his hand away from mine. 'This is why I haven't told you. Sean knows he's made the biggest mistake of his life. He finished things with Samantha before she died. He wanted to put it behind him.'

'Nothing is clearer, is it?' I say. 'We still don't know who murdered my sister.'

SIXTY

My sister torments my thoughts as I drive back. Ezra needs to hear the truth. But as Max said, it's not my place to tell him.

'Things will get better, darling.' Max squeezes my knee. 'I promise you. I'm going to book us that holiday.' A traffic jam around the M25 hampers our journey home. The aftermath of an overturned lorry that took the emergency services a few hours to clear. Still, it allows us a chance for a proper catch-up.

I drop him at the police station. 'How can I face Nisha?' I say before he gets out.

'You have to, Annie. You can't let on.'

'I wish you'd never told me.'

'You gave me no choice.'

'I guess not.' I sigh. 'If I thought you wouldn't be long, I'd hang around, but it's getting late, and we're pushing our luck with Lola.'

'Go home and get her settled. I'll call you once they've finished with me.' He leans over to kiss me. The light casts a shadow over his vulnerability. There's a fluttering in my stomach. The same as when I first met him at my sister's wedding, and he told me about his first wife and how he had raised his two kids alone. The same two kids who have driven a wedge between us. 'I can get a cab back.'

'It's fine. I'll pick you up.'

I drive around the block a couple of times, putting off the inevitable of facing Nisha. To kill more time, I stop at the express supermarket to pick up a contribution towards the food. Feeding another four mouths is expensive.

I wander around the store in a trance, filling the basket with random snacks and drinks. I add packets of strawberries and blackberries and a large bunch of bananas. From the fridges, I select a giant carton of milk, before heading to the baby aisle, where I pick up a packet of nappies. Balancing Lola's car seat in the crook of one arm and the shopping basket in the other, I head to the checkout. I wait in the line, listening to two women in front of me excitedly discussing a night out they have planned for the weekend.

Despite what Max told me, I feel compelled to tell Nisha the truth. I pull out my phone and google what to do when you discover your best friend's husband has had an affair. Various articles offer different and opposing advice. Lola starts whining. I throw the phone back in my bag. For now, I have to keep this newfound information to myself. But the nagging doubt that has been hammering away in the background since Max made me party to this affair won't leave me alone. Did Sean play a part in Samantha's murder? But Max said he was with him the whole day. He could've been lying. I immediately dismiss the thought. If he thought Sean had murdered my sister, there's no way he would keep quiet about it.

The smell of garlic wafts from the kitchen when we arrive back. Maisie runs up to us, accompanied by Bonnie, who is barking at my feet. 'Can I take her?' She tickles Lola's chin, who stops fussing and giggles at her newfound friend.

'I need to give her a bottle first,' I say.

'I'll do it.' Maisie shakes her fists in excitement. 'Can I? Can I?'

'Sure. Let me get it ready.'

Maisie jumps up and down. 'Annie said I can feed Lola, Mum.'

Nisha smiles. She is stirring the contents of a large pan with a wooden spoon. Bonnie hangs around her ankles. 'You're back late,' she says. 'I thought you'd decided to wait for Max at the station.'

'Bad traffic on the M25.'

'I've made a sausage casserole. A one-pot dish. A family favourite. I thought it'd be easy. If you don't fancy it, I've got some pizzas in the freezer.' She takes the spoon and lays it on the lid of the pan.

I stare at her, wishing I didn't know about her husband's affair, but then the truth was impossible to escape. 'I've picked up some groceries.' I hand her a bag of shopping.

'You didn't need to do that.'

'Yes I did.' Looking at her makes me want to cry. She is such a beautiful woman, inside and out. I can't understand what made Sean turn to my sister. 'We have to make a contribution.'

I open the fridge and find Lola a bottle. I wish Max had never told me about Sean and my sister. It has only muddied my thoughts and dumped another dilemma on my shoulders.

After I've warmed the bottle, I settle Lola in Maisie's arms. I'd rather feed her myself, but I can tell how much this means to Maisie.

'I've opened a bottle of wine,' Nisha says. 'Help yourself.'

'Thanks for the offer, but I'm picking up Max later. The police have finished at the house, by the way. We can go back tomorrow.'

'How do you feel about that?'

That's the problem with having a close friend who is a therapist: they ask that question all the time. *How do I feel about that?* I can't answer her. And I can't sit here and talk to her. It feels wrong.

'Would you mind supervising?' I nod over to where Maisie is feeding Lola. 'I've got a splitting headache and need to lie down.'

'No worries. Sean's just gone for a shower. He'll be finished in a bit.'

I can't hang around to talk to her. And I certainly can't face Sean.

SIXTY-ONE

It's been five days now. Five long, lonely days since I last saw my sister. The pain is no less, but still I can't cry. People grieve in different ways, Nisha told me. Situations can paralyse our emotional responses. But it still doesn't feel right that I can't shed a tear for the person I adored so much.

We arrive back at Max's house to find the builders shifting the supply of sand that was delivered on Wednesday around to the back of the house. I look up at the house with its tall, narrow windows with arched tops, and the turret bays. The thought of going back inside is wholly depressing.

I opposed the builders being here today. We need to settle back in without the chaos, but my protests came too late. Max had already arranged it because Jigsaw told him the project is now at a crucial stage. It risks being set back a few months if they can't compensate for the time they've lost this week. They have another job they need to start.

For once, the twins agree with me. 'No way! What are they doing here?' Jasmine protests. 'Can't we have a day without people all over the place?' Jacob concurs with a nod of his head.

Max hits back. 'I'm afraid we need to put up with it. The

sooner we get it done, the sooner the renovations will be finished, and we can move on.'

I'm drained. After Max finished at the station last night, I met Nisha's friend, a criminal lawyer. He was meant to accompany me for another round of questioning with DI Pitman and his colleague, but oddly, the DI ended up postponing the meeting.

The twins help Max unload our luggage and take it inside. I cautiously follow them with Lola's car seat hooked over my arm.

It's cold and damp as if our absence has sucked all the warmth out of the air. Or is that my sister's murder? In the car, Jasmine said being away has made her feel homesick, but for me, it's the exact opposite. There's an emptiness inside of me, a hollow chamber of grief my sister left that I can't fill. I'm sick to death of this house.

I walk into the kitchen and survey the room. To be fair, the police have made an admirable job in keeping it looking as it was before what I can now only refer to as the murder. I stand at the patio doors in a trance, holding Lola in my arms, her head on my shoulder. Cameron and Jigsaw are on a mission, quickly unloading wheelbarrows of sand onto a sheet of tarpaulin and soldiering back to the pile at the front of the house to repeat the process. Max is right. Not that I have anything against the builders, but we need them gone now.

Lola has fallen asleep, so I take her upstairs to her cot so I can get on with unpacking. Max has beaten me to it. The suitcase lies open on the bed. He has already emptied more than half the contents and put them away. My eyes linger on the door to the en suite.

'Are you sure you want to stay in here?' he asks.

We already had this conversation in the car on the way back from Nisha and Sean's house. My feelings are cut in two. Half of me doesn't know if I can stay in this room with what happened behind that door. The other half still wants to be close to where my sister last was. 'Yes,' I say.

Max stops to wrap his arms around me as if reading my thoughts. 'We can get the whole room gutted and start again. Change it around. New everything. Or we move into one of the other bedrooms when the renovations are finished. Let's do that.'

I attempt a smile, but it falls way short. I go to ask him if he has considered my suggestion we find another house to buy but keep quiet.

That's a conversation for another time. We made love last night. It was the first time since Lola was born.

There's still a distance between us, but we're closer than we have been for a long time. I don't know how long it can stay that way. Only the DNA test results can answer that.

SIXTY-TWO

I strap Lola to my front in the new baby carrier I bought from Amazon. The disorientated sense of exhaustion has returned. I slept dreadfully last night, and it takes all my concentration to work out how the straps work. It's this house. It drains me.

Lola loves the new harness and, for a while, is content strapped close to me while I go about mundane jobs lost in my thoughts. Thoughts about my sister, and Nisha, and Ezra, who has gone to stay with friends.

The twins are at school for a music performance rehearsal, and Max has holed himself in his office. He's dreadfully apologetic, but he has to catch up on the work he has missed this week. I'm not bothered. I'm happy to have the time alone with Lola.

In the living room, I snatch up an odd sock of Jacob's, an unopened letter addressed to him, Jasmine's school pullover and a set of sketching pencils she has left lying around. The twins must be the untidiest humans I've ever encountered. Or perhaps it's me. The only person I've lived with besides Max was a computer programmer named Peter, who was as clean and tidy as a freshly laundered bed.

Lola coos, staring up at me with her beautiful blue eyes, as I take the discarded items upstairs. I drop the sock and letter by Jacob's door before crossing the landing to Jasmine's room.

I've only been in her room a couple of times. It was when I first moved in and used to leave clean laundry and all the crap she'd left lying around the house on her bed. It caused an argument, where she bluntly told me I had no right to go into her or her brother's room. Max told her she was being rude. I was only doing her a favour. But that only heightened her exasperation. We agreed she would try to be tidier, and I would leave anything meant for the two of them by their respective doors. I was the only one who kept to their side of the bargain.

Her door is ajar. She usually makes a point of slamming it shut every morning as if to remind me I can't go in there. I push the handle. The hinges creak ominously as the door slowly opens. The sound echoes along the dark hallway. My heart pounds, my conscience telling me she'd go mad if she were here. But the elbow of curiosity nudges me into the room.

Her White Musk perfume's clean, sweet scent overrides the smell of used cups and dirty plates and the mountains of clothes strewn across the floor and furniture. I glance around the walls decorated with photographs, paintings and canvases of her work and artistic embellishments. There must be at least one hundred pieces across the four walls – far more than when I was last in here. It's a shrine to her personality. The photographs are mainly of her and her friends, her life story through the years, but there are some of Max and Jacob, and many of her mother, too.

An open portfolio draws me to her desk. I walk towards it, the bare floorboards creaking underfoot. I turn the pages. The quality of the paintings suggests it's not her most recent work, but still, it's impressive. Art was a subject I never enjoyed. Mainly because, despite trying my best, I wasn't any good at it. But Jasmine is incredibly talented. The date below her autograph in the bottom left-hand corner of the pages confirms these are paintings from her early teens. I can't resist perusing through them. My heart thumps, each heavy beat a reminder that what I'm doing is wrong. I'm in my stepdaughter's bedroom, nosing through her stuff.

Around two thirds of the way through, I stop and stare, my mouth agape. I quickly turn the pages in dismay. Staring back at me is a series of pictures depicting fires in different situations. Some are innocent – a blazing bonfire burning rubbish in someone's overgrown back garden, a loved-up couple sitting in front of a roaring fire. On closer inspection, I believe the man is Max. The woman must be her mother.

Lola starts fussing as if to remind me what I'm doing is wrong. 'Just give me a minute,' I say, kissing the top of her head.

Other paintings are more disturbing. Extremely disturbing indeed. One shows a wooden house on fire, flames ripping through the cladding with trapped people hanging out of the windows. A woman is dangling a young child from the attic window. Jasmine's attention to detail is remarkable. She has depicted both the woman and child's haunted expressions so well that fear leaps from the paper in abundance. I turn the page as an uneasy feeling passes through me. The painting portrays a woman engulfed in flames running frantically through a cornfield. What is her fixation with fire? I think back to the incident in the kitchen. The fire everyone thinks I started because I left that pan of rice on the cooker.

I turn the next page and gasp out loud. There's a picture, dated last week – the day after the fire – of just that: a fire in our kitchen.

What the hell?

I look around the room, shocked to see a painted canvas on the wall, lost in the vivid display of the surrounding pieces. It's only a small one – the size of an iPad – an abstract painting of a man and a woman tossing a crying baby between themselves. There's no resemblance to Max or me, but it's clearly Lola. She's clutching the pink teddy bear the twins bought her for Christmas.

I need to speak to Max.

SIXTY-THREE

I hurry downstairs and burst into Max's office. 'We need to talk.'

He's on the phone. He shoves his hand over the receiver and shakes his head, mouthing, 'I can't talk at the moment.'

I return upstairs and put Lola in her cot for a nap. I lie down, too. What I've seen in Jasmine's room has shaken me. Before I know it, Max appears, sitting beside me holding Lola. He startles me. I look at my watch. I've been asleep for over two hours.

He looks tired. 'I left you sleeping while I picked up the twins. You didn't hear Lola crying.' He caresses my shoulder.

I yawn, flattening my hair as I sit up. 'I was sound asleep.'

'You must've needed it. What did you want to talk to me about?'

A knock at the door from downstairs interrupts our conversation. 'That'll be the builders.' He stands up. 'I'd better go and see what they want.'

I take Lola from him. 'I'll be there in a minute.'

When I get downstairs, Max is chatting with Cameron in the kitchen. Max hands me a cup of coffee. 'I need to send a quick email, and then I'll join you outside,' he says to Cameron.

He turns to me. 'Jigsaw wants to ask some questions about the electrics.' He picks up his cup of coffee. 'I'll be back in a while.'

Cameron looks drawn, not his usual upbeat self. 'I'm sorry to hear the shocking news about your sister, Annie. It's dreadful.'

'Thanks.' I swallow hard. 'It's been a tough time.'

'I was just telling Max the police questioned all of us builders who have been on site these past few weeks.'

I sip my coffee. 'What did they ask?'

He shrugs. 'General questions. Where we were at the time. If we'd ever met your sister. That kind of thing.'

'I'm sorry you've all been pulled into this.'

'And I'm sorry for everything you're going through. It can't be easy. Are they any closer to finding out who did this?'

I shake my head.

'If there's anything I can do for you, let me know. I wish we could've helped, but none of us were here when it happened. Although...' He hesitates.

'What?'

'It's nothing.' He turns to leave.

I pull at his arm. 'Don't go. What were you going to say?'

'Nothing, seriously, it was nothing.'

'You wouldn't have implied there was if there wasn't,' I say. 'Please, Cameron. This is important.'

'Jigsaw said he heard Max shouting at your sister that day.'

'What about?'

He shrugs. 'He couldn't make out. He was just walking past the window of his office and heard the noise.'

'And?'

'It's just Max must feel bad.'

'Did you report this to the police?'

'Jigsaw did.' He points to the door. 'I really need to get going.'

. . .

After dinner, Max takes Lola for a bath and the twins go to their rooms while I clear up. I haven't had the chance to speak to him about Jasmine yet. As I stand from loading the dishwasher, my head spins. I take an involuntary step backwards. The plate I'm holding slips from my fingers and crashes to the floor. The room sways out of focus around me. My stomach spasms. I lean on the countertop until the feeling passes. But it doesn't.

I struggle to reach the armchair by the patio doors, where I sit and put my feet on the coffee table. I've felt well since staying at Nisha and Sean's place, and now I'm back here, and the symptoms have restarted. 'I'm allergic to this house,' I mutter. Ridiculous. How can someone be allergic to a house? But it can't be a coincidence my symptoms have come back since returning here.

The need to sleep is overwhelming, but I've already slept for two hours this afternoon. It's not right to feel this tired. My stomach turns. Not from nausea, but from the thought that something is very wrong with me. I feel like I'm dying. I can't die. My baby needs me. The familiar mist of doubt overcomes me as a disturbing thought enters my confused mind.

Someone is poisoning me.

That would explain why my bloods showed abnormal liver function readings.

Someone wants to get rid of me.

SIXTY-FOUR

My skin turns clammy. It can only be someone in this family. It's one of the twins. I'm sure of it. I wipe beads of sweat from my forehead as an even more disturbing thought enters my head. While Max was away, I was feeling increasingly better.

I stagger upstairs, holding onto the handrail for support. My mind is in overdrive. I want to pack a case and get away from here, but I'm in no fit state at the moment.

Max is dressing Lola on the bathroom floor. She is giggling as he sings to her. 'You OK?' he asks as I pass. I ignore him and go to lie on our bed.

He appears with my clean and fresh baby. 'Did you get her bottle?' he asks, frowning.

'I need to talk to you,' I say.

The creases in his forehead deepen. He perches on the edge of the bed. 'What's wrong?'

I quiz him on the pictures I found in Jasmine's portfolio. It isn't the right time for the conversation. Lola is fussing. A sign she wants her bottle. But I have to have it out with him.

'What are you trying to get at?' he asks.

'She seems to have an obsession with fire.'

'I wouldn't call it an obsession, more of a therapy. She doesn't like to talk about it, but when she was younger, about twelve, I think, one of her friends' mothers died in a house fire.' He tells me how much it affected her. 'Painting was her therapy while she was an ear to her friend.' His jaw clenches, ever so slightly, but it does. 'Please don't go in her room again. It'll only cause an argument.'

Sleep brings no respite. The nightmares return with a vengeance.

They're getting darker and darker. I run after the faceless person hounding me, breathless and bewildered. I can't catch them, but I feel like I'm getting closer. In one, Jacob is holding me down while Jasmine stands above me, slaying my stomach with an axe. But the latest one is the worst ever. Max is standing at her side, ordering her to drive the weapon further up my body to my neck.

I wake up drenched in perspiration. My eyes are wide with fear as the images from the nightmare stick like glue in the forefront of my mind. I scan the room, holding my neck as I gasp for air as quietly as I can. Max is snoring gently. I don't want to wake him.

In the morning, I see Zoe arrive from the utility room window where I'm loading the washing machine with one hand, while trying to comfort a grizzling Lola on my hip with the other. Max has gone into his work office today, which is a relief. It will give me time to think.

I need to get away from here. If only for a few days to clear my head. But I can't seem to get my head straight. Everything is a gruelling effort.

Zoe stops to chat to Cameron, who is unloading bricks into

a wheelbarrow from a pallet at the edge of the garden. Their carefree laughter sends a pang through me, a craving for when life was much less complicated. If I'd never met Max, I'd probably be planning my next big trip away or out with friends having a laugh like the pair of them in the garden. But then I wouldn't have Lola. I kiss the top of her head. She lets out a sudden loud cry. I flinch.

'Oh, man! What a big noise from such a little one.' Zoe enters like a breath of fresh air. Throwing a rucksack and a drawstring bag inside the door, she takes Lola from me, comforting her with whispers of her soft accent. 'What have we got planned for you today? How about swimming?'

My baby's balled hands relax and she immediately quietens. Her eyes fix on this fairy godmother who has landed on our doorstep with an invisible magic wand that seems able to silence my daughter every time she waves it. Lola utters sounds as if she's trying to speak.

'I thought I'd take her to the local pool today.' Zoe rocks my baby in her arms. 'I worked with a family once who had a colicky baby and it really helped him. There's a suitable session for babies at the leisure centre at eleven thirty.'

Lola giggles, her small hands waving as if she understands what her new fairy godmother has in store for her today.

Zoe points to the drawstring bag. 'I've brought my swimming costume. Does she have a swimsuit?'

I shake my head. 'I've never got around to taking her swimming.' It's something I've thought about but never got around to organising.

'That's cool. I'll grab some swim diapers from the supermarket and see if I can get a swimsuit at the shops for her. It may be difficult at this time of year. They may have one at the leisure centre. I'll check it out. If not, we could order one online, and I'll take her tomorrow. I'll keep you posted. There's an under-ones session at the ballpark I can take her to instead.'

It will give me time to get myself together. 'I'll get some money for you.'

'Cool, all set.' She lifts Lola into the air. My baby lets out a squeal of laughter. 'There's a café, so we'll take a bottle and grab lunch there.' She swings Lola gently from side to side. 'We're going to have a blast together. Also, when I was reading up on colicky babies last night, it said massage is great. I'll give it a go if you're happy for me tò.'

I flinch as the guilt of motherhood gives me another slap across the face. I should be doing more of these kinds of activities with my daughter. I will when things settle down. I'm going to be the best mum in the world.

A knock at the door startles me.

I open it to a guy holding a parcel. It's here.

My heart races as he scans the barcode on the parcel and hands it to me before marching back to his motorbike.

My hands shake as I hold the brown package against my chest and stare at my baby.

'Are you OK, Annie?' Zoe asks. 'You seem...' She glances at the parcel. 'I know you've a lot going on, but you seem very troubled.'

'Just tired.'

She gives a sympathetic smile, her eyes flitting between mine and the parcel. 'Try to have a rest while I'm out.'

I feel pathetic and weak, a ghost of the strong woman I once was. It's as if every day, I'm wading through a muddy maze and keep coming across dead ends. With each step I take I'm sinking deeper and deeper. A sudden sense of unease strikes me. 'What time will you be back?' I ask.

'If the weather holds, perhaps we could stop at the park on the way back and feed the ducks.' She turns to Lola and taps her nose. 'You loved that the other day, didn't you?' She looks at me. 'Early afternoon, sometime. Is that good for you? Ready for her afternoon nap.'

'I think she needs a change,' I say.

'No problem. I'll go and do that, feed her and then play with her for a bit before we go.'

She takes Lola upstairs, and I rush to the kitchen to open the parcel. With trembling hands, I open it and read the instructions. This will tell me if Max is my baby's father. If I'm about to lose everything.

'All done!' Zoe appears with my giggling baby.

I stuff the instructions back in the box and place it in my handbag. 'Help yourself to a croissant before you go out.' I point to the leftovers from breakfast.

'That's kind of you. I'll have it when I've fed this little one.' She smiles at Lola and stares at my handbag.

Lola coos. Panic rushes through me. I don't want Zoe to take my baby out.

My head's in a spin, but desperation overrides my unease and weariness.

I need to trust her.

Because I don't trust anyone else around here.

SIXTY-FIVE

After Zoe leaves with Lola, I boil the kettle to make a cup of tea to take to my office. I search the Airbnb app on my phone. I want somewhere relatively near as I don't trust myself to drive too far. I feel better than I did last night, but a deep sense of confusion is still playing with my head.

It's cold but bright outside. The morning fog chills the air, nipping at my bare skin.

Jigsaw appears. 'Hey, Mrs C. Is Max around?'

'He's gone to work,' I say. 'Can I help?'

'I'm just wondering when the floor tiles are due to arrive.'

'Floor tiles?' I didn't even know we'd chosen them.

'For the playroom. Max said he ordered them a couple of weeks ago.'

I can't understand why he would do that without consulting me. 'I'll call him and find out.'

I hurry to my office and unlock the door. It's freezing in here. The automatic heating hasn't come on. I fiddle with the radiator but can't get it working. I slam my fist on the dial.

Leaving my coat on, I sit down, peering around at the boxes of stock lining the walls. I need to close the business temporarily. The thought is depressing. I worked hard to get it up and running and it's been a struggle keeping it going these past few months. But all I care about now is getting away from here. I'll pack up the outstanding orders today and get them dispatched. There were thirty-two when I last looked. And I'll put a notice on my website to say I'm taking a break, but I'll be back. It'll take me most of the morning, then I can pack a case for me and Lola and head off as soon as Zoe returns with her.

My teeth are chattering. I fiddle with the radiator dials again and switch it off and on, but I still can't get the damn thing working. I can't work in here like this. I'll freeze alive. I leave the office and march up to Cameron, who is transporting planks of wood on his shoulder into the shell of the extension. 'Cameron,' I call out. He turns. The plank of wood strikes the side of the house. 'Are you busy? Sorry, that's a silly question.'

He tips the plank of wood and leans it against the brickwork and runs his hands through his blond curls 'What's up?'

'I don't suppose you can spare me a minute to look at the radiator in my office? It's not working, and it's freezing in there.'

He follows me back to my office, where he inspects the radiator. 'Often with these things, it's the power supply.' He glances around the room. 'Do you have anything else electric in here?'

'My computer. My phone charger.'

'Try the computer.'

I try to turn it on. 'It's not working.'

'Perhaps a fuse has blown. Where's the circuit breaker?'

'In the utility room.'

'Go and check the fuses.'

I briskly walk to the house, my arms wrapped around my body to thwart the cold. In the utility room, I open the circuit box. The breaker for the office has clicked to the 'off' position. Something has tripped it. I reset it and head back.

'It's come on.' He stands up, brushing dust from his hands.

'Thank you.'

'Are you OK, Annie? You look super pale this morning.'

I touch my cheeks. 'I'm fine.' I adopt his accent in jest. 'Just super cold.'

He doesn't laugh, just frowns before turning towards the door. 'Look after yourself, all right?'

My phone rings. It's Max. I ignore it. Picking up my cup of tea, I take a sip. It's now lukewarm. I gulp it down. Max keeps calling. I answer the phone after the fourth ring. Only because I fear he'll come back here if I don't. 'I've been trying to get hold of you,' he says. I can't tell if he's irritated or concerned. 'Don't do that to me. I've been worried.'

My breaths fog the air. 'Why did you order floor tiles for the playroom without consulting me?'

'We did talk about it, Annie. We discussed this a few weeks ago. We looked through the brochure Jigsaw gave us. You chose the white marble-effect ones. Don't you remember? I wanted to go with carpet, but you said we had to think of the future. It wouldn't always be a playroom, and for now, we could get a large rug.'

I recall him saying that about the rug. 'I don't remember choosing those tiles.'

He lowers his voice to a whisper. 'Is everything all right, darling?'

'I'm fine.'

'You're slurring your words. Where's Lola? Do you want me to come home?'

He's gaslighting me again.

I have to get away from here.

My stomach cramps. I rub my hand along my lower abdomen. 'No.' My voice is too stern. 'You have work to do. And so do I. I'll see you tonight.'

I end the call and find the number for the GP surgery. The recorded message tells me I'm number four in the queue. I catch myself talking aloud, telling myself I should've got away from here weeks ago. *You're number three in the queue.* Only I can stop myself from slipping further down the black hole I've been sliding down for weeks, months, even. *You're number two in the queue.* It's now time to be brave. *You're next in the queue.* I need to find somewhere to stay for a while. When I finally get through, I ask the receptionist if the results are back from my blood test. They're not. She tells me to call back in a few days. I end the call in frustration. I was hoping they could tell me what's wrong with me before I leave.

A charge of nausea turns my stomach. I yawn as if it's nine at night, not nine in the morning. I fire up my computer and log on to Airbnb. A familiar feeling stirs within me. The excitement of booking a holiday. Only, this is no holiday I'm booking. I'm planning a getaway to save myself and my daughter.

SIXTY-SIX

.

I book a one-bedroom cottage in west Essex with a small garden, securing the reservation with my personal credit card. I can get there in under an hour. I'd go now if it were just me, but there's Lola to consider. I need a travel cot and a supply of nappies, wipes and formula so we can lie low for a few days until I consider my next move.

The room starts spinning and so does my stomach. I clutch hold of the desk until the feeling passes. The voices I usually hear at night now infiltrate my ears, telling me I'm being crazy and paranoid. I blink several times. I can't listen to them. I was feeling much better when I was at Nisha and Sean's house. Now I'm back here I feel as if my body is full of poison. I need to at least get away for a few days to try and decipher what the hell is going on.

I begin preparing the dispatch notes for the orders I need to fulfil, but the room spins again. My computer screen blurs into a whirl. The floor shudders beneath my feet. I rest my head on the edge. I'm going to be sick. I can't be ill again. Not now. I need all my strength to get away. The radiator is now kicking out an influx of heat. It's boiling in here. I rip off my coat. I'm melting like an ice cream on a summer's day. And I'm tired, so very tired. 'You're a psycho,' a voice screams into my ear. I clutch the sides of the chair and stand. A fleeting pain tightly grips my stomach. I pick up my phone and call the doctor's. They need to tell me what the hell is wrong with me. But I hang up when the recorded message tells me I'm number nine in the queue.

I return to the house. My arms are so weak I struggle to open the patio door. I stop to breathe. This is how I felt the afternoon my sister died. I press my fingers over my eyes. Thinking about her makes them sting. I tug at the door again. The damn thing won't move.

'You all right there, Mrs C?' The glass reflects Cameron approaching. His body moves in aggressive waves, undulating with a menacing sway. He appears deformed, much bigger than usual, like a monster coming at me with a vengeance.

'Mrs C?' His voice is warbled.

I flinch as I turn to face him, my eyes blinking excessively. He doesn't look deformed at all. 'I can't get this door open.' I frantically give the patio door another tug.

'Here, let me.' He wraps his hand around the handle and pulls. The door opens with ease. He frowns at me. 'You sure you're all right?'

I wish people would stop asking me that.

My knees buckle as I struggle upstairs to my bedroom. A quick lie-down and I'll feel much better. My heart sinks. That's what I thought on the evening of the fire. And the day my sister died.

The door of the en suite is wide open. Someone has been in there because it wasn't me. It must've been Max. Or perhaps one of the twins intentionally left it open to spook me. Something draws me to walk inside. Samantha's face flashes before me. I stare in the mirror. The builders were right. I look a mess. Recent events have paled my face and the skin around my eyes is as black as darkness. It looks like a frightening zombie is staring back at me.

A faint banging sound commences. I flinch. It's as if my sister is knocking on the walls, desperate to tell me who murdered her. I put it down to my distressed imagination until the sounds grow louder, and I realise it's the builders, their hammering and drilling echoing through the walls. I sit on the toilet, staring at the radiator where I found my sister hanging and think back to that night as batshit thoughts swirl around my head.

Could it have been me?

Could I have murdered my sister?

The walls bend and distort. I fix my eyes on the floor to try and ground me. A clammy sweat engulfs my body, and the room darkens as if someone has turned off the light. My baby is my last thought as everything turns black.

SIXTY-SEVEN

The face in my dreams flashes their eyes before falling into the shadows. I chase them, clutching their shoulder to turn them around. But they are too strong for me. And too fast. They run and run until once again, they're merely a speck on the horizon.

I awake with a start. At first, I don't know where I am, and then I see the green wall tiles above and know I'm lying on the floor of the en suite. A strike of lightning flashes across the mottled glass windowpane, followed by a clap of thunder that echoes around the small room. It's such a change of weather since this morning.

A smell, a vile, acrid stench makes me gag. Dazed, I sit up, trying to figure out what I'm doing here. Slimy clumps of hair matted with vomit cling to my face. I retch and drag myself towards the toilet, heaving over the basin, but there's nothing left inside of me.

I haul myself up. Smears of sick cover the sleeves of my hoodie where I must've wiped my mouth, and there are splatters across the thighs of my jeans. I slip my phone from my back pocket and check the time, gasping sharply. It's almost two in the afternoon. I must have been lying there for hours. I could've died, choked on my own vomit. This isn't good.

I dial the number for the GP surgery. Their recorded voice tells me I'm number seven in the queue. I hang up.

I need to clean myself up before I see Lola. I strain to listen, but I can't hear her and Zoe downstairs. Perhaps she's taking a nap. Struggling to the landing, I call their names, only to be greeted by silence. I strip off my clothes, discarding them in a pile to take to the utility room. The loud shrill of my phone breaks the silence. I grab it. It's Max. I can't speak to him. Not like this, standing naked with vomit caked in my hair. But there are five missed calls from him and two texts.

Why aren't you answering your phone? xx

I'm getting worried, Annie. Are you all right? Is Lola all right? Please call me. xx

I need to get to him before he comes home. I steel myself and call his number. He picks up straight away.

'Annie! Finally. I've been worried sick.'

Sick. Hearing the word intensifies the putrid smell around me.

'Why haven't you been picking up your phone?' He sounds genuinely concerned. My rationale questions whether I've got him wrong: the man who was so kind and gentle when I met him. Is it my psychotic state that is distorting my feelings towards him? Getting away will give me some much-needed time to get my head straight.

I force cheeriness into my voice. 'I'm sorry. I've been in my office working all morning,' I say, my tone unwavering and determined.

'Where's Lola?'

'Zoe took her swimming.'

'Swimming? Is that a good idea in this weather?'

'In the baby pool, Max! It's heated. She's joining a class with other babies.'

'I'll be home soon.'

'You don't need to be. Everything is under control here.'

The smell of vomit wafting from my hair makes me gag. I end the call, dash into the family bathroom and jump into the shower, washing away the putrid smell with three rounds of shampoo and bodywash. My phone rings again. I need to answer it. It could be about Lola. I suddenly want to see my baby. The protective instincts so sorely lacking in the early days are now raking through every fibre of my body. Call it mother's intuition, call it whatever, but I need to see my baby. Inexplicably I feel I should never have let Zoe take her out. My baby should be with me.

I burst out of the shower and grab the phone, but it's only the bank asking if I have a minute. That is the most stupid question to ask a working mother. I tell the caller it's not convenient and to contact me another time. But I can't remember what I was doing. I slap my cheeks. That's it. I need to pack. I scramble into clean clothes, jeans and a fresh hoodie. And I need to pack a bag for Lola.

Everything's an uphill slog. As if someone has opened me up and replaced my bones with bricks. I'm running out of time. I want everything packed up so I'm ready to go when Zoe returns with my baby.

I pull my old travel bag out from beneath the bed, briefly thinking about all the places this well-used leather bag has been with me. We've travelled the world together. I throw in enough clothes to last me a couple of days before running to the airing cupboard and scrambling through the layers of dried clothes, pulling out items belonging to Lola. But strangely, there's only one sleepsuit and a dress of hers in there. I must have already put everything else away. I can't remember doing that. But I can't remember doing many things lately. I clutch my head. I've been treading water for so long, but I now I feel as if I'm drowning.

I take the sleepsuit and dress to the bedroom and throw them in the bag before grabbing the charging cord plugged into the socket behind my bedside cabinet. I open the top drawer of the tall chest where I keep Lola's clothes. I pause. The drawer is mostly empty. I must've packed her stuff in the wrong one. I open each drawer, one by one, getting faster as I reach the bottom one, but they are full of my and Max's clothes. There's not one single item of hers in any of them. That's odd. I try to recall what I've done with all her clothes. I can't leave here with only one sleepsuit and a dress. They must be in that uncontrollable pile of washing working its way to the ceiling in the utility room.

I head downstairs to collect the rest of Lola's clothes. A noise is coming from the kitchen. It sounds like the fridge door opening. It's at odds from the sounds of Lola I was hoping for. Perhaps one of the twins has come home early. Or Max. But I would've heard them. Besides, the twins have music rehearsals after school and won't be back until later. I creep down the rest of the stairs and tiptoe towards the kitchen. My sixth sense tells me something isn't right. The sense that's been nagging me with the same thought for weeks now, months even.

A gurgling noise follows the sounds of water splashing in the sink. I step into the kitchen, but stop, my foot halfway through the door.

Someone is tipping the contents of a bottle of one of my vitamin drinks down the sink.

Someone who shouldn't be there.

SIXTY-EIGHT

I stand there incredulous as he takes what looks like a piece of folded paper towel from the zipped pocket of his fleece hoodie. Unfolding the edge, he produces a thin syringe full of clear liquid and plunges the contents into the bottle.

I blink and shake my head in disbelief, momentarily thinking I must be dreaming. 'What the hell are you doing, Cameron?'

He slowly and purposefully spins around. A brutish smirk curves his twisted lips. He looks so different. Menacing. I'd go so far as to say, evil. It's as if he was expecting me. 'Ah, perfect timing.'

The hairs on my arms stand to attention like an army of soldiers ready to do battle. It's always a signal of danger for me. I remember the day Lola was born, when my abdomen was inflamed and pulsing with pain. Each follicle pricked my skin with fear, and I couldn't stop shivering.

But this is crazy. I'm crazy. Cameron's only ever been a friendly face around here. But today, his gaze is cold and calculated, chilling me to the bone like the weather.

I stare at the syringe. The tension in my shoulders releases as the realisation strikes me like a punch in the stomach. I'm not going crazy. In a terrifying moment it all comes crashing down on me. I haven't got postnatal depression. And there's nothing unreliable about my narration. He has been drugging my drinks, poisoning me.

It's all falling into place. The blood test results showing an abnormal liver function, and why I've been feeling so crap for so long. I thought it started when Lola was born. But, thinking back, it didn't. It began when he joined the team of builders. That's why I've been out cold on the en suite floor for hours. He must've dropped something into the cup of tea in my office this morning when I came in here to check the circuit breaker.

A gust of wind slams the utility room door against the catch. Cameron leaves the sink and rushes to close it, smacking it shut with a thud.

'What time is Max due home?' He points the syringe in my direction.

I can almost taste the trouble brewing, tart and toxic on my tongue. 'You've been drugging me, haven't you?'

He ignores my question. 'I need to speak to Max.'

'You can speak to me.'

'I need to speak to both of you.' His voice has changed. His casual, unhurried voice is clipped and stilted, delivering his words faster and aggressively.

'What about?'

Fear races through me as the memories come flooding back. It's like I can now slot the pieces of the confusing puzzle my life has become into the right places with considerable ease.

I clutch the doorframe.

The face in my dreams.

It belongs to him.

SIXTY-NINE

'Why? Why would you do that to me?' I retch as the thought suddenly dawns on me. 'Wait. It was you, wasn't it? You murdered my sister.'

He laughs, a hoarse chuckle that grates against the silence and rebounds off the walls. 'She got in the way.'

For a second, I think he's joking. This is all part of an act. I can't work out what's going on. What motive could he have had to kill my sister? He didn't even know her. He's bluffing. 'In the way of what? Drugging me?'

He holds up the bottle of juice as high as his hand can reach before releasing it. It drops to the floor, exploding with a shattering bang, strewing splinters of glass and the remaining liquid across the tiles.

This is mad. He's mad.

He digs a small object out of the pocket of his cargo trousers. I panic until I realise it's a cheap and tacky phone that lacks the glossy finish of a modern one. I've never seen a burner phone in my life, but that's how I think of one.

He snarls. 'Let's wait until Max comes home, and we can talk about it.'

A flame of rage fires through me, anger for what he has done to my sister and my family. I step towards him and shove him. 'Why did you murder my sister?'

He reaches out and snatches a handful of my wet hair, twisting my neck and drawing my face to his. 'Don't you touch me.' Milky-coloured spittle shoots from his mouth onto mine.

I cringe and swipe my hand across my mouth, wiping his spit from my lips. He yanks my head. I look at him in contempt. Excruciating pain shoots down my neck. I try to scream, but fear supresses the sound, trapping it tightly in my throat. I lash out. I strike his chest with my fists with all the force I can muster. 'Why did you murder my sister?'

He grabs my flailing hands. His strength is too much for me. His arm loops around my neck and cinches me in a vice-like grip. I choke, the air wrenched from my lungs as his muscly forearm compresses my windpipe. I try to fight him, clawing at his arm, but I don't have the power against this human tower of a man. 'But you weren't even here that day,' I struggle to say between choked breaths. 'You'd all gone when she was murdered.'

He releases his grip and throws me to the floor, smirking. 'That's what you told the police.'

I fall on my side. A shard of glass cuts my cheek. I touch it. Warm drops of blood ooze from the wound.

He looks at it mesmerised, fascinated, and a smile contorts his face.

'I thought you'd left for the day. I saw you leave.'

'But did you see me come back?'

'You tricked me. I gave you an alibi.'

He nods. 'Thanks for that.'

I want to wipe that smirk off his face. 'Why did you do it? What did my sister ever do to you? You didn't even know her.'

He drags me off the floor and transfers his hand over my

mouth. 'You don't want to get yourself hurt, Annie. Just do as I say, and you'll be fine.'

'What do you want from me?' My voice is muffled.

'Nothing,' he says. With his other hand, he lays his phone on the kitchen counter, stabs the keypad and selects the speaker button.

Panic rises through me as visions of my darling baby girl flash before me. I can't let him kill me. My baby needs me.

The dial tone rings until Max answers. 'What's up, Cameron?'

I try to scream, a signal to my husband that I'm in danger. But this beast's hand is so tightly packed over my mouth that I can't even emit a whimper. My words are a prisoner that can't escape. He tightens his grip. I can't breathe.

He shunts me to his side still holding me close and lowers his head towards the phone. The gritty smell of concrete mixed with sweat makes me retch into the coldness of his hand. 'I think you should come home,' he tells my husband.

Max's concerned voice fills the kitchen. 'Has something happened?'

I'm petrified Cameron is going to suffocate me. Succumbing to the pressure, I remain still, not making a sound, praying for relief from the force of his hand over my mouth.

'I think she's been drinking,' Cameron says. 'She's vomited over the kitchen floor. I've helped her up to bed, but she's asking for you.'

My husband sighs heavily. 'I'll be there in ten.'

'I'll stay with her until you get here.'

'Thanks, Cameron, I appreciate it. Thanks for looking out for her. I'll be right back.' I sense the desperation in my husband's voice and imagine him scurrying around for his keys and wallet and grabbing his coat to leave in a hurry.

'No worries, Max. It's all cool. I'll look after her.'

He stabs the screen, ending the call. 'Now you.' He releases his hold and shoves me towards the kitchen door. 'Into that bastard's office. Now!'

SEVENTY

He tails me along the hallway towards Max's office, punching his fist into the small of my back. 'Get a move on.'

Fear overwhelms me as I trip and stumble along the floor. My legs are still heavy from whatever he put in my tea earlier. I grab the wall to steady myself and to fall in line with his stride. It's bizarre, unreal. 'What do you want from us?' I dare to call out. 'What've we ever done to you?' I rack my brains, trying to think why he would be doing this. Why he would end my sister's life so abruptly and cruelly. But I can't think of a single reason.

He rams his fist into me again, a kidney shot. It's excruciating. 'Shut it.'

'You've played us, haven't you? Hiding the keys and Lola's bottles and formula.' I shake my head. 'Tripping the electrics in my office. Tripping the security. It was all you, wasn't it? All to make it look like I was going mad. Why? Why?' I never suspected a thing.

'Shut up. Just shut up.'

'And the wine. You were pouring away wine to make it look like I was drinking it. How could you have acted so innocently?'

I look towards the front door, considering if I can make a run for it. I decide in a breath. Throwing all of my energy into my legs, I bolt along the hallway. Four effortful strides, and I lunge for the door, thrusting it open to a storm that's now raging. The chilling late-afternoon air strikes me with a hint of freedom.

But I'm not quick enough.

Cameron catches me by the scruff of the neck. 'I don't think so.' He drags me backwards like a rag doll and over the threshold to Max's office, where he slams me to the wall with force. The impact winds me. I struggle for my next breath. 'Stay there and don't move.' His face is so close to mine I can smell stale cigarette smoke on his fetid breath. And I can smell the sweaty waft of fear, but that's coming from me.

I gulp in as much air as my lungs can take. 'What's all this about, Cameron? I don't understand. Do you want money? I can get you money. Name your price.' I want to ask him about my sister, but I'm scared bringing it up again will anger him even more. I bite my lip. My best bet is to stay quiet until Max comes home.

He grabs Max's laptop from the desk. It's a top-of-the-range MacBook Pro that Max recently treated himself to when he knew the business was almost sold. With the flick of his wrist, Cameron rips the cord from the socket in the wall.

I glance from him to the computer as I try to fathom what is happening here, but I'm stumped. Nothing I can come up with can explain what's going on.

He wraps the cord around the laptop and grabs my arm, roughly pushing me back to the kitchen, where he shoves me into the armchair in the corner where I fell asleep on the night of the fire.

'Did you start the fire that night?' I cry.

'Stay there!'

'You did, didn't you?'

He smirks. Releasing the laptop onto the kitchen counter, he lifts the lid and attaches one end of the charging cord into the port at the side. He plugs the other end into the wall socket and presses the switch, before walking towards me with deliberate steps.

I inhale sharply, struggling to fill my lungs with air. I clutch my throat and concentrate on breathing, telling myself I have to survive this, whatever *this* is. My baby needs me. I stare at the shattered glass from the bottle of juice. The neck sits vertically in the middle of the floor, its edge serrated from where it broke away from the rest of the bottle. A potential weapon I could use to protect myself. I consider leaping across the room and grabbing it. But I know he'd only get the better of me. My only choice is to remain silent and wait for Max to arrive home.

Digging into the pocket of his hoodie, he produces a coil of rope.

My pulse races. He's going to tie me up. He's a frickin' psycho. 'No, Cameron. You don't need to do this.' I jump out of the chair. It scrapes across the tiled floor and rams into the wall behind. I need to get away from him. Max, please hurry up. A fleeting thought passes through my mind. Is this a set-up, and he's just doing Max's dirty work? But to what end, I can't work out.

Cameron uncoils the rope and strides towards me. 'No one runs away from me.' Holding an end in each hand, he tugs the rope taut as he reaches me. 'Hold up your hands.'

In defiance, I do the opposite, dropping both hands around to the base of my spine.

'Don't make things difficult for yourself, Annie.' His heavy hand slaps me hard across the face. I nearly topple over. 'Believe me, it won't be worth your while.'

Slowly, I lift my hands. 'What do you want from us?' I hold his glare with a blend of venom and abhorrence.

His lips tense, and his cold eyes return my glare with a

fierce look of determination. 'You shouldn't have tried to run away.' He roughly smacks my wrists together. I wince as the force of his hands crushes the bones in mine. Wrapping the fibrous rope around my wrists, he gives the ends a mighty tug, securing them with a knot.

The cord cuts into my wrists, each fibre like a needle piercing into my skin. 'That's too tight,' I protest. 'You're going to cut off my blood supply.'

But he isn't interested. 'Sit down and wait,' he roars. He paces up and down the room, his movements haphazard, muttering like a deranged lunatic. His heavy breathing echoes around the silence of the room. Even the builders outside are quiet.

I turn my eyes to the garden. The builders. I sit up straight, searching for one of them to help me.

'Don't get any ideas. They've all left for the day. The weather has worked nicely to my advantage today.'

I meet his gaze. Who is this guy? I can't understand how we could have let such a maniac into our lives. 'What are you trying to achieve here, Cameron? Who are you?'

'Shut up.' He thwacks his hands on his forehead. 'Just shut up, will you, huh?' He continues pacing, his strides lengthening. Suddenly, he stops. He stares at his phone for a while before he makes another call. 'Pick up. Pick up, will you.' He waits as the phone dials out.

He's not working alone. Jigsaw enters my thoughts. Cameron tries to make a call again, but still no one answers. This time he leaves a message. 'He's on his way back now. Everything's going to plan. How's everything at your end? Call me straight back.' He draws a deep breath, aggressively stabbing the end call button and tossing the phone on the kitchen counter. Max has spoken too freely about the sale of the busi-ness and the dreams the money will allow him – us – to achieve. Yes, it's always been about our dreams, our plans. And now

Cameron and Jigsaw are working as a pair to strip all that away from us.

I glance at the kitchen clock. It's nearly three o'clock. The twins should be home soon. And then I remember they have music rehearsals after school. They aren't going to be back until later. Zoe. She should be back anytime. I will her not to come back before Max. I don't want my baby subjected to this madman.

I think back over the past few months as the lunatic paces the room, wondering what he intends to do to me. For so long, I thought it was the twins who had it in for me, who were tormenting my life to get rid of me. And more recently I believed that my husband had a part to play in this horror story as well. I even considered I was to blame. I've always been such a good judge of character. But with a lunatic like him drugging my discernment, I've got it all terribly wrong.

A car pulls into the driveway. Its tyres skid along the gravel as it abruptly stops in front of the house. Within seconds, the front door bursts open, and I hear my husband pound up the first few steps of the staircase.

'Max,' I scream. 'Help me.' He pauses before retracing his steps and making for the kitchen.

Cameron strides over to me and digs his hand into the pocket of his hoodie.

I gasp as he draws out a knife, my fear notching up another rung of the ladder of terror he is pulling me up. He holds the long, slender blade against my neck, such a small tool but with the power to kill with a millimetre of movement. He runs the cold, sharp blade along the side of my throat, just below my jawline. Each beat of my heart pounds against the pressure.

Max's footsteps quicken into a run along the hallway and into the kitchen. His face is a picture of confusion as he confronts the sight of me tied up in the corner of the room.

The knife nicks my skin. A warm drop of blood trickles down my neck.

'What the hell—?' Max shouts, running towards us.

Cameron lets out a long, low chuckle. 'Hello, Dad.'

SEVENTY-ONE

Cameron waves the knife in Max's direction. 'Stay where you are.'

Max stops dead, one foot in front of the other. His eyes lock onto mine, intense and urgent. He turns his gaze to Cameron. 'Dad? What the hell are you on about?'

Another chuckle comes, this time much louder, teeming with disdain. The sound cuts through the air like the knife against my neck. 'You're clueless, aren't you, huh?' Cameron shakes his head, emitting low snorts through his flared nostrils.

'What's all this about, Cameron? Put that bloody knife down.' Max's jaw locks as if he's trying to suppress his anger for my sake. His eyes flit between Cameron and me. I've only ever seen him like this once before, and that was when we were arguing about the twins.

'All this time, we've chatted about the renovations, drunk beers together in here, and you still haven't got a clue.' He slowly shakes his head and euphorically screams, 'You're my father, Max.'

Max's eyes flit again from him to me, this time in confusion. 'Don't be so ridiculous.'

'Let me paint the picture for you. Cast your mind back to 2001. Where were you?' Cameron's voice is now riddled with savagery.

Max raises his eyebrows, his face a vivid painting of absurdity and bewilderment. He shrugs. 'I can't remember,' he says hesitantly as if waiting for the memory to surface.

'Let me help you out a little. Be a little more specific. June 2001.' Cameron's hand begins to tremble. The knife tremors against my skin.

'I'm none the wiser,' Max says. He looks at me in a blank desperation as if he doesn't know what to do for the best.

'You need a little more help, huh? San Francisco.'

Max blinks.

Cameron lets me go and flings me onto the floor. 'Let me try and trigger your memory.' He produces a photo from his pocket. The edges are curled. I steal a glimpse of a young man standing with a woman holding a tray of drinks in her splayed hand before he throws the photo at Max.

'The three-day IT conference at the Carlton Hotel where you were staying. Remember now, huh? On the last day of the conference, they held a party. A waitress was working there that night. Remember her, Max? Melody Hickman. Mel, you would've known her as.'

Max breathes in deeply through his nose. His shoulders tense.

'It's starting to sink in, Maxwell Carpenter, huh?'

Max's hands ball into fists.

'You took her back to your room. You treated her well, she always said that. You were a decent guy. Or so she thought. Until she wrote to you and told you she was pregnant, but you never even bothered to reply.'

Max's face freezes, his eyes wide and no longer blinking.

I can't believe what I'm hearing.

'What kind of person ignores word of their children?' He

jabs the knife in Max's direction. 'Hey, Max? What kind of sick person does that?' He raises his voice to a roar. 'Tell me.'

'I never received any letter.' Max steps towards me. 'Anyway, this has nothing to do with Annie. Let her go. At once.'

Cameron grabs me, steps backwards and yanks me with him. 'Stay away.'

I squirm as the side of the blade digs into my flesh. Max gives me a look of despair. My whole body is shaking now. I will my legs to take my weight. If they give way, that knife has the potential of sending me to join my sister.

'Mum tried again four months later when your children were born. She sent you a picture of us in incubators in the ICU. Seven weeks early, we came.'

'Children?'

'Twins, Max. You fathered another set of twins that you abandoned like you did our mother.'

SEVENTY-TWO

Max's eyes avert from Cameron to me. 'I never knew. I swear I never knew.'

Cameron scoffs. 'I don't believe you.'

'It's true. I never received any correspondence from your mother at all. Never.' Max raises his hands. 'I swear.' Beads of sweat line Max's forehead. He throws off his coat.

I turn my head an inch, managing the slightest of glances. When you look closely, there is a scant resemblance in the straight bridge of their noses and the bone structure of their jaws. But it's only visible if you're looking for it.

Cameron tightens his grip around me. 'Our mother died, you know. Mel died.'

'I'm sorry to hear that. Honestly, I am.'

'She busted a gut to give us the best she could. She struggled, Max – worked three jobs for years. Never invited another man into our lives.' Cameron throws out his spare hand, sweeping it around the room. 'Meanwhile, you've been rolling in cash, living the high life. Two vacations a year, taking my half-brother and half-sister skiing in the winter and to the beach in the summer. Private schooling. And what did you do for us? Jack shit, that's what.'

I feel as if I'm at the cinema watching a movie I never wanted to go and see in the first place. I will Max to keep quiet. This psycho killed my sister, and he won't think twice about driving this knife into me. I never thought it possible to hate another human being so much, but for now, I need to concentrate on staying alive.

Max's lips twist to the side, signalling his thoughts concur with mine. We need to get out of this situation alive. He lowers his voice as if trying to placate this crazed man who has infiltrated our lives. 'Listen, Cameron. You've got to believe me. I never knew. Your mother and I—' He looks at me and mouths, 'I'm so sorry.' He turns back to Cameron. 'Your mother and I spent the night together, as consenting adults. I never knew about the outcome.'

'I often asked her over the years who our father was. Do you know what she said?'

Max shakes his head. He looks at me, his soul begging for forgiveness through his regretful eyes.

'She always said you was a kind Englishman, but she never told us she only met you once. She pretended you were around, but that you died when we were little. But on her deathbed, when she was heavily medicated to stop the pain, she confessed the truth. You were very much alive. She found you through the company you worked for back then – Digital Central – and she kept track of you, which, of course, got easier with social media. When the time came, she decided we had the right to know about our siblings. Turns out we have three! My mum died of cancer in January, in case you're interested.'

'I'm sorry. I truly am.' Max squints. 'Where's your brother in all of this? Does he know you're doing this?'

Cameron erupts into a disconcerting bout of laughter. 'You really need to catch up, don't you?'

Max shakes his head. 'You're talking in riddles.'

My heart contracts in my chest. I know what's coming.

'My twin is female. And she's with your daughter as we speak.'

'My daughter?' Max says. 'Which one?'

'Lola, of course.'

SEVENTY-THREE

I let out a low scream. 'No!'

This is my worst nightmare.

Any mother's worst nightmare.

My baby is my life. And I've given her over to another lunatic. We should never have taken Zoe on. But everyone told me I needed help and Max insisted, and I was desperate.

Cameron laughs.

I want to hit him, tear his eyes out. But I know I have to suppress all emotions for my daughter's sake. We need her alive. I can die. But she can't.

'Zoe's my sister, Max. So, essentially, you employed the two children you never knew you had. And let me tell you this. If you think I'm crazy, you've seen nothing yet. She may come across as innocent and playful, but no one crosses my sister.'

Max puffs out a large breath. 'Jeez. What do you want from me?'

'Don't worry, Max. We don't want a relationship. We're too good for you. All we want is the money our mother deserved all these years.' Suddenly, Cameron lets me go and pushes me.

With my hands still tied, I stumble and fall with a thud, my head hitting the floor.

Max rushes over, falling onto his knees to help me. He tells me how sorry he is for subjecting me to this madness, while surreptitiously loosening my bindings. 'Where's Lola now?' I scream at Cameron. The need to see my daughter safe is all-consuming. 'What have you done with her?'

Max scrambles to get up and launches himself at him.

Cameron steps backwards, escaping Max's attack. 'Careful, you're going to get yourself cut. No more funny ideas. If you harm me in any way, you don't get your daughter back.'

Max's placid nature fails him. 'You bastard.'

'That's right. And whose fault is that? Who made me a bastard, Max?'

My heart thunders in my chest. I take a deep breath. 'Please, please don't hurt my daughter. She's innocent in all of this,' I say gently, attempting to appeal to his better nature. Who am I trying to kid? This guy has no better side. He's a rotten apple, evil to the core.

'Well, that's up to you.' Cameron nods towards the laptop. 'Log on and transfer a million dollars to this account.' He digs into the large pocket of his cargo trousers and produces a folded piece of paper.

'So this is all about money,' Max scoffs incredulously.

I dig my teeth into the knot of the rope tied around my wrists. It loosens. I tug it some more. It falls free. Cameron notices but doesn't seem interested. He's too busy with Max. He must've had his goal in sight for a long time. Now he's close to the finishing line.

Cameron unfolds the piece of paper and hands it to him.

'A million dollars.' Max laughs cynically. 'You're kidding me. I can't just do that.'

'Yes, you can. I know how much you sold your company for. I've seen the papers in your office. You have the money. I think we're being pretty reasonable. For the amount you're going to get, a million dollars is not too much to ask.'

'That's true. And you can have every last penny I have to return our daughter safely. But it doesn't work like this. I can't just transfer such a large amount. There would be security checks.'

'It'll be fine. We've looked into this. Where's your mobile phone?'

Max pats the pockets of his jeans before removing his phone from the back one.

Cameron grabs it. 'Your bank will most likely call and ask some security questions and if it's a valid transaction. Be prepared for that. If you give any indication it's not, you can say goodbye to my baby sister.'

How dare he refer to my baby as related to him in any way, I want to scream at him, but I bite my lip. I don't trust myself for what might come out of my mouth.

'How do we know you'll bring Lola back?' Max says.

'You're gonna have to trust me on that one. We—'

Max intercepts. 'What's the plan here, then? How do we get her back?'

'You transfer the money, and I'm out of here. Tomorrow morning, as long as you haven't called the police, and we've arrived safely at our next destination, we'll text you the details of where you can find her.'

I can't believe this is happening.

'Where is she now?' Max wears a mask of boldness. He's putting on a brave face, but inside, he's falling apart.

Cameron taps the kitchen counter beside the laptop with the blade of the knife. 'Money, first, Max.'

'He's bluffing,' I scream. 'He killed my sister, and now he's going to kill our daughter.' I'm panicking, terrified of what's going to happen. All I want is to hold my baby girl.

Max looks at me incredulously.

'He admitted it.' My voice breaks. 'Before you came home. I caught him drugging a bottle of my juice from the fridge. I'm not going crazy. I'm not depressed. I've been drugged all along, Max. And he murdered—' My voice breaks again. 'Samantha.'

Max turns to Cameron. 'What the hell?'

'I wanted to make you suffer, Max.'

'Then why not drug me? Murder me?'

'Because we needed you around. You had to get your business sold. No sale. No money. But it's sure been fun watching the stress this has caused you all in the process.'

SEVENTY-FOUR

'Fun?' Max roars. 'You did all that to my wife for fun? What kind of sicko are you?' He turns to me, his eyes wide with shock. 'I've been going out of my mind with worry. I've thought there was something seriously wrong with you.'

'Why Samantha?' I say to Cameron. 'What did she ever do to you?' I'm trying to stay calm, but it's impossible.

'I've already told you. She just got in the way. Which is a shame, because she was a really classy lady.'

'How did she get in the way?' I ask.

'She found me messing with your drink. Caught me red-handed. Just as you found me this afternoon. It could've been your sister standing there at the door, almost in the identical position.' He laughs. 'Quite ironic, huh? She'd come back, something about losing a necklace. I was otherwise occupied.' He laughs scornfully. 'She was on her way upstairs that afternoon to tell you.' His eyes are like steel, hard and rigid. He is terrifying. 'We couldn't have that. We hadn't got our money. So I had to get to her first.'

'You strangled her and then tried to make it look as if she'd taken her own life. You're evil. Pure, pure evil.'

He notices the rope on the floor. I wonder if it's the same piece of rope that killed my sister. He doesn't care that I've released myself. He's going to get what he wants, and he knows it.

I can't help myself; I lunge for him. But he's too strong for me. His muscled arm swats me away like a fly.

'Stop, Annie. Think of Lola,' Max shouts. Reaching out, he grabs me and takes me in his fold, his strong arms around me like a welcome cloak of protection.

Cameron waves the knife in my direction. 'You come for me again, and you'll be on the receiving end of this.' He raises his voice. 'Money, Max. Now.'

I unfold myself from my husband's arms. 'Just do it. Get it done.' My voice is a desperate cry. 'Then we can get our baby back.'

Reluctantly, Max logs on to his computer.

Cameron hovers over him, watching each click of the keyboard like a hawk.

Within minutes, Max has transferred the sum from his bank to the account detailed on the piece of paper. 'Done.' Max shuts the screen. 'Now tell me where our daughter is.'

'Steady. Steady.' Cameron picks up his phone and types a message. 'I need to wait for clearance. Zoe will message me when the money is safely in our account.' He walks to the fridge and pulls out a beer as if he owns the place. 'Drink, anyone? A glass of wine, Annie?' He cackles at his own jest.

Max sucks his lips into his mouth as if he doesn't trust himself to speak.

Cameron rummages around in the pocket of his cargo trousers and pulls out a bunch of keys with a bottle opener attached. He flips the top off the beer bottle, takes a swig and wipes his mouth with the back of his hand.

I concentrate on my breathing, swallowing words that could jeopardise the chances of getting our daughter back.

Max takes my balled hand into his and squeezes tightly. 'I'm so sorry for everything,' he whispers. 'I'm going to make it up to you. I promise. Just keep it together.'

How can he be so calm? But it's in his nature, even in the darkest of situations. I berate myself for doubting him for all these months. His phone rings.

'Careful what you say,' Cameron calls out. He stands opposite Max, twirling the knife in his hand, the blade spinning freely between his palm and fingers.

I can tell by how Max answers a series of questions that it's the bank on the other end of the line, as Cameron correctly predicted.

Max speaks calmly and clearly as he relays his date of birth, his mother's maiden name and account details, revealing nothing about the dire situation playing out at this end of the line.

Cameron nods his head slowly and deliberately.

I perch on one of the breakfast stools beside my husband, trying to work out how this is going to play out. If Cameron does what he said, I won't see my baby until tomorrow morning. I can't think about it.

I need to do something.

And I need to do it soon.

SEVENTY-FIVE

'There, it's gone.' Max thrusts the computer screen towards Cameron. 'Done.'

'Nice.' Cameron picks up his phone and makes a call. He paces a few steps one way and then the other. 'Come on. Come on. Where are you?' He must be trying to get hold of Zoe. But she evidently doesn't pick up as he ends the call with a frustrated scream.

I'm beside myself, as anxious as he is to hear a connection. I need to know Lola is safe.

He has a one-sided conversation with himself. 'The money's gone. I've seen it with my own two eyes. It must've got there. I'm done here. But what if it hasn't? She'll be real mad with me.' He shakes his phone. 'Where the fuck are you, Zoe?' He firmly nods his head and appears to make a decision. He slips his phone into the pocket of his fleece with one hand, flicking the blade of the knife in our direction with the other. 'I'll be off then.'

He wields the blade near to my face and then hovers it in front of Max. 'Let me be quite clear. Any police, then it'll be' –

he draws a pretend line with the knife inches from Max's throat – 'goodnight for your darling daughter.'

I can feel my facial muscles twitching with a rage so intense I'm close to bursting. He can't leave. I jump up from the stool. It crashes to the floor, the sound loud in the silence of the room. 'No way. You tell us where our daughter is first.'

He sneers. 'As soon as my sister and I are well away from this shithole, you'll get a message.'

All I can see is my baby's vulnerable face. I can't let him go. Not without knowing where she is.

'You can't leave us like this. Please, Cameron. She's your baby sister,' Max tries to reason.

My chest tightens as if the muscles are going into spasm. A crazed rage pulses through me. I missed the best days with my baby because of this man, because of the drugs. With every word that comes out of his mouth, the rage inside of me intensifies. The desire to wipe the sarcasm from his mocking face consumes me.

'Catch you later.' Cameron mocks a salute with the blade to his temple and walks towards the kitchen door.

I can't contain my anger a moment more. I explode into action. Wrestling my hand from Max, I propel myself towards Cameron. Max tries to stop me. But he can't. I'm too far gone. A moment of insanity overrides my judgement. I can't see beyond stopping this animal and forcing him to tell us where our baby is.

Max jumps off his stool. 'No, Annie, don't!' he shouts.

But I'm not listening. And I'm too quick. I launch myself at the psychopath. When he turns around, I claw at his face like a woman possessed.

Unaware of the approaching frenzied assault, he screams in agony. I gouge his eye sockets, my nails digging and scratching. He staggers forward, one hand holding his face, the other thrusting the knife towards me. I turn my body, parrying his attempt to plunge the blade into me.

Losing his balance, he tumbles forward, faceplanting onto the cold, hard tiles. A guttural howl emerges. It echoes around the room with a haunting intensity. For a fleeting moment, I think it's Max, but then I see Cameron sprawled out, holding his face with one hand. The other is feeling for his groin, where a deep crimson pool of blood seeps through his trousers and onto the floor.

The grim realisation of what I've done sets in. I panic. It's as if someone else took control of my body and carried out this attack, and I'm a bystander watching it all unfold. I can't believe what this man has driven me to.

The storm outside amplifies the commotion inside. The antiquated house lights up intermittently with each flash of lightning, and rolls of thunder crash through the early evening sky like a heavy drumbeat.

I stand frozen. Max springs into action, kicking the blade away before dropping onto his haunches. He flips Cameron over and grabs the collar of his hoodie. 'Tell me where Lola is!'

Cameron's eyes move downwards, the colour in his cheeks fading fast. 'Fuck!' His other hand rushes to his leg. 'Look what she's done. I'm bleeding out.'

'No! Look what you've done! Not her.' Max leans backwards. 'Tell me where Lola is, or I won't help you!'

'Look what she's done.' Cameron is shaking unconsolably and whimpering like a small child. 'You've got to help me.' His voice weakens. 'Please help me, Max.' He's losing strength.

Unfazed, Max is steadfast. 'Tell me where our daughter is, and I'll call for help.'

'I beg you.' Cameron's eyes roll into the back of his head. 'What father lets their child die?'

'You're no son of mine.' The venom in my husband's voice is palpable. 'Tell me!'

Moments lapse. Cameron's eyelids flutter.

'You're bleeding out. Tell me!' Max roughly tugs on the collar of Cameron's hoodie, drawing his face close until their noses are touching.

'St... station... France... I...'

'She's taking her to France?' I scream. 'Is that what you mean?' The thought of my baby being taken abroad is unimaginable. The urgency of the situation sinks in. Adrenaline courses through my veins like some sort of amphetamine. I shove his shoulder. 'Which station?'

'Pancras. Great.' His eyes close.

'Don't let him die,' I plead with Max. I need to get my daughter back. And whatever this monster has done to me and my family, we can't have his death on our consciences for the rest of our lives. 'If he dies, we'll never get Lola back.'

'Get me a towel,' Max shouts at me urgently, applying pressure on Cameron's inner thigh.

I rush to grab the first available cloth, a used tea towel with a picture of Jasmine and Jacob covering the front. I throw it towards Max.

Cameron is fading alarmingly fast. As is the weakness, the sickness, and the confusion I've felt for months now. The adrenaline rushing through me has put me back in control. I can't quite make out what he is trying to say. 'North. Nord.' He becomes delirious. Then silence.

Max places the compression on the wound to try and stem the flow of blood. 'I think he's gone.' Max looks at me, his hands covered in his son's blood.

SEVENTY-SIX

'We need to call an ambulance,' Max yells. 'And the police.'

His words mirror those he said the night I found my sister. 'No way! Remember what he said. If we involve the police, then who knows what Zoe will do.' I'm frantic. 'She's taking Lola to France.'

'Calm down. She's not. She can't.'

'How can you say that?'

Max doesn't answer me. He's too busy ripping off his shirt. He tears the material of Cameron's bloodied trousers and stuffs the shirt over the wound, now leaking blood like a river.

'Is he dead?' I ask.

A red stain oozes through the whiteness of Max's shirt. 'Check for a pulse,' he says, frantically trying to contain the blood.

I reach to Cameron's neck, placing two fingers on the artery. 'No. There's a faint beat.'

'Wake up.' Max slaps Cameron's face. 'Stay with us.'

Cameron's upper body jolts. His eyes open and close as if he's drifting in and out of consciousness.

Max can't control the flow of blood. 'Get me some clean tea towels,' he orders.

I feel like I'm in a dream, another one of my nightmares. It's surreal. Ironic. Only a week ago, my husband was trying to save my sister. Now he's trying to save the man who murdered her.

'Tea towels, Annie. And then an ambulance.'

'What about Lola?' I cry.

Blood covers his hands as he presses his shirt against the wound. 'We need to sort this and stop the blood. Then we'll be able to get more information out of him. Get the tea towels.'

Part of me doesn't want to. The part that remembers the night I found my sister and the following days as I've tried to navigate through life without her. I want this beast to die. But then I'd be no better than him and we'll never get our daughter back.

I dash to the unit to the left of the sink and grab the stack of clean tea towels from the bottom drawer. Rain is still hammering on the window and streaking across the patio doors. There's an unopened packet of dishcloths in the drawer. I grab them as well, tearing open the packet as I rush back to my husband.

He snatches them from me. Discarding his shirt, he replaces it with the cloths, pressing them on the wound. 'Get my phone.' He nods to where he left it by his laptop.

But it's not his phone I go for. I drop onto my knees.

'What are you doing?' my husband cries.

I reach into the pocket of Cameron's trousers and pull out his phone. I stab a finger at the screen. A series of messages appear.

'Get my phone, Annie! Tell them we need to call for help.'

A sudden banging noise startles us. Max and I both turn to a voice.

Jasmine appears, standing at the door in her school uniform and black puffa jacket. Her face mirrors mine, terror and confusion wrapped into an abject look of fear. She drops her school bag. 'Cameron!'

'Call the police and an ambulance,' Max orders her. 'Now! Be quick.'

'What do I tell them?' She looks so young, so innocent and vulnerable, as her fingers punch the screen of her phone.

'We need help urgently. A man has seriously injured himself with a knife.'

Jasmine looks from Max to me, her confused expression asking many questions. 'What's happened?'

'I'll explain later. Just do it!' Max orders.

I quickly scroll through the chain of messages on Cameron's phone as Max struggles to contain the blood pouring from Cameron's leg. 'I need your help here, Annie.'

I continue scrolling.

'What are you doing?'

'Trying to work out what's happened to our daughter.'

SEVENTY-SEVEN

For once I have clarity. I can't stay here. My daughter needs me more than ever. I must do something.

Not bothering with a coat, I grab my car keys and bolt out of the front door into the torrential downpour with Max calling after me. Rain immediately seeps through my hoodie, soaking into my skin. My trainers squelch across the ground. Mud splatters the front of my jeans. Not that I care. There's only one thing on my mind now. And that's getting my daughter to safety.

I unlock the car and get in, slamming the door hard. My hands are cold and trembling uncontrollably as I fumble with the keys to start the engine, and my foot is shaking so much I can only just get the car into gear. The engine stalls three times. A banging sound startles me. At first I think it's the rain pounding the roof of the car, but I turn to a face at the window. I scream. My thoughts are so confused, I think it's Cameron. The face from my nightmares. A voice calls out my name, a rumble of sound against the rain. It's Jasmine. She thumps her fist on the window again. I can barely make out what she's saying. Something about her dad. I open the window.

'Dad said to come back in. He's called for an ambulance. And the police are on their way.'

'Why did he do that?' The panic in me intensifies. 'We can't involve the police. Cameron said no police. I can't wait. Lola needs me.'

Rain soaks her hair, sticking the corners of her bob to her face. Streaks of mascara smudge her cheeks. 'Let me come with you.'

I consider her offer. 'Where's your brother?'

'He went to his room. He doesn't know what's happened.'

I've doubted this young woman for so long that it's hard to trust her. But stronger together, two of us must be better than one. 'Get in.'

'I need to tell Dad.'

'There's no time.'

She dithers, glancing from the house to the seat waiting beside me.

I rev the engine. 'I'm going now.'

She darts around to the passenger side and jumps in. I reverse out of the driveway before she has even shut the door. 'Steady on,' she says, anchoring herself with a hand on the dashboard.

'Get your seatbelt on, quickly.' I want to get away from here before Max comes after me. I don't know if he'll ever forgive me for this, but I can't wait for the police to arrive. No police. That's what Cameron said. Her seatbelt clunks into place. 'Call your brother. Tell him to get downstairs to help your dad.'

'Do you think that's a good idea? It'll freak him out. You know what he's like.'

'Your dad needs help.'

'What's happened?'

I brief her as I race up the road, fiddling with the satnav.

'Cameron! Zoe! Twins? Dad's kids?' she cries. 'Our half-brother and half-sister? No way. Seriously?'

'That's right. Your dad never knew, though.' I honestly believe that. 'He was as shocked as me.' I approach the junction leading to the main road, debating whether to stop. A car is approaching, forcing me to.

'I never liked Zoe. She tried to befriend me, you know. I thought there was something weird about her.'

'You should've said something.'

'I did. I told Dad.'

'Why didn't he say something?'

'He told me I was being awkward. And that you needed help, and we had to support you.'

Her words sadden me. I should never have mistrusted him.

'If she does anything to hurt my sister, I'll kill her myself. I mean it.'

I thump the palm of my hand against my forehead as if I'm trying to punish myself. 'I should never have let her take Lola out of the house.'

'Don't blame yourself,' she says matter-of-factly as if she's talking to a friend. 'Why don't you let the police sort it? They have skilled officers who can deal with this kind of incident.' She's remarkably calm. Much calmer than me.

'You weren't there, Jasmine. You didn't witness what he said. If we involve the police' – my voice breaks as I relay Cameron's words – 'I'll never see my baby again.'

I find the satnav and locate the destination search.

'You've cut your face.' Jasmine digs in her pocket and fishes out a tissue. 'Here, let me.' She holds up the tissue. 'It's clean!' She places the tissue gently on the wound and holds it there. It's the kindest gesture she's ever made towards me. 'Where are we going, by the way?'

'St Pancras station.' I keep my eyes focused on the road. The wipers are swiping on maximum, but visibility is poor. 'Cameron said they're heading to France. I'm guessing on the Eurostar train to Paris.'

'With Lola!' she cries out.

'No! I don't think so. They're going to leave her somewhere.'

'He told you that?'

I nod.

'How do you know he's telling the truth?'

'They're not interested in Lola. They wouldn't want the hassle of taking a baby out of the country. They're only interested in the money.'

I hope to heaven I'm right.

My phone rings. 'It's your dad.' I answer it.

Max's voice booms through the speakers, reverberating around the car. 'He died.'

SEVENTY-EIGHT

'Cameron's dead,' Max adds.

Jasmine and I simultaneously gasp. His son is dead, and I'm relieved. I can't ignore my deep hatred for that maniac who has wreaked havoc on our lives and robbed me of my motherhood journey. I can't believe we've descended to this. There's another dead person in our house. 'Has the ambulance arrived yet?'

'No. Is Jasmine with you?' he asks.

'She is,' I reply. I can't believe I'm saying this, but it's a relief to have her here with me. 'We're going to St Pancras. I have to be there, Max. I must be there when they find Lola.'

If they find her.

I bat the negative thoughts from my mind. There's no room for them.

'I'll tell the police everything,' he says. 'They'll get onto it straight away. They'll find her.'

'But he said no police.' My voice weakens with acceptance. His actions can't be undone now. 'You heard him.'

'We can't not involve them, Annie. It's for the best. They'll call through to the station and get straight on the case. We're wasting time by not telling them. There're officers specially trained in this kind of stuff.'

The two-tone siren of an ambulance wails in the background. 'They're here,' he says. 'I'll call you back as soon as I can. Text me the number Cameron was conversing with on his phone. It might help the police find her.'

'I'll do it. I love you, Dad,' Jasmine calls, but it's too late. He has already ended the call. 'He's right,' she says.

I nod, hoping to heaven he is.

Jasmine's fingers deftly flit across the keyboard of the satnav as she takes over typing into the destination search. She's surprisingly composed. 'It says thirty-six minutes.'

'But you know what traffic can be like, especially in this weather. It's going to be rush hour soon, too.'

I fumble in my pocket for Cameron's phone and toss it into her lap. 'Read the text exchange on there. See if there are any more clues as to what they've been planning.'

Frustratingly, the poor weather conditions force me to drive slower than I want to. My heart beats furiously. I'm still woozy from the drugs earlier, but the fight-or-flight response has kicked in. My hands clasp the steering wheel with a fierce intensity as I slow to stop the car aquaplaning on the pools of water from the deluge.

'From what I can make out, they were planning on taking the Eurostar to France,' Jasmine says.

'That's what I thought.'

'And then travelling across France to Switzerland. How did they think they'd get away with this?'

'You should've seen him.' My breathing is still erratic. 'He was an absolute lunatic.'

'There's CCTV everywhere at a big train station like that. The police would easily hunt out someone with a baby.'

'Which makes me think she hasn't taken her there. She's already left her somewhere else.'

'Should I send a text? Pretend to be Cameron and say he's on his way.'

'I don't know. She could detect something's amiss. She wasn't picking up when Cameron was trying to call her earlier.'

'Let me read through the messages again. I need to get the tone right.'

'When did she last send a text to him?' I ask.

'Earlier this morning. Then nothing.'

Fear spreads within me like a virus I can't control.

Jasmine's fingers tap the phone. She reads out her reply as she types, 'Just leaving. This storm is something else. Should be there in an hour. What time's the train?'

We wait, but there's no reply. 'Doesn't look like she's picking it up.'

'What – complete radio silence? That's what Cameron was frustrated about. What is she up to?'

Jasmine shrugs. 'She doesn't say.' She types, reading out her message again, 'Keep me in the loop. I'm worried about you.'

Jasmine screams. 'Watch out!'

I hit the brakes, screeching to a halt as the car in front suddenly brakes.

Jasmine slams her hand on the dashboard. 'Jeez, Annie. We won't make it at this rate.'

The driver behind me beeps their horn. Several others do, too. The brake lights of the car in front fade. The driver pulls away. I glance at the satnav and let out an anxious sigh. There's still fifteen minutes to go. I try to imagine what Zoe is doing with my baby right now. There's a part of me keeping the faith. That Cameron was bluffing, and Zoe is not as bad as he made out. But knowing she's so deeply involved in this plot, my hope is fading fast.

'I'm sorry,' Jasmine says, opening the doors to the discussion I've been thinking about having with her.

I turn to her. Light from the street shines on her face, She looks so young, so vulnerable sitting there with her hair stuck to her head and mascara-blackened eyes. 'This isn't your fault.'

'No, I mean, for giving you such a hard time since you met Dad. I was jealous. And I was wrong. We seriously thought you were crazy. We thought you started that fire.'

I'm stumped. Where's the moody, stroppy teenager I've grown to loathe and distrust this past year? 'Cameron drugged me that night. He slipped something in my drink, and started the fire when I fell asleep.'

'He could've killed you, and Lola. And us.'

'I don't think he would've let it get that far. Lola was his collateral. You know, I've felt dreadful for so long, it's a relief to know it's nothing serious.'

'Dad was always telling me I needed to be kinder to you. I should've been.'

Guilt hits me. All along, Max has been on my side. 'I'm sorry as well. I overheard a conversation you had with Priti when we were at Nisha's. Your dad and I should've been more sensitive to you and Jacob.'

'I shouldn't have said those things.'

'No. But you were right. We should've involved you and Jacob more in the decision to move me in.' I take her hand.

'He really loves you, you know. Dad really loves you.'

I slowly nod. 'I thought it was you two, you know. It sounds crazy now I can see clearly, but all along, especially when I was drugged, I wondered if it was you and Jacob, as mad as that sounds. As it turns out it was two stepchildren I never knew existed.'

SEVENTY-NINE

Max calls again, updating us on the situation through the speaker. His voice rumbles around the car like the wind outside. The transport police have taken control. Max has given them Zoe's phone details and they are putting a trace on her straight away. They want to speak to me. 'I'll pass the officer over to you.' His voice is as panicked as mine. He puts them on the phone as the line goes dead.

'Damn. Call him back, can you?' I say to Jasmine.

'There's no signal.'

'It must be the weather. It'll come back soon.'

The remainder of the journey proves a challenge. The rain continues falling, creating a stream out of every road I turn into. The satnav detours us onto a different route, adding seven minutes to the journey.

Seven minutes we don't have.

'Anything more from Zoe?' I reach out my hand and tap Cameron's phone sitting in her lap. 'Check again.'

'I'm checking every second. There's nothing, but that could be the bad signal.'

'Tell her he's here and ask what she's done with the baby.'

'Don't you think that'll look suspect?'

I shrug. My nerves are in tatters. I don't know how much more I can take of this. 'We need to know where she is.'

'Where would you leave a baby in her situation?'

'I don't know.'

Funny enough, I've never stolen a baby and had to think about it, I nearly say but keep quiet. This isn't the time for sarcasm. I slam my sweaty hand on the steering wheel as the traffic lights ahead flash amber. The car in front continues through them. I debate picking up speed to do the same before they turn red. A rash decision makes me ram my foot on the accelerator. But I'm too late. I jump a red light. Usually that would stress me out, but I'm past caring.

'From what Cameron said, they weren't planning on letting you know where they'd left her until tomorrow, so they must be leaving her with someone. You can't leave a baby alone for that long. She'll cry.'

I groan as a thought occurs to me. 'If they're considering leaving her for so long to allow them a safe getaway, they would have to drug her. The same as they were drugging me.'

I've never felt so useless or terrified in my whole life. I should've protected my baby.

'Come on, think. Where would you leave a baby if you were her?'

'I don't know,' I say, exasperated. 'Where would you?'

'Think about it logically.' She checks Cameron's phone again. 'If they think you might go to the police, they don't want to risk being seen with a baby at a big railway station. So, I reckon she's left her somewhere else before going to the station. Somewhere safe and warm.'

I can't work out if she means that or if she said it to reassure me. 'Perhaps they don't even care about safe and warm. Perhaps they've left her in an alleyway somewhere.'

'No,' Jasmine says adamantly. 'She'll start crying and attract attention. So, yes, they have probably drugged her. And I reckon she's either left her with someone they know – but that doesn't seem likely – or she's left her in a hotel room or somewhere like that.'

The thought of my baby all alone is breaking me. 'I'm out of my depth here.'

She pats my shoulder. 'You're doing great, Annie.'

I can't believe how mature she's behaving. This is not the same person I've lived with for the past year. 'Check the phone again,' I say.

She bows her head to look at the screen. 'Radio silence.'

'Prepare a message to send when the signal comes back. Ask her something. Anything. She may come back online.' I'm clutching at threadbare straws of hope, but we have to try everything.

'What should I say?'

'Say he's looking for her. It's very busy. He can't find her.'

The phone clicks as she types. 'Is this all right?' She reads it out to me. '"Made it. Super busy here. I can't find you. Where are you?"'

'Send it.'

'There's still no signal.'

I groan angrily.

She points to the windscreen. 'Look at that sign – half a mile to go. We need to find somewhere to park.'

'I don't care about parking,' I say frantically. 'I'll just leave the car in a side road.'

The satnav detours us up a narrow street. 'This will do.' I slam on the brakes slightly ahead of a metered parking space and clumsily reverse into it. As I turn off the engine, my phone rings again. This time it's from an unknown number. 'We're back in signal,' I tell Jasmine. 'Send that text.' I answer the call. 'It's your dad again.'

'What happened?' he asks.

'The weather is atrocious. We lost signal.'

'I'll put the officer on again.'

Another call rings through. I tell Max to hold.

The caller introduces himself as Superintendent Crone from the British Transport Police. 'Is this Annie Carpenter?'

'Yes.' My teeth chatter from the cold as the heating dies. 'My stepdaughter is on the line, too.'

He briefs me on the situation, his voice firm with an air of superiority and confidence. For the first time since this nightmare began there's a shimmer of hope, like the sun peeping through the clouds on a winter's day. But that sun soon disappears as he tells me his officers are still looking for Zoe and Lola as he speaks. 'So far, there's been no sighting of either of them. That's not to say we won't find them very soon. I understand you're on the way to the station. Where are you now?'

'I've just parked the car in a side street.'

'Please don't enter the station, Annie.'

'I have to.'

'I know you want to help, but if Zoe sees you, she'll panic, which could jeopardise my officers' operation.' He goes quiet before adding – as if I need to give another reason to follow his orders – 'And put your daughter's life at risk.'

EIGHTY

The superintendent gives directions to a pub nestled around the corner from the station. It's only three streets away. One of his officers will meet us there.

'You need to follow his instructions,' Jasmine says. 'These people know what they're doing.'

'I hope so.' I open the car door, resigned that I must leave this to the professionals. 'Let's go.'

The weather conditions haven't improved. I get out of the car, ignoring the sting of the rain across my face. I hurry across the road, zigzagging between traffic. Jasmine cries out for me to be careful. When she reaches the other side of the road, I grab her arm, and we run hand-in-hand through the wind driving the rain horizontally across the streets.

The pub has two floors. Downstairs is a traditional British boozer – low beams and an inglenook fireplace – and the upstairs houses a cocktail bar. I scan the crowd, not knowing who I'm looking for, but spot a guy, mid-thirties with a comb over, sitting at the corner table, nursing a bottle of orange juice. He sees us and waves. I head over to him, navigating through tables and wet umbrellas half-opened to dry, turning to check Jasmine is behind me.

'Annie Carpenter?' he asks.

I nod, lost for words.

'Take a seat, and I'll bring you up to speed. First, can I get you a drink?'

We drop down on the two old wooden chairs opposite him. 'No, thanks.' Jasmine also declines.

'Are you aware Cameron has passed away from his injuries?'

He is hard to hear above the enthusiastic chatter from the crowd of people enjoying an early evening drink. I nod and ask about my daughter. I don't give a damn about what's happened to Cameron, however shocking the ordeal we've suffered. 'You have to find her.'

'Rest assured, our team is doing everything possible to get your daughter safely back to you. We're holding the next Eurostar train on the platform and currently have officers searching the carriages. If she's on there, she will be found.' He picks up his bottle of juice and slurps a mouthful through the striped straw.

My throat is dry. I swallow hard. 'Please tell them to be quick.'

He nods sympathetically. 'We've got a pretty good description of Zoe from your husband. But he doesn't have any photos of her. We wondered if you have?'

I shake my head, berating myself for this. I should've taken a photo of her.

'I do,' Jasmine pipes up. She reaches into her pocket and pulls out her phone.

'From when?' I ask.

'I took it the other day as I thought she might be interesting to paint someday.' I watch in amazement as she scrolls through her phone before turning it to face the officer. 'Here you go.'

'Fantastic,' the officer says. 'Could you send that to me?'

Jasmine AirDrops the image to the police officer.

I grab the phone to see the photo. It's of Zoe smiling as she holds a giggling Lola in the air. Evidently she hadn't noticed Jasmine taking the photo. I break into a cold sweat and turn my eyes away from the image in disgust.

A call comes in on the police officer's mobile. He holds up a hand to us and pops a finger in his ear.

'What's happening?' I ask urgently, desperate for any information. Any morsel of hope that my baby is still alive.

He places his hand over the mouthpiece. 'Zoe's phone has been traced. They've found it in a bin near the station.'

I let out a low, broken groan.

'That's why she hasn't been picking up,' Jasmine cries.

The police officer stands up. 'I've got to take this outside; I can't hear a thing. They've had to let the train go. No sign of Zoe or Lola. Wait there. I'll be back in a moment.'

I lace my hands and place them on top of my head. I've never felt so useless and scared in my life. 'I can't bear this.'

'Think back to after Cameron collapsed. What exactly did he say to you?'

I rub my forehead. 'I could just about make out the station. St Pancras.'

'Think hard. There must've been more. Even the slightest word, phrase, utterance. Think! Think!' Jasmine is showing a level of maturity way beyond her years.

'He said... I don't know. He was delirious. Something about it being great.'

'Go on. Anything else?' Jasmine types on her phone.

'He said the word *nord*. He was mumbling at that point. I couldn't work it out.'

'Got it!' Jasmine's eyes sparkle. 'I typed "great nord St Pancras". This is what I got.' She turns her phone towards me.

'The Great Northern Hotel St Pancras. That's where you'd hide a baby, safe, warm. I bet she's there.'

'I know it. Your dad and I stayed there one night. It's worth a shot.' Anything is worth a shot. I stand. 'Come on, let's go.'

'What about the police?'

'No police,' I say. 'They're looking in the wrong place. I just want Lola back. And if I can possibly lay my hands on Zoe,' I say, 'so much the better.'

EIGHTY-ONE

'The hotel's only a few streets away from here.' Jasmine has already sourced its location. 'I still think we should wait.'

'No. Come on.' I throw my bag over my shoulder. 'You coming?'

She stands up.

As we exit the pub, the police officer is huddled in a corner with his back to us, still in deep conversation on his mobile. We skit along several back streets with Jasmine directing while referring to Google Maps. Within minutes we arrive at the elegant townhouse hotel. We bound into the palatial lobby adorned with artwork, and a wrought-iron staircase that curves up to the floors above.

A smartly dressed woman is checking in a couple at the opulent reception desk. I consider the best way to approach this. We're both a drenched mess, a far cry from the neatly attired staff and clientele of this five-star hotel.

'What should we do?' Jasmine whispers.

'She could've booked a room. Let's ask her if she's had a woman with a baby check in here today,' I say. 'On second thought, look at the state of us. She's not going to tell us. Look.' I point to a sign for the toilets. 'It's worth a try.'

We head past the reception desk through a cloud of expensive perfume and stop in unison at the entrance to the female toilets. Jasmine barges in. I follow her into the fragrant smell of rose petals. Soft music is playing. With bated breath, one by one, I push the doors of the five cubicles, starting with the disabled toilet that doubles as a baby changing facility and is large enough to take a buggy.

Nothing.

A cry escapes me. There's no end to this torture. 'What now?'

'Come.' Jasmine grabs my hand – not for the first time – and drags me from the room. 'Who are more observant, men or women?' She pulls me into the male toilets.

Thankfully no one is standing at the urinals. The room is warm – warmer than the ladies. The heating must have been turned up a notch. We repeat the process cubicle by cubicle until we come to the disabled facility. The door is locked. We can't see underneath it as the door carries right down to the ground.

'Here, let me.' Jasmine rushes into the adjacent cubicle, climbs onto the toilet, heaves herself up the dividing wall and bends her torso over the top.

'Annie. Annie. She's here. We've found her!' She acrobatically flips herself over the wall, her boots landing with a thud on the tiled floor. There's a pause. 'She's alive.' She scrambles to open the door.

I rush in, and there she is, my baby, sleeping blissfully unaware of the drama playing out around her. I check her pulse.

'Has she been drugged?' Jasmine asks.

'Quite possibly, but she is breathing.' Tears stream down my face. Tears of regret. Tears of relief. And tears for my sister that I haven't yet managed to shed.

I lift my baby out of the buggy and hold her close to me. 'We need to get her straight to hospital.'

Jasmine throws her arms around me. 'She's going to be OK,' she says. 'Everything's going to be OK.'

EIGHTY-TWO

Jen

I stand at the station, peering up at the digital departure board.

It was a half-a-million-dollar gamble. But I couldn't risk my brother's erratic behaviour any longer. A frosty chill slices through me. If there's one thing I miss about home, it's the weather. I can't wait to be in a sunnier climate again. My eyes scan the departure times. My next train is delayed. It's not leaving for another thirty minutes.

I find a small café along the concourse that welcomes customers with the intoxicating smell of rich coffee and buttery pastries. It's inviting after the stench of the unkempt guy I had to sit next to on the train from Paris. I ask the barista for a muffin and a filter coffee. I should have something more substantial. The next train will take four hours. But my nerves have stolen my appetite. I couldn't be more excited, though. Portugal has been on my bucket list since forever.

A heady mix of excitement and anticipation rushes through me, and fear, of course. I can't deny that. But I keep telling myself, I'm gonna be fine. If I stay chilled, everything's gonna go according to plan. No one's searching for a woman with long black hair who blends into the crowd with her dark coat and beige pants. They are looking for someone with a blonde pixie cut... the old me. That's if they've even started looking, yet.

I ask the server to add a sandwich to my order. 'Club sandwich, madame?' he asks in a strong French accent. 'Ten minute. Kitchen busy.'

I don't have time. I scan the ready-to-go counter and point to the display of Brie and apple baguettes. 'I'll have one of those, instead.' What a strange combination, but I'm up for it. This is the new me, trying new foods, exploring new places. And meeting new people – eventually.

I tap the glass in front of a tray of salami and pickle baguettes. 'And one of those.' It's been a long day. And it's going to be a long night until I reach the hostel I've booked into under my new name: Jennifer Taylor. I'll shorten it to Jen for the new people I meet. I've always loved that name. Jen. It has a ring of calmness to it. Zen Jen, that's who I'm going to become known as.

I take my purchases to the middle of the café, where I sit at a table next to the large window fronting the concourse. It's crowded in here. Despite the melodic mix of light jazz music, I can hear the conversation of the couple sitting next to me. Not that I can understand it. French was never an option to take at the kind of school I went to. Most kids had only just mastered English. I bite into the Brie and apple baguette, realising how hungry I am. I haven't eaten since that croissant Annie gave me this morning.

Poor Annie. I don't like what Cam did to her. Totally not cool. That wasn't part of the plan – not the plan he shared with me, anyhow. When I got to England, I was clueless about all that had gone down with her. Cam told me we were just gonna get back at the dude who ditched our mom when she was pregnant with us. Hurting someone else was never part of the equation. And then he went and committed murder. The damn idiot! But that's Cam for you; he's always been volatile. He knew if he'd told me about everything he'd done, I'd never have agreed to be part of it. He even involved me in the game with the baby formula. What the hell! Just a total jerk. Which is why I'm here in South-West France, waiting for a train to Portugal. And he's looking for me at that station in London to head to Switzerland via Paris.

I hungrily take another bite of the baguette, listening to the hustle and bustle of the hurried commuters grabbing a bite to eat.

Annie got me thinking this morning when that parcel arrived for her.

She was totally shaken up. And it was the way she held it against her chest and the tense look on her face that told me she had something to hide. Only when I looked at the box when she went upstairs did it all fall into place.

Why, despite thinking Lola was my half-sister, I never felt the same connection to her as I did to Jasmine and Jacob. I could be wrong, but I rarely am.

That parcel does hold a secret.

Annie's secret.

I wonder how I can use that to my advantage.

I open my belt bag. Unzipping the inside pocket, I remove the cream-coloured cloth wallet and flick through the wad of cash, checking it's all there. I don't know why I keep checking. It must be my nerves.

I sip my coffee, the porcelain cup clinking as I replace it on the saucer. I love how the Europeans use these dinky cups and saucers. I count the notes to pass the time. Five thousand euros – that should keep me going until I can access the million dollars now working its way through the international banking system. Who would've thought? I was always considered a dunce at school. Zoe the ugly one who left with not a qualification to her name. But it's not what you know but who you know. To be smart, you have to mix with smart people. And one thing I quickly learned in life is that most people will do anything for the right price.

I met Brandon in a bar. A wannabe Wall Street trader who never managed to strike his dream job but proved them all wrong when he started up on his own. He now owns an impressive pad in Bel Air and a yacht he keeps in Marina del Rey that he sails every weekend. We clicked straight away. On a business level, that is. He wanted more, but he wasn't my type. Real smart dude, but way too flashy for me. But he settled for a five per cent cut to make a million dollars untraceable in the international banking system and to secure a false set of papers to give Cam and me new identities. It seemed a reasonable deal to me.

I check my phone. The new pay-as-you-go I bought solely for the purpose of conversing with Brandon. It'll end up in a bin as soon as he confirms the safe receipt of my funds. The same destiny as the burner phone Cam arranged for me that's now in the garbage somewhere in the backstreets of London.

I open my passport, smirking at the photo. I did a good job with my make-up before Cam took this one. TikTok has a lot to answer for. I found a woman called Transformation Tina, a make-up artist who regularly posts about how to use cosmetics to transform your appearance. She was impressive to watch. I practised dozens of times before perfecting the look I wanted, applying lashings of concealer to obscure the mole on my cheek and pencilling on a set of heavy eyebrows. And I found prosthetic pieces online to change the shape of my chin and nose that make me unrecognisable. The exact make-up regime I followed when I arrived in London earlier today. It's so easy. But isn't everything when you know what you're doing?

Poor Cam. Despite being a total jerk most of the time, he has always loved me. But I couldn't love him back. He operates too far on the wrong side of danger for me. He always has done. I wonder what he'll do when he turns up at that station and can't find me. And how long he'll wait until he realises I'm never going to turn up and the million dollars we agreed to split is no longer in the account he forced Max to transfer it into. But I don't care now. Cam has got what he deserves.

I look out of the window, alarmed to see two policemen enter the café. I look downwards at my passport, taking momentary glances up. My heart pounds as they pass the counter and walk towards me. This can't be happening. They approach me. One of them puts his hand in his pocket. I can't look. My hands tremble as I replace the passport and money into the belt bag waiting for them to stop at my table.

But they don't. They carry on past me and sit at the table three rows down.

I need to get out of here. I gulp the remaining coffee and pack the untouched baguette and muffin into my rucksack for later.

Leaving the café, I inhale deep breaths as I head towards the platform to catch my train. My new journey to starting over.

EIGHTY-THREE

I run the tape dispenser across another cardboard box, sealing the top with a heavy sigh. 'Another one done!' I guide the box with my foot to join the others lined up at the side of the room.

Nisha pulls up the spaghetti strap of the top she's wearing. It falls again. She's lost a lot of weight these past six months. But, then, she's had a lot to deal with. Discovering your perfect life is not so perfect and your husband was having an affair with his business partner who was then murdered is enough to shatter anyone. 'You haven't labelled it.' She throws a marker pen to me. 'Here you go.'

I catch the pen and write LIVING ROOM in big letters across the side of the box. 'Which one do you want me to start on next?' I ask.

She points to the cabinet below the TV. 'Why don't you pack the board games?' She reaches for another flat-packed box. 'I still can't believe it.' Her sorrowful eyes observe the box. Since Sean told her about the affair, she hasn't been herself. Understandably. But she'll get there, she insists. She's seeing a therapist, a friend of hers, to help her heal. 'Twenty years, and it's all come to this – selling the home I thought I'd live in for the rest of my life.'

My phone rings. It's Jacob. He tells me how his exam went today and asks what time I'm coming home. Home is now a modern four-bedroom house on a new estate at the far end of town we moved into a week after the 'incident', as we now refer to it as. We signed an annual rental agreement with a six-month break clause while we search for our forever home, as Max calls it. He couldn't be sorrier for everything that happened, and he spends every day trying to make up for it.

I stare at my beautiful daughter asleep in her car seat. 'When Lola wakes up, I'll come back,' I tell my stepson. There's no chance of getting anything done with her crawling around. She's the most inquisitive of characters.

'I'll cook dinner,' he says to my delight. The love of cooking I had when I was single has never returned. Cooking for a family is a burden, I've decided. One likes this, another one doesn't. One wants peas. The other one wants carrots. Jasmine likes mash. Max and Jacob hate it. It does my head in. 'I'll make that pasta sauce Lola likes,' he says. 'Is that all right?'

'Sounds perfect,' I say. 'Thank you.'

He ends the call telling me he'll make dessert, as well.

'He really has come into his own since moving out of that bloody house.' I slip my phone back into my pocket. 'So has Jasmine.' The twins and I have grown close while still respecting each other's unspoken boundaries.

'So do you think they'll ever catch Zoe?' Nisha asks, wrapping an ornament in a sheet of bubble wrap.

I shrug. 'She could be anywhere.'

'What about the private detective Max wanted to hire to find her?'

'He's finally given up on the idea.' Thank goodness. It took me a while to persuade him that the stress was killing me and that we needed to let it go.

'A million dollars, though! The woman took a million dollars. I'm not sure I could let it go,' Nisha says.

That was Max's view at first. But I pointed out that the business sold for eighteen million dollars in the end. Split three ways, we've got more than enough money to live comfortably for the rest of our lives. His daughter got one of those millions. So what.

I say the same to Nisha as I said to Max six months ago, 'We have to put it all behind us and move on.'

I had no choice.

I received a call from Zoe only days after she disappeared. She knew Max wasn't Lola's father; the DNA test confirmed it too.

'You make sure everyone leaves me alone, and I'll leave you alone,' Zoe hissed down the phone before hanging up. I had no other option but to convince Max to give up on his idea of hiring the private detective.

Because, now I've seen what life could be like for Lola, coming from a broken home, I decided to keep my secret.

Despite the genetics, as far as I'm concerned, Max is Lola's father. And she won't end up like Zoe and Cameron. I even lied to Nisha and told her the results came back a match.

I'll just have to live with my guilt.

For now, it's time for us to enjoy our baby.

A LETTER FROM AJ CAMPBELL

Dear reader,

I want to say a huge thank you for choosing to read *First-Time Mother*. I loved writing Annie's story. If you enjoyed it and want to keep up to date with my latest releases, just sign up at the link below. Your email address will never be shared, and you can unsubscribe anytime.

www.bookouture.com/AJ-Campbell

In doing so, you will also receive a copy of my gripping short story *Sweet Revenge*.

As for all authors, reviews are the key to raising awareness of my work. If you have enjoyed this book, I would be very grateful if you could leave a short review on Amazon and Goodreads. I'd love to hear what you think, and it makes such a difference in helping new readers discover one of my books for the first time.

I often get asked as an author where I get the inspiration for my stories. And the simple answer is they come in a whole variety of ways. They sometimes come from stories I read through numerous online news channels, where I ask myself the question, how could that have possibly happened? From there, an idea is sparked, and I start plotting! Other times, inspiration hits when I'm out and about, and I see people interacting in their everyday lives. Sometimes, I think of a hook sparked from an abstract thought and develop the idea over time. The idea for *First-Time Mother* came to me in the shower! This then developed from the renovation work being carried out at a house at the end of our close. I wondered what it would be like for my protagonist – Annie – to live through all that chaos with a newborn baby.

All my novels undergo a rigorous editing process, but sometimes mistakes happen. If you have spotted an error, please contact me so I can promptly correct it.

I love hearing from my readers – you can get in touch via my Facebook and Instagram pages, or my website.

Best wishes,

Amanda X

www.ajcampbellauthor.com

 facebook.com/AJCampbellauthor
 instagram.com/ajcampbellauthor

PUBLISHING TEAM

Turning a manuscript into a book requires the efforts of many people. The publishing team at Bookouture would like to acknowledge everyone who contributed to this publication.

Audio
Alba Proko
Sinead O'Connor
Melissa Tran

Commercial
Lauren Morrissette
Hannah Richmond
Imogen Allport

Data and analysis
Mark Alder
Mohamed Bussuri

Editorial
Natalie Edwards
Charlotte Hegley

Copyeditor
Janette Currie

Proofreader
Becca Allen

Marketing
Alex Crow
Melanie Price
Occy Carr
Ciara Rosney
Martyna Młynarska

Operations and distribution
Marina Valles
Stephanie Straub
Joe Morris

Production
Hannah Snetsinger
Mandy Kullar
Ria Clare
Nadia Michael

Publicity
Kim Nash
Noelle Holten
Jess Readett
Sarah Hardy

Rights and contracts
Peta Nightingale
Richard King
Saidah Graham

Made in United States
Orlando, FL
01 May 2025

60943083R00187